The Protector

The Fall and Rise of Oliver Cromwell

The Protector

The Fall and Rise of Oliver Cromwell

Tom Reilly

**TOP HAT
BOOKS**

Winchester, UK
Washington, USA

JOHN HUNT PUBLISHING

First published by Top Hat Books, 2022
Top Hat Books is an imprint of John Hunt Publishing Ltd., No. 3 East St., Alresford,
Hampshire SO24 9EE, UK
office@jhpbooks.com
www.johnhuntpublishing.com
www.tophat-books.com

For distributor details and how to order please visit the 'Ordering' section on our website.

Design: Stuart Davies

UK: Printed and bound by CPI Group (UK) Ltd, Croydon, CR0 4YY
US: Printed and bound by Thomson-Shore, 7300 West Joy Road, Dexter, MI 48130

We operate a distinctive and ethical publishing philosophy in
all areas of our business, from our global network of authors to
production and worldwide distribution.

Also by Tom Reilly

Cromwell was Framed
ISBN: 978 1 78279 516 2

Chapter One

1599

Monkeys were unpredictable creatures. Elizabeth knew that. Everybody knew that. But nobody ever expected the bulky, domesticated chimpanzee to suddenly swipe her baby from his oak cradle. Even if anyone did, fewer still could have predicted that the monkey would scale the ivy-clad façade of the old stately home with the child. From the tranquil social gathering on the front lawn, Elizabeth looked on in disbelief. Her five-month-old son was clumsily tucked under the primate's upper left limb. The gathered family watched in horror as Caesar clambered up the old limestone wall. He skillfully used the chunkier ivy vines to hoist his sinewy, simian body upwards. He seemed to know instinctively which vines would hold his weight and which wouldn't. The remaining three limbs provided the dexterity he needed to gain elevation. The beast displayed a natural deftness reminiscent of his days in his natural arboreous environment. In seconds he had gained a height from which a fall would certainly cause the baby's death.

Caesar was familiar with this terrain. Free to roam around the precincts of Hinchingbrooke unrestrained for the recreation of its occupants and their guests, he had made this ascent innumerable times a day. Caesar had never strayed too far from the family home. There was food and succour within the manor house demesne. He had learned that imitative behaviour of his human owners often triggered extra culinary rewards. But today, for whatever reason, he was wayward. Where this escapade had always been a sight of mild amusement to the human onlookers, it was now a terrifying prospect to behold.

It may have been the fact that the Cromwell family (alias Williams) had visitors. There were more people around to see

1

Caesar's frolics. So far this afternoon, his exertions to impress had yielded three tasty peaches. The patriarch of the estate house, the now chair-bound 62-year-old Sir Henry Cromwell had been engaging in a convivial afternoon with his son and close-by neighbour Robert and daughter-in-law Elizabeth. The parents were accompanied by their brood of four children, the youngest of whom was now dangling from Caesar's right hand by the leg, two storeys up. It was Sir Henry's father who had abandoned the name Williams and chose to adopt the name Cromwell instead, in honour of an uncle, Thomas Cromwell, chief minister to Henry VIII.

As the capricious child abductor ascended the wall, Caesar hesitated slightly with the challenge that was presented to him when the awkward protrusion of the battlements and the diminution of the ivy halted his momentum. This new conundrum was obviously due to the passenger he seemed disinclined to discard since he had not encountered it before with such a burden.

The house Caesar was climbing was built on the site of a former nunnery, and the rooms spoke of ghosts; some were even rumoured to be peopled with more malignant forces. The very well-connected Sir Henry Cromwell, who was known locally as the Golden Knight considered talk of the supernatural mere melodramatic piffle. In 1564, Queen Elizabeth I had visited Hinchingbrooke and Sir Henry had spared no expense in order to make the visit memorable for everybody concerned. The queen had been on her way to Scotland. The promise of lavish hospitality at Sir Henry Cromwell's Hinchingbrooke estate was simply too good to pass up. The entire episode was a thorough success. It was one that Sir Henry had hoped to repeat sometime in the future, despite the pecuniary extravagance.

From his deep slumber in the tepid, early-afternoon September sun, under the shadow of the big house, only seconds earlier, the baby was now wailing hopelessly. His young life, now in the hands of his histrionic animal captor. His father, Robert, quickly positioned himself directly below the mischievous climber, ready to catch the child, should he fall. The suddenness of the impossible act had stunned the company below. The placid, jovial scene had instantaneously become a chaotic one. The usually stoic Elizabeth began a scream on impulse that was both primal and animalistic in its timbre. Her eldest child, Joanie, now seven years old, had been cavorting among the late summer roses with her younger sisters Elizabeth (4) and Catherine (2). She could not fully absorb the terror embodied in her mother's screams because of the innocence of her age.

Little Joanie had been playing mother to her younger sisters. She loved to mimic the adults in their grown-up activities. Afternoon tea on the lawn at Hinchingbrooke was the perfect opportunity to pretend that the children's world was just as important as the adults. Well, of course it was. She was Robert and Elizabeth's firstborn. She could never understand why people insisted she had her father's eyes and her mother's nose. She had her own eyes and her own nose, that much was very certain. She didn't much like the long walk from their home in Huntingdon High Street to her grandfather's home, just outside the town. But she loved the wide-open space that she had to play in when she was there. She loved to pretend that she was her new baby brother's nursemaid. And now, here he was being carried along the roof of the house by Caesar the monkey, who she thought, was just so amusing. It irritated Joanie that the baby was once again the centre of attention, when the adults really should be listening to her and her sisters and smiling at their every playful move. Curious to see what would happen, she moved closer to the house to watch the adults in their fright. This was very unusual. Very unusual indeed.

Sir Henry's firstborn son, Oliver, suddenly emerged from the front door, once traversed by the Queen of England. He was astounded at the scene that now confronted him. Above his head, Caesar had successfully prevailed over the architectural hindrance that had impaired his climb. He was now bounding along the top of the flat, lead-capped wall, with the crying child back in his brawny arms. At 39 years-old and cutting a dashing figure, Sir Oliver Cromwell was well used to crisis situations. He was imbued with considerable *savoir-faire*. Having occupied the position of Sherriff of Huntingdonshire, he had been the captain of musters during the Spanish Armada threat. Queen Elizabeth had dubbed him a knight bachelor, just a year previously. By nature, he was a savvy soldier and a quick thinker. In true military style, he immediately took command of the drastic situation. Rushing towards his father, who was still seated on his chair due to his infirmity, he dragged the lap blanket that was covering his father's knees. Fixing his glare at the bizarre and horrifying circumstance now unfolding on the roof, he barked at his brother:

'Seize the other two corners, Robert, and pull the blanket taut. Now, let us follow his every move and do not remove your gaze from the animal!'

The two brothers ran to where Caesar had positioned himself on the wall up above them. It seemed to the observers that Caesar was enjoying the ghastly game. Perched between two battlements, child in his arms, he began to ejaculate screeches as if to taunt the would-be rescuers. Elizabeth turned her head away. She could no longer bear to look. It was coming on two years now since she had lost her first son, Henry. Named after his grandfather, young Henry had been a strong boy, of robust constitution but influenza gripped him when he was just five years old. When he died, Elizabeth thought smiling again was simply an impossibility. The disease, when it came, was ruthless. It started with a slight cough and mild sweating. Within a week it had engulfed the boy and he breathed his last breath in his mother's arms.

And now her new son and heir was up on the roof in the arms of a monkey. The joy that the birth of this latest child had brought to their lives was consummate. The aspirations that herself and Robert had conceived for their second boy in their many idle hours since his birth were immeasurable. Like they had done with Henry, the family would depend on this child to carry their branch of the Cromwell name into the future. He would ultimately inherit the modest estate of his father. He would provide for the family when the parents had passed. He would achieve a station in life that was befitting of the illustrious Cromwell family. Even the prospect during the pregnancy, that after three healthy girls, this might in fact be another boy was all-consuming for the parents during the entire gestation period. The elation when a boy was born was unbridled.

The very idea that the helpless infant could, at any second, simply tumble from the monkey's arms and fall to the ground was simply unconscionable. Yet, it was reality. At this very moment, right here, right now the uninhibited optimism that she had nurtured over the last five months for the child to fulfil the modest expectations of his parents might easily be brutally taken away. This appalling prospect overcame Elizabeth in that moment. The unrestrained noises of the captor, the captive, and his protectors began to fade from her consciousness. A fit of dizziness engulfed her and she fell to the ground thoroughly insensible.

Oblivious to the condition of his wife, Robert was trying to calculate the possible trajectory of the tiny body with each startling movement the primate made. If the feckless monkey were to cast the boy in any direction, he was ready to follow as swiftly as he could. He knew he could depend on his burly brother to do the same. More portly than Oliver, at 37 years old Robert had not yet begun to feel the infirmities of his years. He was confident he could cover ground quickly if need be. However gallant his thoughts were, the vastness of the roof and the speed with which Caesar could traverse the built landscape was patently the biggest problem the two now had. And yet, Caesar did not seem inclined to take his burden far from the view of the onlookers. He remained in full sight as if he was revelling in their predicament.

When the moment came it was as shocking as it was sudden. From his lofty position, now above the rectangular bay window, Caesar made an instant decision to scale the slender chimney tower that rose elegantly above the ornately-carved stone battlements. In that moment he released the child from his grip. The child began to plummet. In one swift movement of resolve, the two brothers quickly adjusted their position. They just managed to catch the falling infant in the blanket. They both seemed to instinctively know to allow for slack should the tiny body inadvertently spring from their makeshift safety net.

As instantaneously as it had begun, the abduction had ended. Apart from a few minor scrapes, the baby seemed otherwise unharmed. Robert lifted the child into his arms. He turned towards where his wife was last standing only to see her limp body lying on the freshly-cut grass.

'Elizabeth!' he shouted, running towards her and realising that there was now a new emergency to deal with. 'What happened to her, Father?'

'The shock seems to have overtaken her, and she has collapsed, Robert. I'll wager it is merely a giddiness of the head. She will recover,' replied Sir Henry reassuringly.

It was Oliver who reached Elizabeth first, and having some experience of military medical emergencies, he raised the upper half of her body from the grass and the movement was enough to trigger a gradual opening of her eyes.

'My child?' she exclaimed regaining her faculties. 'What has happened to my child?'

'He is perfectly well,' said Robert calmly, placing the baby in Elizabeth's arms. 'Oliver and I managed to save him from that despicable creature. The Lord saw fit to allow him to live.'

'Oh, thank God in heaven!' said Elizabeth as she held the baby close, both to stifle his cries and to experience the sensation of his tiny body against hers once again. The danger was now over.

'That monkey will have to go, Father,' said Oliver to Sir Henry. It was impossible for the father to argue with his son's decision. Not that Sir Henry had ever fully embraced the idea of a domestic chimpanzee roaming around the house. It was a fashion in estate homes in the locality, but he had really only agreed to providing a home for Caesar to appease the grandchildren. They had derived so much pleasure from the monkey's antics. Until today, that was.

Impressed safely into his mother's bosom, the baby's loud cry was now reduced to muffled whimpers. Robert assisted Elizabeth to her feet. She managed to sit on one of the chairs that had been brought from the study for the occasion. For ten minutes she caressed the boy, feeling the composition of his frame and the texture of his soft young skin, as if to confirm that he was still fully intact.

'Is the baby dead now?' asked Joanie nonchalantly as she plonked herself down beside her mother. 'Is he gone to the Lord?'

'He is very much alive, Joanie! You will have to give him very special kisses now following his trials on the roof this afternoon.'

As the heart rates of each of the adult family members gradually returned to normal, within thirty minutes Sir Henry's first footman had returned with Mr Simcott the local physician. He knew the families well. He had been present at the births of all of Elizabeth's children. Indeed, he had been present at the birth of many of Huntingdon's citizens. He could have been forgiven for thinking that he had seen it all. It was only five months earlier that he had delivered this particular baby into the world. He remembered the occasion well as it had been at 3 o'clock in the morning when he was called out. He had only just retired an hour or so earlier due to a Simcott family celebration.

Having listened to details of the awful affair in total shock, and after examining the kidnap victim, the physician concluded that there were no broken limbs, that the child was extremely fortunate to be alive and that it was the mother who now needed some rest. He added that he had never heard of such an incident happening before. He was perfectly happy to admit that the entire episode had sufficiently unnerved him.

Receiving a glance from his wife, turning towards his father, Robert said, 'I think, Father, we might take our leave and return to Huntingdon at this juncture, if you will kindly beg our pardon. After such tribulations I feel that the time for idle conversation has well passed.'

'Of course, Robert. As you wish. Perhaps, Oliver, you would be good enough to call the footman to procure the carriage.'

'Oh Mother, do we have to leave so soon?' squealed Joanie. She sensed the afternoon was about to take a turn for the worse as her Uncle Oliver disappeared towards the stables to call the footman. 'But Father, baby Elizabeth and Catherine have not eaten all of their honey cake yet,' she added despondently.

But her futile questions to each parent in turn hung in the air as the adults began to prepare for their departure from Hinchingbrooke. The absence of an answer usually meant submission to the flowing tide.

As the carriage rattled and swayed its way down the avenue towards the main gate and the handsome medieval town beyond, little Oliver Cromwell fell fast asleep. He was nestled snugly into the folds of his mother's cloak and the aroma of motherhood. He had cheated death this afternoon. Both Elizabeth and Robert thanked the Lord for this blessing on the short journey. His downcast eldest sister wasn't impressed. Of course she would have preferred to be frolicking by the roses still. She would be yet, had Oliver not spoiled the day.

As always, Joanie needed to direct her parents' attention to her, so in the compact confines of the carriage she thought she had the perfect stage, so she began:

To market, to market, to buy a fat hen,
Home again, home again, jiggety-jig.
To market, to market, to buy a fat hog,
Home again, home again, jiggety-jog.
To market, to market to buy a plum cake,
Home again, home again, market is late.

There were other verses that Joanie knew well. But her parents clearly weren't engaging with her entertaining rhyme, so she turned her face away. Instead she began to count the horse's steps and sing the rhyme to the clippity cloppity rhythm now in her head. As it happens, neither Elizabeth nor Robert even noticed that she was singing. They were preoccupied with baby Oliver. Nor did they even notice that all afternoon Joanie had been coughing or that now her petite seven-year-old body was glistening all over with sweat.

Chapter Two

The principal face of Hinchingbrooke house looked to all intents and purposes like it had been fired on by an eleven-foot barreled demi-culverin with several 30-pound shot for numerous hours. That is, to judge by the amount of rubble and smashed dressed-stones that now littered the entire house forecourt. The dining room at ground level and the bed chamber on the first floor were completely exposed to the elements. Stone masons with calloused hands unfurled blueprints and discussed window jambs, carved mullions and leaded glass amid the dust of the dismantled wall section of the house; the very part of the wall that Caesar the chimpanzee had once climbed so effortlessly four years earlier. Now demolished. Not, however, by accident. Very much by design.

Just two days previously the Golden Knight had conceived of a rather precarious notion. A notion that was now highly time-sensitive and to most people nigh on impossible to accomplish. When they learned of it, the majority in the town were of the opinion that it simply could not be done. His house staff and the gardeners were of the same mind. All this upheaval for naught? Cynicism prevailed wherever the subject was raised.

Queen Elizabeth I had died childless on 24 March, 1603. It was now the beginning of July. With the surreptitious assistance of Sir Henry's cronies within the royal court, he had just learned that the date of the coronation had been set. King James VI of Scotland would soon be on his way from Edinburgh to London to be crowned King James I of England, Ireland and Scotland on the twenty-fifth of the month. The royal train would be passing the gates of the old house en route. The temptation to inveigle the king and his entourage to stay overnight was impossible for Sir Henry to resist.

The first royal visit had been such a spectacular success for the family. That was almost forty years ago now. The house looked tired. It needed rejuvenation. But there was an immense obstacle – there were just three weeks to go before the king was due to travel. The serious concerns that were being voiced almost universally to make Hinchingbrooke appear and feel palatial, in just three weeks, seemed very well founded. Because right now, the manor house looked like a besieged fortification that was ripe for storming by armed forces on a chaotic war-torn battleground.

The first four years of Oliver Cromwell's life had passed uneventfully. Despite reaching his sixty-sixth year, and being severely constrained by various age-related ailments, his grandfather, Sir Henry's mental health had not deteriorated. His intellectual faculties were as strident as ever. But deep down he knew that he was no longer fully capable of organising the momentous event himself. He had certainly not lost his ability for foolish impetuosity. But there were limits. Limits he needed to acknowledge. Back when Queen Elizabeth had visited, he was thirty-nine years younger.

To be done to his satisfaction, Sir Henry was well aware that royal visits made quite a dent in the Cromwell family coffers. But this time he really wanted to impress his august guests. He knew that the benefits would bristle through the coming years. He knew the family would reap the societal rewards. The respect that hosting a royal visit can command in aristocratic circles was, in his opinion, simply unparalleled. His plans to impress were commendable; he would construct a semi-circular bow window. This would be more appropriate to the character of a house that would accommodate royalty once more. The principal rooms would also be refurbished. The king would sleep in the chamber overlooking the lawns with the new window framing a fresh vista of his modest estate without. However, the challenge of the short timeframe had the potential to thwart his plans. But it was much too late now to go back on his decision once it was made. He simply needed to focus on a solution to ensure it would be completed in time.

Toying with his clay pipe, he sat in his withdrawing room. The dining room furniture had been temporarily installed there due to the building work. For the size of the house, the room was compact. The dark oak panelling on each wall incorporated classical Italian elements; two large pilasters gave the appearance of supporting columns on either side of the fireplace under which two caryatids were placed to support the generous oak mantle above. Three smoothly-carved arches sprung from the mantle high up over the fireplace and emphasised the European influence on the woodcraft. The geometric framework of square-shaped panels at accurate intervals around the entire room completed the wooden ornamentation. To the right of the luxuriant fireplace a hanging tapestry depicting Adam and Eve in the garden of Eden added a bright visage to an otherwise austere ambiance. Gazing out towards the front lawns, Sir Henry was swimming deeply in a sea of thoughts about the work that was to be carried out in the coming weeks. What if he were to fail? What then? He got quite a start when his son Oliver entered the room with a suave, wide swing of the oak panelled door; his usual flamboyant entrance.

'What has been the delay in your coming? It is past three hours now since I sent my note. You must realise that our time is limited!'

'I apologise, Father, I had some matters to attend to.'

'Harrumph. There are no matters more considerable than this one. The mason and his men say they will need to work day and night. The carpenter has asked for more money. I have ordered more beeswax candles to facilitate the work. Brayfield, the chandler, will bring them this afternoon. We cannot afford to waste even one hour.'

'Beeswax? Would tallow candles not suffice? Have you considered what the total outlay of the undertaking will be as of yet?'

'Hmm,' said his father formulating his thoughts. 'Sit, Oliver.'

Oliver strode dutifully across the heavy elm floorboards, placed his felt capotain on the convex of one of twelve damask-covered walnut chairs around the table, and sat as instructed. He knew by his demeanour that Sir Henry was about to answer this basic question more effusively than the asker had intended.

'How old were you, Oliver, when our glorious Queen came to stay? Three summers? Four?'

'I have no memory of the occasion, Father. I was but an infant of two years. Yet, I am aware that the occurrence has acquired a celebrated status in the entire Huntingdonshire area.'

'This could be another momentous time for we Cromwells, Oliver. How many families in England can lay claim to hosting a royal guest, much less *two* royal guests? It would be very few, let me say it. There are many happy prospects to be foreseen when one has played host to a reigning monarch. This family's reputation has been enhanced through the years since Good Queen Bess slept in the chamber that would become your very own bed chamber. How covetous do you think the Montagus have been of our legacy? How do you think we have gained so much ground in the theatre of governments and policymaking? This opens doors my son. It opens them wide. To the royal court. To the seats of power. To the makers of policy themselves. The Lord has seen fit to present us with another opportunity for preeminence. And we must seize this chance. The investment we make now will be paid back tenfold as the years pass. And it will be *you* who will harvest the dividends.'

'Then may all the candles be of beeswax. Let the Montagus tolerate the tallow!'

The two men laughed heartily at this, but mostly because of the relief they felt that they were each of the same mind. In that instant Oliver knew that his father's audacious concept was the right thing to do. This wasn't about a three-week disruption to normality. It was about decades of attainment. And it would emphasise yet again, that the Montagus were the subordinate titled family in the area. They would remain that way for some time to come, should his father's design come to fruition. There had always been tension between the Cromwells and the Montagus because of an ancient land dispute and the scars had never healed. He began to be amused by the idea of informing Baron Montagu of nearby Kimbolton that a monarch would be accommodated at Hinchingbrooke for a *second* time. Envy, he reflected, was one of the seven deadly sins.

'Well then,' replied his father, 'You must know that I have to step back, and you have to step forward? This will be your legacy, Oliver, not mine. I am old. You and your children are the ones who will reap the rewards of this occasion. You must take control of this undertaking and ensure that it happens.'

'Yes, I am inclined to agree with you, Father,' said Oliver who had clearly foreseen this conversation. He was glad it was Sir Henry who had raised the subject and not he. 'Let me be about this business. But if it pleases the good Lord above, you will be with us yet for many years to come.'

'That would indeed be a blessing! And three weeks hence, on the happy day, you can look directly into the eyes of Edward Montagu as we feast with royalty and you will see what form resentment really takes. Of course Baron and Baroness Montagu must be among the company. All the nobility in the county shall be invited!' replied Sir Henry.

The following three weeks were fraught with a vast multitude of challenges as the building of the bow window and the refurbishment of the primary rooms at Hinchingbrooke were carried out as expeditiously as humanly possible. Despite his administrative acumen there were many moments when Sir Oliver feared that he would let his father down. Extra financial demands were made by some of the rogue tradesmen as they preyed on the time limitation anxieties of their employer. But during those moments, Sir Oliver was always there to provide a solution to whatever the obstacle. The project proceeded unabated throughout every single day. Thanks to the beeswax candles, throughout every single night. Hindrances were overcome with the solicitation of more money. It took over fifty men almost twenty uncompromising days to do it. By 22 July, just one day before the king was due at its front gates the now perfectly resplendent Hinchingbrooke House was ready for its regal guests.

It was just before noon on 23 July when the royal retinue reached the manor house in the warm midday light. Sir Oliver had chosen to greet his auspicious guests at the main entrance. Sir Henry was seated to the right of the main portico, next to the new bow window. The cortege consisted of over a hundred personnel. Courtiers, their servants and royal guards fussed about as the royal carriage, drawn by four white mares made its way along the main avenue towards the house. Queen Anne's ladies-in-waiting were ushered around the back to enter the house furtively. The principal carriage halted on the forecourt.

Sir Henry had the presence of mind to absorb the scene. It was one that he never thought would happen again in his lifetime. Soon they would be feasting, making merry. They would be indulging in stimulating conversation with the man who will be crowned king of England in two days from now. As well as the expense of the bow window and the other rooms, he had procured lavish gifts to present to the royal couple. Horses, hounds and a large golden chalice that was inscribed to mark the occasion. He was convinced that the outlay would be outmatched by the dividend.

Sir Oliver stood to attention on the doorsteps with his immediate family around him. He hoped that the expenditure would be worth it. He patiently waited for the king and queen to alight from the royal carriage.

Robert and Elizabeth Cromwell and their four children stood

to the other side of Sir Oliver. It was four years now since little Joanie had died. Influenza was a ruthless child killer. Doctor Simcott had done his best for her. But the Lord must have wanted Joanie more than Elizabeth did. That was something that Elizabeth could still not comprehend. On the day of her death, a feeble and frail little Joanie had kept asking when she was going to the Lord. And what would she ever say to him? She had hoped that there would be other children to play with in heaven. But she would certainly miss her mother and sisters quite a bit. Through her intolerable pain, Elizabeth had tried to assure her beautiful, ebullient daughter that herself and her brother Henry would have a wonderful time with the Lord and his angels; that Henry would be glad of her company and that the Lord would love her just as much as her parents had done. She had also reminded Joanie that herself and her father would be looking forward to joining them as soon as they had completed the Lord's work here on earth. What Elizabeth hadn't been prepared for on that fateful day, however, was the way Joanie's final words in this world completely ripped her heart asunder. Leaning over her delicate little frame and clasping both of her hands as tightly as her infirmity would allow, she watched as little Joanie had smiled at her mother, and then slowly began her last rehearsal to make the Lord smile:

> *To market, to market, to buy a fat hen,*
> *Home again, home again, jiggety-jig.*
> *To market, to market, to buy a fat hog,*
> *Home again, home again, j i g e t y – j o g.*

She had then gone limp and closed her eyes. Despite the futile screeches of her devastated mother, she had departed her short life on this earth, and, Elizabeth hoped, entered into the Kingdom of Heaven.

It had been just two years later in 1601 that Elizabeth had

given birth to Margaret. Baby Anna was born in 1602. Today the Cromwell children were all dressed in their Sunday finery. They were under strict instructions to behave as the royal couple stepped down from the royal carriage and approached Sir Oliver. The company were now bowing to meet his gracious majesty the king and her gracious majesty, the Queen.

While all of the adults in the assembly were focusing on their airs and graces nobody noticed the three-year-old boy pull away from the hand-grip of one of the female servants. He proceeded to walk impishly towards Elizabeth and Robert's children. The strange boy's black hair was neatly tied up and he had a crisp white ruff around his neck. He wore a white slashed doublet with lavish gold braiding on the front that was pointed at the waist, white silk trousers with gold motifs on each outside leg, with points at the knee and a tiny pair of folded-down suede leather boots.

The four-year-old Oliver Cromwell, whose attire was much more dull, wore a black sugarloaf hat, a dark brown jacket with no adornments but with plain white linen sleeves On his feet he wore wide-topped brown leather boots that were scuffed at the toes.

Little Oliver had never seen such a child as this. Where did he come from? What was he doing here? Would this odd-looking new boy be able to play games like his sisters would sometimes play with him? As he was thinking about these things, the precocious boy dressed in gold and white came over closer to him. The child then said the word 'dirty' and slapped Oliver on the side of the face, leaving his cheek stinging sharply. In response, Oliver punched the boy directly on his nose with a clenched fist. The child fell back with the force of the blow. A stream of blood ran down the child's silk doublet.

It was the first time that Oliver Cromwell had caused Charles Stuart's blood to spill. The second time would shock the entire world.

Chapter Three

The day that Oliver Cromwell almost died for the second time in his young life, began like any other school day. He was by this time eleven years old. The afternoon lesson was in full swing. The school master was a fiery man with eyes, gestures, words and a religious zeal that could stir the souls of his pupils into a burning fever. 'And then, imagine this, children; the ill-fated Cathars, men, women, children, boys and girls just like you, and poor little defenceless babies were all cut down by the Church's crusaders. Massacred in cold blood. The cold steel blades of the cruel attackers' swords cutting through the soft, warm flesh of the mere innocents. There was no mercy shown by the Pope's followers. No mercy whatever.'

The tiny Huntingdon Grammar School stood facing on to the town's market square and directly across the street from the All Saints Church. The one-roomed building was all that was left of a former medieval hospital that once occupied the site. Its convalescent past as a much larger edifice meant a number of arches and architectural embellishments high up on its walls seemed grossly disproportionate to its now reduced size.

Educator Thomas Beard stood in the centre of the classroom with his fifteen pupils a captive audience. In the slanted, dusty sunbeams with shafts of afternoon light pouring into the rustic old room, they were transfixed on his every word. His voice rose to a crescendo and fell to a hushed whisper as he paused for a few seconds to let the final message sink in. 'The entire village was laid to waste. The streets flowed red with blood. Those they did not slay by the sword they burned alive in the marketplace. And all because the Cathars would not conform to the Roman Church!'

The children knew by the way the school master had constructed the tale that a ghastly finale was inevitable. It was yet another account of fire, brimstone and atrocity committed by the Church of Rome from the repertoire of the Huntingdon clergyman. And all in the name of God! These juvenile lives were malleable yet. He would purge them of any present and future complacent ways. This was the time to do just that. This was their impressionable years. Their years ahead would be dictated by the Old and New testament. They would not need a pope, or a bishop, or a priest in their lives. They just needed to be 'pure' and have a close relationship with God. It was his vocation to set them out on this path to righteousness. Clearly Puritans were God's chosen people.

Beard stood aloft and engaged his audience. 'Now, is it not the verdict of history that popes were murderous tyrants? Is that much not certain? We cannot argue with the facts that antiquity has bequeathed to us. But what of bishops? What can be said of bishops of the Roman faith? Surely, they were beyond reproach as servants of God?'

Oliver sat at a double desk with his friend Valentine Walton. The Waltons lived on the outskirts of the town. Even though Valentine was five years older than Oliver, the latter looked up to the former with boyhood admiration. They had gravitated towards each other and discovered that they had so much in common. Every so often Oliver would find himself in a dark mood. It was a regular occurrence. There wasn't always a reason for it that he could put his finger on. But Valentine never seemed to mind it. So they bonded very well. Despite the clear message contained in the eighth commandment, outside the classroom, the two friends were gaining quite a reputation locally as the orchard thieves. Boys will be boys. There wasn't an orchard around that hadn't been raided by the duo. They enjoyed the adrenaline rush. The apples were just the means to the end.

The pupils were familiar with Dr Beard's descriptive portrayals of the transgressions of the Roman faith throughout history. Oliver was even more familiar with Beard. The school master cleric had become a close friend of the Cromwell family over the years. Today Oliver knew that he was about to describe what he considered were more abhorrent offences of the Roman bishops: simony, nepotism and absenteeism. Oliver also knew that Beard would use evocative detail to elicit the revulsion of his pupils. Beard had done this often before. Even at his young age, Oliver was familiar with Beard's book *The Theatre of God's Judgements*, in which Beard contended that sinners and persecutors will be punished in this world as well as the next.

When Beard had finished talking, the imaginations of his listeners were filled with images of the cruel Roman clerics effecting a policy of destruction and wanton murder all over the world. He had taught them that the Pope was the ultimate despot. The Pope was not in fact pro-Christ but was the anti-Christ. They simply couldn't understand why anybody would want to follow the doctrines of such a tyrant. The words 'popery' and 'Catholic' would conjure up all sorts of images of evil; images that Thomas Beard had expertly crafted and then delivered to their fertile imaginations. According to Beard, they were to be very thankful that Henry VIII had cut England's ties with Rome. And that Catholicism was no longer tolerated by right-minded people in the country any more. They were also to be wary of those who would support such a despotic regime should they encounter any in the outside world.

When the lesson had ended, as he did every day, Oliver fetched his sisters' capes. Elizabeth, now 15, Catherine, now 13 and nine-year-old Margaret were much better students than Oliver was. But he was a dutiful brother. Bidding their goodbyes to Dr Beard, they stepped out of the school and on to a bustling Huntingdon High Street. The daily sensation of freedom with this simple act would never diminish over the entirety of their formative years. The market was in full swing. It was populated by preoccupied adults who experienced freedom all day long, every single day. Now out of sight of the school master the horseplay could begin. Oliver pulled the hat from Valentine's head and pretended to fling it into the street.

'What will we do if we meet the Pope on the way home?' asked Margaret as they began to walk. 'Will you be able to get Father's sword, Oliver, and chop his head off before he gets us?'

'Oh, don't be concerned, Margaret, the Pope doesn't live in Huntingdon,' replied Oliver as he passed the hat back to Valentine.

'Maybe he does, Oliver,' interjected Valentine toying with the girls. 'Perhaps he's positioned at his potato stall over there, in the market, dressed in disguise.'

'Now, don't pay any attention to young Mr Walton's fantasies, Margaret. I think we would know it, if the Pope lived in Huntingdon disguised as a market hawker,' said Oliver.

'But he didn't live in France either, Oliver,' chimed in Catherine. 'And look what happened to the children in Beziers!'

'It is most unlikely that we will ever meet the Pope in Huntingdon,' repeated Oliver trying to reassure them. 'But wait, is that a Roman bishop I see chasing along the street behind us?'

The girls screamed with delight and broke into a run. The four darted along the cobbled street laughing loudly. Oliver pretended that the bishop was following. Valentine chased Margaret to the other side of the street passing two men who were out for a stroll. He shouted, 'Run, Margaret. There's two more! There are bishops everywhere!'

'They're gaining! Quicker! We must be quicker now,' shouted Oliver at the giddy girls as they reached the front door of their High Street home. The Cromwell residence was literally just a stone's throw from the Huntingdon Grammar School further along the street. It was six years now since Oliver's grandfather Sir Henry Cromwell of Hinchingbrooke had died. The manor house and the abundant parkland domain had passed to Sir Oliver. Oliver's father Robert's dwelling was a modest, half-timbered, two-storeyed house with a small farmholding at the

21

rear. This was the land that Robert cultivated to provide for his family. A small brew-house was located by the edge of a brook called the Hinchin that cut through the land. The brook loaned its name to Sir Oliver's recent property inheritance. One of a handful in Huntingdon, the brew-house produced beer that was sold to the local populace to supplement the family's income.

Robert had once stood in the local elections and became a Member of Parliament for Huntingdon. But politics did not suit his calm disposition. He served one term only. Robert preferred the tranquil fields of Huntingdon to the noisy halls of Westminster. He loved to stroll among the gorse hills of an evening where foxes gave chase and grouse and pheasants rustled in the hedgerows. To him, the plough was king, and he was happiest while working amongst the hay. Some years, if he applied himself to the work steadfastly, he could yield an annual income of three hundred pounds. This meant that the wolf was not a frequent visitor to the Cromwells' door. He constantly hoped that his only son, Oliver, would take an interest in the farm, but that had not happened thus far. It was wild oats that his son seemed sure to sow in the coming years. Oliver's interest in his school books was cursory. His interest in recreation was not. But surely that was bound to change.

'Good day to you, Father,' said Oliver as the party of five encountered Robert in front of the house toiling over his scythe with a well-worn whetstone. From his bowed position, Robert raised his knee from where he had the tool pinned down. He looked up at the welcome troupe and smiled. Before he could say anything, Margaret burst out, 'Oh Father, Father, one of the Pope's cruel bishops has followed us home. And the Pope himself is selling potatoes in the market square! You must come now with your scythe and chop both of their heads off, or I will never be able to sleep again!'

'I think I understand,' said her father, smiling at Margaret and moving his focus towards the two boys. 'Well, gentlemen.

What mischief is this? I suspect one, or both of you is responsible for the prank at play here?'

'Yes, it was our trick, Father. Dr Beard's last lesson of the day was about the evils of popery. Valentine and I played a hoax on the girls to take advantage of their fright. It was really very humorous.'

The elegant farmer leaned down towards three girls. Their clear eyes were wide, and their breath was still short from the exertion. 'You must never worry, girls. Your mother and I are always here to protect you. No ill shall ever befall you as long as we have breath left in our bodies.' The girls seemed reassured with their kind father's words. He was the destroyer of their fears. Their leveller of mountains.

'Now, Oliver. Please run to the market and establish the cost of the Pope's potatoes. I am very curious to learn it!' joked Robert.

'With your permission,' said Oliver when the laughter had died down and the girls had disappeared into the house, 'Valentine and I have planned to seek swans' eggs by the river this afternoon. I expect I will return before we dine. May I go, Father?'

'I would have preferred that you helped me with the crop of barley in the second field, Oliver. But I understand that the ways of young boys are now different to what they were in my time. Of course, you may go. But you know you must be careful at the river. It is never as docile as it seems.'

Emboldened by the adult's permission for an afternoon of abandon, Oliver and Valentine made their way back along the High Street. They passed the school heading towards the river at the end of the town. They managed to resist the temptation of the tangy fruit delights in the orchards they passed. Today was not a day for stealing apples.

'How do you manage with so many girls in the family, Oliver?' asked Valentine as they walked. 'Will you have to approve of all of their suiters?'

'Oh, I expect so. I think I might ask each of them to take one of Dr Beard's examinations before allowing any of them to walk out with any one of my sisters,' joked Oliver. 'But really, Valentine, I don't know why any man would want to marry any of them. They can be so peevish and vexing.'

'Do you really believe so? I cannot agree. I think they are all charming. Indeed, captivating. You are very fortunate to have such appealing kinfolk.'

'Am I ?' said Oliver sarcastically. 'Well then, since I have such a surplus, and you have such a dearth, I am happy to discard one or two. How many would you like? Three? Four?'

'You'll understand when you're older, Oliver, that girls have many traits, and while peevish and vexing might be two minor ones, there are many others that are very desirable.'

'Minor ones? You have so much to discover! I have a feeling that you have strangely forgotten that swans' eggs are also very desirable, Master Walton. And that this is our undertaking for today. You are free to take as many of my sisters as you desire away. But not this day. On the morrow! Now, let us away to the river!'

The three-hundred-year-old bridge just beyond the town crossed over the sleepy Great River Ouse. The bridge was built of stone throughout. It had six pointed arches with cutwaters and refuges on both sides. As they approached the bridge, they could see a young man standing on its crest, leaning against the wall and staring into the waters below. Dressed in a black ankle-length cassock, which the flush of his youth seemed to belie, he appeared not much older than Valentine. The two orchard thieves approached the man, slightly irritated that he was standing in their spot. They both knew immediately that this was a stranger.

'How now young gentlemen?' said the young man.

'Greetings,' replied Valentine. 'Will you be standing there

for much longer? We need to observe the movements of the swans and the point where you stand is the finest location from which to do this.' Wary of the religious attire, Oliver was happy to allow his older partner-in-crime to engage with the stranger.

Amused by their impudence, the young man decided to tease his interrogators. 'And when you catch one of these swans, will you fly all the way home on its wings?' he asked. Immediately taking a liking to the stranger, Valentine couldn't help asking what his business was in the area. 'Are you passing through? Or is Huntingdon your destination?' asked Valentine.

'Well, if you must know everybody's business, I am the new curate at All Saints Church, and I should be very grateful if you could tell me where I would find this house of God,' the curate said.

As the curate was of the Protestant faith, he had passed the subconscious examination that Oliver had subjected him to. Oliver pointed back the way they had just come. 'Proceed along the High Street and when you come to the market square, All Saints Church is at its furthest end, near the Falcon Inn,' said Oliver. 'It is the only building with a high tower, so it would be difficult to miss,' he added with a wry smile. 'Or you could simply summon one of the swans and have it take you there over the rooftops,' added Valentine with a laugh. Pushing away from the wall, the curate said, 'I thank you both for your wit and your direction and I expect and hope that I will be experiencing your acquaintance again soon.'

The curate started towards the town and the would-be egg robbers immediately got to work. 'I think if I was to stand on the parapet and if you were to hold my legs, I could see deeper into the rushes,' said Oliver excitedly and up he jumped onto the wall of the bridge. Valentine was distracted by the sight of a swan that was flying way off in the distance. He hadn't realised that by now he should have been holding on to Oliver's legs.

It all happened very quickly. The stone capping crumbled

away. Instantaneously Oliver lost his balance. There were several primary sensations that he felt as he tumbled from the bridge into the river. Firstly, came the stumble from the wall. Then the powerless loss of control with nothing now beneath his feet. The dreadfully helpless feeling of weightlessness as he fell through the air anticipating the hostility of the cold water. The utter shock that engulfed him when he crashed through the calm surface of the Great Ouse. In the short time he had had to evaluate his predicament, he hadn't expected the landing to be painful. But he had smacked through the water on the flat of his back. A sharp pain ricocheted through his body. Totally disorientated, he began to flail about in the dark, muddy river. After some long seconds beneath the surface, he managed to get his head out of the water.

Oliver could not swim. Frantically flapping about, his head went under again. He had no idea how to prevent it. The powerful, languid current of the river was fast sweeping him away from the bridge. Managing to surface again, he desperately looked to see if there was anything he could cling on to. Nothing. He had landed in the middle of the wide river. Both shores were too far away. His young body was fast getting tired. With the thrashing about, he wasn't sure if he had the strength to get his head back up, if he were to go under one more time. Up on the bridge, Valentine was screaming Oliver's name. Valentine could not swim either. In that moment of panic he could see no obvious way to help Oliver. He froze, panic-stricken.

Oliver's head disappeared beneath the river surface a third time. This time he swallowed a lot of water as he submerged. Fighting against the heavy, wet clothes that prevented free movement, he was now exhausted. He simply couldn't give up. But he was just an eleven-year-old boy against the colossal forces of nature. As his head disappeared, his hand remained above the water. It was just enough of his body for the curate to clutch. Oliver felt himself being pulled up. He burst out into the air again with a guttural deep breath. In a swift movement, the curate turned him on his back, hooked his arm under Oliver's neck and somehow dragged him to the shore.

It might take some time, but the curate would eventually look Oliver in the eye and tell him that he regretted his actions of that day.

Chapter Four

An eighteen-year-old Oliver sat directly in front of the prostitute. Their knees were touching. There were no words. The commotion from the tavern below was radiating through the fissures in the ancient timber boards of the old wattle and clay building. To the encouragement of raucous cheering, a vulgar female voice from below could clearly be heard singing,

As I walked forth one summer's day,
To view the meadows green and gay
A pleasant bower I espied
Standing fast by the river side,
And in't a maiden I heard cry:
Alas! alas! there's none e'er loved as I.

Oliver was way beyond perceiving any of the din from below. His breeches lay redundant on the floor next to him. His head was rolled back, partly to avoid the odour of the wench's matted hair, partly as a coping mechanism to disengage from the lewd act; the incredibly pleasurable lewd act.

The pace of the prostitute's strokes was steadily increasing, and Oliver knew that the moment was not far off. He tried to control the uncontrollable urge. He wanted it to endure longer this time. Now past her prime, his lady friend was completely in tune with his objective. Eager to relieve her next client of his tuppence, yet showing no signs of impatience whatsoever to her present one, she deftly loosened the strings on her red- and white-laced bodice. Then, with her free hand she released her two breasts from their confinement. As intimate partners often do, her companion intuitively realised that she had raised the stakes by her movements. He looked down and fixed his gaze on her breasts now bouncing liberally in the dim candlelight. The length of the cleavage creases that had now become clear only troubled the seller, not the buyer. When she twisted both of her nipples, he felt the inevitable transformation in his exhilaration and his breath began to quicken. She sensed he was now very close at the sight of her stimulated glands as he stiffened in her hands in response to her bawdy performance.

She gripped him firmer, caught his eyes and stared assertively into his lecherous soul. The confident glare, coupled with the nakedness of her breasts, tipped him over the edge. Within seconds he stood up and she pointed him towards the open room. Abruptly he let go and the entire viscous release splattered across the floor. His body shuddered spontaneously in the fleeting moment of concentrated gratification. Quivering, he made an attempt to steady himself by putting his hand on her shoulder. 'No touching! You ain't allowed to touch!' she roared. Oliver remembered that his budget had only stretched so far. The conditions of sale had indeed been made very clear to him not five minutes earlier. As always, this was the exact point where the guilt of the covenant between the two struck him intensely. It was over again until the next time he could afford it. Despite this stabbing feeling of remorse on every occasion, he knew he would be back for more. The addiction needed to be satiated. His licentious acquaintance knew it too. And for now it was. Oliver had the potential to become a decent customer.

It was six years now since Oliver had almost drowned. His father had managed to partially engage him in some few agricultural pursuits in the intervening period, although Robert wished it were more. It was just three years since Robert and Elizabeth concluded that Oliver's interest in the family brewhouse patently superseded that of his interest in the farm. To avoid future familial complications they had closed the business down. It was the farm that yielded the bulk of the income, so the decision came easily. Two more girls had been added to the Cromwell family in the meantime; Jane was born in 1605 and

Robina in 1607. Elizabeth had given birth to another boy, Robert in 1609, but apart from Oliver, her sons seemed destined not to survive. Robert died of the dreaded influenza after a few weeks. Elizabeth often wondered if it was the fact that Oliver was the only boy among six sisters that resulted in his disorderly behaviour. Were it not for so many heartbreaking setbacks in her married life thus far, she would have been confident that the Lord will surely intervene. She still hoped He would. Her and Robert's pleas to the Almighty for the rehabilitation of their only son were impassioned, and this was the only way she knew to a satisfactory resolution. Preaching directly to the boy had proved futile.

Meanwhile, on 23 April, 1616, two days before his seventeenth birthday, the younger of the Huntingdon orchard thieves had become a student at Sydney Sussex College, Cambridge. Part of the statutes of the college stated that the Masters and the Fellows must be amongst those who abhorred popery. The university was well chosen. One of the first escapades he engaged in to impress his new friends was to leap from the first-floor window of his college accommodation on the north side of Hall Court above Sydney Street to his horse below. He received quite an amount of acclaim on campus when it was understood that he achieved the feat at the first time of asking. Inevitably, rather than take a deep interest in his studies, Oliver found that the extra-curricular activities on offer attracted his attention more. For instance, he proved more than a match for his opponents in any game of cudgeling. The football field was a place where he could release the tensions of the day. He also took part in plays that the students put on and even played the part of the king in one particular production. After a year in the place, he had gained a reputation for being quite the university reprobate.

But it was activities beyond the college gates that interested him more. Now a thickset-bodied adolescent of eighteen years and of considerable strength and average height, Oliver was very attracted to the wider city of Cambridge. There were appreciably more opportunities to pass the time in the university city than in his home town of nearby Huntingdon. To add to that, there were thousands of testosterone-fuelled like-minded young men with whom to enjoy the vast array of attractions. Free from the shackles of his parents and his old fervent school master, whoring and gambling were just two vices that the young Oliver Cromwell had developed a taste for. He had certainly discovered the traits of the fairer sex that Valentine had once spoken of and then some. Other glorious iniquities must surely lay in wait in the city to be discovered.

Now upstairs at the Blue Boar Inn, Oliver hastily pulled his breeches back up and fastened them. He thanked his coconspirator profusely for fulfilling her part of the contract while she ushered him out the door. On the small, rickety landing outside the room a well-dressed elderly gentleman was doing his utmost to turn his face away. Oliver brazenly held the door ajar and said 'After you, my good man. Or should I say, after me!' and he ran down the stairs laughing to rejoin the rumpus.

The room was full of every kind of fellow that was drawn to the comforts that the dilapidated alehouse could provide to assuage their daily struggles. Most of the common trades were represented. The grey render on the walls had dislodged in several large patches and there appeared to be no attempt made to either repair or prevent the rot from advancing. Several of the unruly assemblage, clasping their tankards of ale, were focused on the only female of the company. She was performing on one of the oak tables rasping out another ditty. Oliver was on first name terms with the warbling proprietress. Rapidly-emptying jugs of ale in various sizes lay on the stone-flagged floor. One or two empty ones were tipped over. A motionless drunkard lay face down and prostrate across one of the tables in front of the large fireplace. In a dark corner beyond the fireplace two men sat at a table with playing cards scattered on the table. They were between games. A hunting spaniel lay sleeping at the feet of one of the card players. A single empty stool was set directly opposite the man with the dog.

'Tempus fugit,' laughed Valentine as Oliver returned to his stool and avoided stepping on the dog as he settled. 'Why, it does not seem like you have been absent for more than a moment or two. Has the deed genuinely been completed, or was the hag too drunk again?'

'I can assure you that the accord was concluded effectually. Unfortunately my funds are not so great after an evening at this table. So prudent negotiations were the order of the day in the room above.'

'Aha. I see now. Well, perhaps your fortunes will change as the evening progresses,' replied Valentine.

'Will you two stop whittering on like old maids and can we please play some cards,' said the man with the dog assertively. I like taking money from foolish students, such as the like of you, I do.'

'Unfortunately, my good man, I have spent my last pennies and I have no more for you to take,' said Oliver.

'But you were playing so well,' sneered the man.

'There will be other days. I will return on the morrow and win all of my money back from you, you'll see that I do.'

'Now, Oliver,' said Valentine. 'Perhaps the ale has affected you more than I had anticipated. You will not be able to return to this tavern on the morrow.'

'Oh, yes! Apologies friend, it will be a week at least before I can relieve you of *my* money,' said Oliver to the man.

'It makes no difference whatever to me young lad. Pray tell me, what is all of this secrecy between you? If you have a mind to, that is,' said the man.

'Tomorrow I will wed one of Oliver's sisters,' announced

Valentine. There was a time when he wanted me to take all six, but I have concluded that one is sufficient for my needs,' he laughed.

'Well, then, that calls for some merriment,' said the man raising his mug of ale and standing on the dog's paw as he rose to make the announcement. 'More ale over here,' he shouted to anyone that would listen. But nobody heard.

It was another two hours and after midnight before Oliver and Valentine arrived back at Oliver's Sydney Street lodgings. The gates to the college were locked. Eventually they had managed to acquire more ale. They were both well inebriated. The penny that Valentine slipped to the porter was enough to gain them access to the safety of the compact upper-floor quarters. The money was worth more to the old gatekeeper than the credit of betraying the offenders to the dean. Tattling bought very little food.

'I wonder if I shall ever marry,' said Oliver, as he slumped down on his bed.

'If you ever do, then you will need to give up all of your vices. I'm sure you realise that money is needed to succeed in marriage, and you have an unhappy propensity to allow whatever little you have to slip through your fingers,' replied Valentine.

'Money is but one aspect. But you, above everybody, Valentine, should know that I am a tormented soul. What possible good could I bring to any marriage? I would only bring suffering and anguish. I have sought the Lord but He has never intervened in my life like He has intervened in the lives of others. Before I became a sinner, I had tried to seek the path to righteousness and because I could not discover it, I concluded that God had abandoned me. I am *not* one of his chosen ones.'

'You are still young. There is ample time for the Lord to show you the path. But you will have to repent your sins and change your ways before He would ever consider you worthy. I have

33

been a witness to many of your transgressions, Oliver.'

'Yes, it was good of you to indulge me on this last occasion. It would not be comely of a man of married status to frequent the dens of iniquity that I have frequented since I came to Cambridge. Your visits here have always been a source of pleasure to me. And I am aware that you disapprove of my lifestyle.'

'Disapprove? Yes, you know I do. But it was much better for me to watch over you on the occasions of my visit. I am well aware of your tendency towards melancholy and the anxiety it brings to you. Your parents are happy that I visit you. But I have never revealed the true nature of your misbehaviours to them.'

'I think it's time we slept. Dawn beckons and that three-hour horse ride! Margaret will take a very dim view of me if I keep you late for your wedding,' said Oliver avoiding any detailed talk of his misconducts.

The following day, the twenty-three-year-old Valentine Walton married sixteen-year-old Margaret Cromwell. The ceremony was carried out by Dr Beard. On the evening of the wedding day while the others made merry, Oliver had another bout of anxiety. They had been friends for a long time now. And while Valentine had been welcomed into the Cromwell family by his father, Robert, Oliver feared that things would never be the same between his friend and himself from this day forward. Oliver stayed at home for three more days after the wedding and during that time, his father inveigled him into helping on the farm. While Oliver found it wearisome, he did not want to disappoint his father.

On the fourth day following the wedding, Oliver rode slowly back to Cambridge. It took him a full eight hours and several detours to get there. Following admonishment from his parents about his lack of academic progress, he was in no hurry to get back to college. He was pensive all day. He stopped at a couple of taverns along the way for refreshment for himself and water for his horse. Returning to his studies didn't seem such an attractive proposition. But he made up his mind that he really should try to turn his life around. Arriving at Sydney Sussex around 8pm and after installing his horse in the college stable yard, he headed for his quarters. At the top of the stairs as he approached the door to his room he could see that it was ajar. 'How now?' he called before walking in. He heard a movement inside the room, but nobody appeared at the door. He stiffened his body and pushed the door open. A figure of a man could be seen in the fading evening light from the street outside sitting on his bed. He could just about make out the familiar figure. Oliver was astounded. It was Valentine. What could possibly have brought his new brother-in-law here? 'Ah Oliver,' Valentine said. 'I missed you along the road. I bring sad tidings. It is your father. After you left this morning, your poor father fell dead. Your time at university has ended. I am to take you home.'

Chapter Five

Oliver's heart was thumping in his chest. The noise around him was deliciously deafening. The circular arena was packed with a baying crowd. Oliver was just as wound up as his fellow gamblers were. He watched the scene below him unfold. It was a frenzied cauldron of chaos. It was a delightful escape from mundanity. The drama of this particular place surpassed any conventional card game. The peril of losing was perennially eclipsed by the glorious possibility of winning. That all too infrequent moment when everything came together. All of the social classes were represented. The spectators were crammed on to tiers of wooden seats that rose up to overlook a spherical earthen floor. In the centre of the floor an enraged bull was tied to a wooden stake. The bull stomped intermittently on the ground, snorting ominously. Three dog owners held their ferocious bullmastiffs on ropes at a safe distance from the bull. For now. A regular punter, Oliver, was familiar with all of the dogs' names: Demon, Beast and Killer.

The dogs had been bred for this moment. Beast and Killer were howling at the bull and frantically trying to break away from their owners. Demon seemed more calm but was stiff with intent and snarled menacingly at his bovine quarry. His teeth were bared. Oliver's money was on Demon. He had won money on Demon before. A silver collar worth ten shillings awaited the winning hound. Oliver stood to gain twenty pounds if Demon was the one to bring the bull down.

At the signal from the bull ring owner, Killer was let loose and leapt towards the bull. Oliver had also won money on Killer before. But he would not anymore. Within seconds Killer was flung high into the air by the animal's horns and he thumped to the ground dead. There was a wild cheer from the majority of the watchers. The excitement was fever pitched. Killer's chest had been gored open by the bull with a deft flick of his head on his first approach. One down, two to go. The brutal spectacle was thrilling. Oliver loved the mayhem of it all. He was revelling in the barbarous pageantry. The odds for victory had now lessened by a third.

In a flash, Beast was loose and was tearing at the bull's hind leg flesh. The bull was kicking and stamping, trying to shake Beast's firm jaws from his thigh. Blood was smeared all over the dog's mouth as he released his jaws. Immediately he attacked the blind side of the bull again mercilessly. He was buoyed up by the cheering mob. Beast was allowed fifteen minutes of ripping the bull's hide to shreds. He was fast. He was agile. He darted at the bull with alacrity. It took three experienced men to pull Beast away.

Now it was Demon's turn. Larger in size than his counterparts, Demon took a different approach. He seemed to sense the length of the rope that held the bull. He ran in circles just out of reach, every now and then snapping at the bull's rear and making a fresh tear. After ten minutes of teasing, the bull was tiring. He went in for the kill. Rushing at his prey, Demon sunk his teeth into the bull's badly lacerated hind quarters. With a wild tug from the hound, the bull lost his balance and he dropped to his knees. Instantly, Demon changed tack and leaped wildly at the bull's neck. He tore the beast's neck flesh ruthlessly. Blood from the bull's veins splashed all over the dog. The crowd went wild. Demon had won. Oliver had won. The bull had lost.

Later that night, back in his bed, twenty pounds to the good, Oliver was still roused by the evening's entertainment. The uproar from the bull ring still rang in his ears. It wasn't until the early hours that the adrenaline level in his body reduced sufficiently to allow him to sleep.

It was three years now since his father had died. With the breadwinner gone, the onus to provide a livelihood for the Cromwell family fell firmly on the shoulders of its only male member. The farm needed attending to. Attending to it was now the future of the only man of the household. Upon returning home, Oliver also had found himself providing emotional support to his widowed mother in the early days after his father's sudden passing. After losing two sons, a daughter, and now her life partner, Elizabeth was yet again grief-stricken. However, despite his proclivities, the relationship between prudent mother and profligate son became stronger. They both grew to understand each other better. Elizabeth came to depend on Oliver more with the passing years. She tried to accept that this was all part of God's divine plan. During daylight hours Oliver did his best to play the part of the obedient son and the eager farmer.

Throughout the intervening years the slowly maturing orchard thief managed to eke out a living for the family from the little farmstead just off the Huntingdon High Street. When she eventually managed to think about it, she was frustrated that Oliver's academic potential had seemed destined to remain unfulfilled. Two years after his father's death, on the advice of his mother, he had tried his hand once more at furthering his studies. He had been accepted into Lincoln's Inn, one of the Inns of Court in London. But after a short while he ended up coming back to Huntingdon. The yoke of husbandry represented the routine stability he had fought so hard to avoid. But he couldn't. If this was to be his lot in life, he would be resigned to it rather than embrace it.

Now spending the summer evenings more readily in the rolling pastures, the winter evenings were a different proposition. As well as the local bull ring, to seek stimulation he found himself more and more attracted to the Falcon Inn in the market square. The ale was good and the gambling better. The stakes for the card and dice games were not as high as those he had once experienced in his Cambridge days. But the prospect of winning was simply too strong to ignore.

One bitterly cold evening, the twenty-year-old farmer stepped from the market square into the vestibule of the Falcon Inn. It was a diminutive space that was really only designed to protect the tavern interior from the Huntingdon weather as it barked acrimoniously at the door of the inn. But Oliver's path was blocked. He was standing cheek to jowl with a large-framed man, whom he did not recognise in the darkened passageway. Oliver immediately stood aside to allow the stranger to pass. But the man remained still.

'Young Cromwell, is it not?' said the man fiddling with his gloves, his tone immediately appearing to be condescending.

'You have me at a disadvantage,' replied the surprised farmer removing his hat.

'I had been informed that I might encounter your good self in this dreary establishment on some occasion and it seems that my information was correct,' said the man, ignoring Oliver.

He tried again. 'I don't believe I've had the pleasure,' said Oliver offering the stranger his hand.

'I hear you play at dice,' announced the man still ignoring Oliver's attempt at salutations. 'I do believe the evening may prove worthwhile yet,' he added, and he turned back inside with a swagger that suggested he was a cut above.

Oliver followed the man inside, hoping that he might be spending some of the offensive stranger's money before he found himself in the vestibule on his outward journey.

'I have returned to the game to give you all a fair chance,' declared the man to the four noisy locals around a table in the centre of the room who were nursing their ales in the middle of a game of dice.

As he turned again to face Oliver, now in the glow of the rush lights attached to the wall of the inn, it struck Oliver that the man's face was somewhat familiar. The name only registered when the dice player spoke.

'Of course, Mr Montagu, please resume your seat.'

Oliver was suddenly pleased that he had decided to venture out that evening. It was a Montagu. And it was a Montagu who wanted to play dice. Oliver had never been directly involved in the Hinchingbrooke Cromwell's feud with the Montagus. He was always at some remove from the enduring quarrel. But he had seen various members of the Montagu family around town over the years. The grudge gave them an unpleasant air, whether real or perceived. This present Montagu was one of the younger generation. Oliver's experience of him to date perfectly fitted whatever perception he might have had of the Montagus. Turns out it was real. Not perceived. Approaching the table, Oliver tapped the purse in his breast pocket. He had to ensure that the coins he had placed there before he left home had not somehow mysteriously disappeared.

'Edward Montagu at your service,' declared the man as he turned and clasped Oliver's hand. 'Oliver, I believe? You have quite the reputation as a ne'er-do-well you know?'

With every word that Edward Montagu spoke, Oliver was taking more and more of a disliking to his soon-to-be dice rival. They both took their places at the table and one of the men took control of the dice as the setter. The game began. They played Hazard. Oliver was two pounds up after just five minutes. Within an hour Oliver had an additional twenty-five pounds, to the money already in his purse, mainly due to the way Montagu seemed to raise the stakes at every opportunity. Three of the dice players had dropped out due to the high wagers. Oliver was on a roll. He knew that the crunch time was coming where he would have to either quit or bet his entire winnings on one game. It was a system he had played often before. When it worked, it was an excellent evening. When it didn't, well, that was gambling was it not? But tonight, he felt that his luck was in.

'You play very well,' said Edward.

'Praise indeed,' replied Oliver.

'I hope you are not considering taking your leave before giving me a chance to recoup my losses?'

This was the opportunity Oliver was waiting for.

'I fear I must be leaving directly. But before I do, I will give you the chance to win your money back. Shall we say, no wager less than five pounds? And just one more play?'

The dice was thrown for the final game and now it was down to just how high the two players were willing to go before one of them capitulated. The five pounds increments soon brought the stake to forty pounds and Oliver's adrenaline was pumping hard. He had no intentions of folding any time soon. When the sum reached ninety pounds he knew that if he lost there was no possible way he could have paid his opponent with the money in his purse. But he was still willing to proceed, the thrill was just so liberating. At one hundred pounds Edward smiled enigmatically across the table at Oliver.

'I think the primary three-digit figure is a civilised mark upon which to rest, don't you, Mr Cromwell?' he said. Oliver was exhilarated. The gamble was exquisite, and he was caught in its talons. 'If you say so, Mr Montagu, if you say so.'

'One more throw of the dice then setter,' said Edward. Oliver needed at least a four. The dice rolled and came up with two dots. Oliver had lost.

He knew it was ungentlemanly to suggest another game. Having experienced losses often in the past, he knew well how to handle the disappointment. Forcing a smile in the direction of his rival he said, 'You seem to have the advantage over me again, Mr Montagu. Except on this occasion, the matter is significantly more weighty. Please accept my congratulations.'

'I trust that you can pay me now?' said Edward. Oliver hated that he did not have the funds on his person to pay his debt, but a wager is a wager and he knew exactly what to do. 'Innkeeper,' he shouted, 'Some wine for the dice table, if you will!' As the wine arrived and Edward was distracted by the activity, Oliver told one of his farmhands that he was to rush to his home and procure thirty pounds from his mother. The man returned within ten minutes and slipped Oliver the money. The debt was paid over as the wine was imbibed. The two men departed through the vestibule together, this time more fluidly than before. Outside, as they were each going in different directions, they stood momentarily together.

'We must do this again sometime soon,' said Edward exceedingly pleased with his evening's exertions.

'I quite agree,' replied Oliver, although not so keen to set a date for a return match as yet. He was still smarting from the substantial loss.

'You do realise that I am aware of the fact that you sent your man for the extra funds, Mr Cromwell?'

'Well, I had not intended to encounter such a formidable dice player such as your good self at the Falcon Inn on an idle Tuesday,' said Oliver. Although he wanted to say so much more. So much more about how Edward repulsed him. About how his family must surely be of questionable integrity. Especially now after such a hefty reverse. 'I think paying my liability was the important aspect of this evening, Mr Montagu. Now, if, you'll forgive me, I will take my leave of you.'

'Ah yes, I understand. The victor and the vanquished. Recreation dynamics are interesting, are they not? Pray tell me before you depart, how is that uncle of yours? How many times has the king now made visits to Hinchingbrooke? I have counted at least three in the last seven years. Accommodating the king is a most expensive business, is it not Mr Cromwell?'

Uncomfortable now with the way the conversation had turned, Oliver sensed a provocation in Edward's question. He was not about to get involved in a conversation about his wider family. Certainly not with a Montagu. 'I bid you goodnight,' said Oliver and began to walk away.

As he was about to make the left-hand turn at All Saints

Church towards home, Edward's parting words made him stop and turn around, stunned. 'Oh, just one final thing. It was providential that I should encounter you this evening. Today of all days. Just this morning I had the absolute pleasure of making your uncle homeless. Too much money spent on entertaining monarchs, it seems. Very foolish. Hinchingbrooke now belongs to the Montagus. Your family will never play host to royalty again. Yes, a very good day indeed. Goodnight, Mr Cromwell.'

Chapter Six

It was Oliver's wedding day. He was at the church. But he suddenly refused to get married.

'It's no good,' said Oliver to his sister Margaret. 'There will be no wedding! I am overwhelmed. I simply cannot proceed.' It was 22 August, 1620. They were standing outside Saint Giles' Church, Cripplegate, London, on a hot August afternoon. The square limestone west tower of the old medieval church rose high above their heads. The guests were all inside waiting for the bride to arrive. As usual, the panic attack came without a warning.

'Now, Oliver, Beth will be here in a few moments. You must gather your faculties and focus your thoughts. Beth is going to be the best wife a man could ever have. Let us return inside and you will feel better then,' said Margaret. None of his sisters could ever fully fathom his disorder. Oliver's breathing was hard. He didn't even hear what Margaret had said. He felt light-headed. He was sweating. He was losing control. His stomach felt sick. In his head something catastrophic was about to happen. There was nothing he could do about it. He tried to tell himself that it would pass. But the feeling of doom took a firm grip.

Oliver had chosen not to tell Beth about the prostitutes. He was also careful not to mention the gambling. Although she had come to suspect something was awry. He did, however, tell her about the anxiety. The bouts of depression that came upon him with no warning whatever. There was no way he could hide that. She totally sympathised with his plight. So that was a relief. It had been a whirlwind liaison. He had never made a connection such as this with any other person in his life. They talked about everything. Sometimes late into the night. They had so much in common. He knew she was a virgin. Noble ladies were expected to behave impeccably. Beth always behaved impeccably. Furthermore, Beth had immediately earned Elizabeth's deference right from the start. The fact that Beth's family were more financially secure than Oliver's also played a part in the betrothal. Beth's father, James Bourchier, was a fur and leather dealer. It was really irrelevant that Beth was two years older than Oliver. It was just over a year now since they had met at a dinner party at his Aunt Joan's house at Little Stambridge, Essex. Oliver hadn't wanted to go, but his mother had insisted. Oliver often wondered if his meeting Beth was really a coincidence. But he was perfectly happy not to challenge the genesis of what, up to now, had been his destiny.

His mother emerged from the church wondering where the groom had gone. 'Well then, Oliver, what say you? Come inside. Your bride will be arriving any moment now,' said Elizabeth not fully appreciating her son's condition.

'I fear he is having one of his fretful moments,' said Margaret softly to her mother. 'He is now saying that there will be no wedding,' she added. Oliver was too preoccupied to register what was happening around him. Elizabeth knew she had to take control of the circumstances. She had invested a lot of time in this relationship. This marriage. Beth was a perfect wife for her son. She was pretty, entertaining and wily. The entire affair was of Elizabeth's own making. In order for the day to progress, she would have to act. She approached the distressed groom who was now visibly shaking. She gently put her arm around his shoulders. 'What is it? Tell me your thoughts,' she said gently. But Oliver could not speak. He was now oblivious to reality. He was chasing his own breath, but he couldn't catch it. His mind was a fault line, and his body a shuddering earthquake. He wanted desperately to get out of it. But he was trapped. The darkness had closed in around him. And right now it was at its peak. Elizabeth had seen this before and she knew she had to try to keep him calm. But he was unresponsive. She turned towards Margaret and asked her to bring a chair from the church. Margaret returned in seconds and placed the chair under Oliver. He sank down on to it, still in his tormented unreality. Some guests began to emerge from the church to see what was happening. But Oliver was dealing with his silent screams. The storm in his head was smothering him. Despite her best efforts, Elizabeth could make no headway.

The open carriage that carried the bride appeared at the gates of the churchyard. Elizabeth Bourchier was exhilarated at the thoughts of the day ahead. She wore a burgundy corset dress with a bell-shaped skirt. Her hair was shaped into a chignon and it was placed high on her head, with even strands of side hair hanging loose. Her husband-to-be was erudite and charming. And he had a droll sense of humour that matched her own. They would have such exciting lives together. Wouldn't it be great if there were children. Happiness beckoned. Her father sat opposite her, looking uncomfortable in his wedding attire. As the carriage drew closer, Beth discerned the scene at the front of the church. A small crowd was gathered around a seated figure. Her imagination accurately filled in the gaps. The carriage had not yet arrived at its designated stop. But she told the driver sharply to halt. Before her father knew what was happening, she had leapt from the carriage and ran across the grass lawn to where Oliver was sitting. With no regard for her wedding dress, she knelt down in front of him. He was totally distracted. She knew exactly what to do.

'Would you all kindly go inside and leave us, please,' she announced. Elizabeth was so proud of her daughter-in-law-to-be at that moment. She turned, assumed her role as the mother of the groom, and ushered the guests back inside the church door. The wedding couple were now on their own.

'Oliver,' began Beth. 'Listen to me. Press your feet into the ground. Focus on your breathing. Breathe slowly. This will soon pass. In moments it will be gone. There is absolutely nothing to fear. I am here now. And I will take care of you.'

Oliver began to feel the ground beneath his feet again. The noose that was tight around his thoughts began to loosen. His breathing became more regular. He was no longer trapped in his private terror. 'Beth!' he said. 'The enormity of the occasion must have overcome me. Then the unease just took hold. And I could not control it. It rose up inside and I could not stop it. However, I think now it is abating.'

'Rest for the moment. We have plenty of time. We have the rest of our lives. The guests can wait. After all, we play the main roles in today's drama, do we not? Without us, there will be no wedding.'

'I must be candid and tell you that I did not think there would be one. When the distress took hold. But with you now by my side, I realise that I was being foolish.'

'Not foolish. Never foolish. This wasn't your fault, Oliver. I know that these things happen and that you can't do anything about them. But you have to remember that I am here now, and I expect always to be around to help you through these dark moments.'

After another few minutes, reassured by his bride, Oliver was ready to get married. 'Just imagine,' said Beth as they walked towards the church door and her waiting father, 'If you had persisted with your decision not to proceed, and I had married another, you would have regretted it for the rest of your life.'

'Another? What other? There's another?' said Oliver with feigned indignation. They locked eyes. Smiled. They embraced. This time for an extra few heartbeats. Everything was back to normal. Everything was as it should have been. Now they could get married.

For pragmatic reasons, the bride moved into the Cromwell home on Huntingdon's High Street. For the first eight years of their marriage they set about raising a family. Their first son came along in October 1621. They called him Robert, after his grandfather. Oliver junior was born in February 1623, a daughter

Bridget in August 1624, Richard in October 1626, Henry in January 1628. During this time Oliver couldn't manage to fully suppress his gambling addiction. Although he did curtail it. Needs must. As an interested member of the renowned family who had often hosted the country's monarch, he soon extended his pursuits to dabbling in the town affairs. He began to attend some meetings of the local corporation and from time to time he signed documents as a material witness. Here was a place where he first beheld social injustices. He watched as the beleaguered fen folk in the area were often exploited by the greedy elite. As a hard-working farmer, Oliver did not like some of the things he encountered in the municipal domain. The cut and thrust of local affairs began to stimulate his curiosity.

With a growing young family, the income from the farm sometimes failed to stretch far enough during those early years. The financial decisions had to be made with frugality in mind. Debts grew but always seemed to be manageable. While Oliver's sisters each moved out in stages to reside elsewhere with their new husbands, the cards, the dice, the bull baiting wagers all took their toll on the household budget. The wolf was becoming aware of the Cromwell's front door.

Having spent all of his life in Huntingdon, Oliver was quite well known in the area. King James had died in 1625 and his son Charles had ascended to the throne. Even though he was just four-years-old at the time, Oliver still remembered the day he had bloodied Charles' nose at Hinchingbrooke all those years ago. It had caused quite a to-do among the adults at the time. Upon the coronation of the young king, the story was revitalised and circulated around the town anew. The word came persistently from Westminster that this new king was proving to be a very divisive ruler. Partisan newspapers began to depict the new monarch as a tyrant. In a short time his subjects were divided on the king's divine right to rule. To some he was wreaking havoc on the country. To others it was entirely his prerogative to do whatever he felt inclined to do. He was the king.

Oliver's once well-aimed blow at the royal nose acquired legendary status. It grew legs. It became an epic tale of a hand-to-hand fight that went on for some time. Oliver was soon credited as being a wild child with mystical strength who conquered one prince and a handful of royal courtiers before he had to be restrained. Soon the story was in wide circulation. A story where good triumphed over evil. Word on the street was that Oliver Cromwell was the one man who was able to put Charles Stuart in his place.

Beth was in the kitchen. She was poring over a large pot that was suspended from a hook in the ceiling. The open, ground-level hearth was sprinkled with debris and faggots from the log fire. Most of the smoke disappeared up the wide red-brick chimney flue. She was cooking a boiled mixture of broken grains, pulses, and vegetables called pottage. The fireplace was conveniently equipped with side niches, which provided a dry place for the saltbox and sugar loaf between use, away from vermin that might have escaped the attention of the house cat. The blaze was kept perpetually alight, for what seemed to be a continuous cycle of cooking. The room was simply furnished, with a table, two benches and a stool, a meat safe on the wall, and an array of kitchen utensils suspended from the walls and hearth. On the opposite side of the room, Elizabeth sat on a carved mahogany dining chair and was engaging with three of the younger children. Oliver entered the room. 'Ladies. I am glad I have found you both in the same location. I have some news. I have decided to stand in the local elections. I think it's high time I went to London to shake up that new king of ours.'

'Well, Oliver, that *is* news,' said his mother, while Beth did her best to interpret the immediate ramifications of her husband's announcement. 'But you don't have any experience in politics,' added Elizabeth.

49

'I have passion. I have zeal. This new king has imposed unfair taxes on his people. And as you know following his coronation – he married a Catholic! There are many abroad in the countryside that say soon England will be overrun with popery. The newspapers convey accounts of his tyranny weekly. This king is not even a shadow of the man his father was.'

'I understand that the situation is a difficult one,' said Elizabeth. 'But you are young yet. There will be plenty of time for you to go to Westminster and do your duty. The family needs you here, Oliver. If you were to leave to go to London, how would we endure?'

'Oh, Mother. The farmhands will still be here. Yourself and Beth know as much about this business as I do. Besides, I will not be gone for that long. And London is only a day's ride away. Can you not imagine it? Your only son. The hallowed halls of the country's seat of power. England's beating heart. I will be following in the footsteps of my father. I would also be entitled to the salary of a Member of Parliament.'

Beth was in full agreement with Elizabeth's line of questioning. She knew she needed to find the balance between maintaining the family stability and encouraging her husband's new aspirations. She just wished he had spoken to her first. Oliver's enthusiasm had already told her that protestations were useless. He was going to stand in the local elections. And there was nothing either her or Elizabeth was going to be able to do about it.

'So who will you be standing against?' Beth asked her husband.

'Well, now. That is a most interesting question. There are others. But I suspect you may have heard of my main opponent. He goes by the name of Edward Montagu.'

'Oh Lord no! But what if he beats you? The Montagus would take so much pleasure in that,' said Elizabeth. 'Could you deal with the ignominy?'

'If the Lord sees fit to choose a Montagu over a Cromwell then so be it. The Lord will have chosen. And I will respect the Lord's decision. But in order to see what His preference will be, I will be delighted to engage in the contest. Who knows? There are just two seats to be contested. God may well choose a Montagu *and* a Cromwell. Is it not a rousing thought?'

The elections were held in June. The Lord decided that Oliver Cromwell and James Montagu were indeed both elected as MPs for Huntingdon. On the day the election results were announced, Oliver discovered that he was bankrupt. The house, the land, everything, had to be sold to pay his debts. He and his young family were now dispossessed of the farm he had inherited from his father. Their only source of income. The wolf was well and truly at the door.

Chapter Seven

Five months later. Oliver was angry. A bead of sweat ran down his right temple. He became aware of just how tight his collar had been fixed. It was uncomfortable. He could feel it constraining his neck. He watched the obnoxious fat man stride around the council chamber pontificating. With every detestable sentence, the Mayor, a Mr Walden, uttered, Oliver's patience condensed. He wanted to interrupt. He wanted to put an end to the speaker's prattling. But he had to bide his time. He had to wait until Walden was finished. He could sense the tension in his body. His sleeve ruffs irritated his wrists as the blood warmed in his veins. Every now and again he glanced at the brass lantern clock on the carved mantel above the fireplace. The Mayor's time would be up soon. Walden had an arrogance about him as he spoke. He needed to rubbish the Mayor's views. The people in the room needed to hear from him. They needed to hear what was right. The Mayor was not right. Oliver was beyond irritated. Beyond agitated. He was incensed.

The town hall was full. Spectators had come to watch the meeting. It was an important day in the history of Huntingdon. They were discussing the recent passing of a new town charter. The essence of the changes from the old charter was that certain aldermen were now elected for life. A clique from which Oliver and certain others were excluded. Oliver watched as the onlookers absorbed the Mayor's words. Suddenly, he couldn't take it anymore. He jumped to his feet, left the council table and strode out into the middle of the floor.

'God's wounds! Do not listen to this shit!' he roared.

The stunned Mayor began to protest. But Oliver wasn't about to let him do any more damage.

'Do you not see what this whoremaster is about?' continued Oliver shouting louder than the faltering Mayor, whose poise was completely lost in the moment. The crowd in the public gallery began to boo and hiss. Oliver's temper was uncontrollable. 'He might alter the rate of our cattle that graze on the commons, with impunity! He and his perpetual cohorts might decide to dispose of this Corporation's land without wholesale agreement! This is what this is about! We must not allow this repugnant windfucker to win the day! (Booing.) Our town would then be a rotten borough! How would it be when these men lose their senses as they grow older? Are we to do what this driggle-draggle say then? (Booing.) How will it be on younger men who will never get a chance to be elected? Younger men who have foresight, erudition, sagacity, insight? Are they to be denied by these old fustylugs?' He spat the words out like they had been causing him a digestive disorder.

Oliver's swearing caused an uproar in the chamber. The spectators revelled in the change of dynamic that had engulfed the room. The aldermen and burgesses were up on their feet remonstrating with him. Most of them didn't support Oliver. Perhaps his dissolute past was catching up on him. He was not considered to be among the Huntingdon elite. His coarse language had just confirmed this to the onlooking Council members.

One of the spectators threw the remains of a tomato he had been eating in Oliver's direction and missed. When one of the overweight corporators slipped and fell on it, pandemonium ensued. A corporation official who had been recording the events tried to calm the upheaval. But his hollow cries were smothered by the yelling of the crowd. Oliver had created mayhem. Most of the town seemed to be against him. Most of the Council was against him. Partisan politics were at play. And Oliver found himself on the wrong side of majority.

Oliver sat back down in his seat. The frantic crowd were still bellowing. They watched as the Mayor approached Oliver, leaned down and said something inaudible to everyone else in the room. But Oliver heard it clearly enough. 'You will come to regret those indecorous words yet, Mr Cromwell. That, I promise you.' Oliver wasn't fazed in the least. As far as he was concerned he had highlighted the skullduggery in the air. He saw the issue as having had a spirited sympathy with the grievances of his friends and neighbours. Others saw it differently.

He felt somewhat isolated that night. When he got home he still felt that he had done the right thing. In his deepest thoughts, he had long since let go of the idea that he was just jealous that he wasn't in the elite circle of local aldermen and burgesses. He passionately believed that this was wrong.

A buyer for the freehold property on High Street had not yet been found. Yes, he was now an MP. And yes, he had been to London and experienced his first sitting of Parliament. But his financial situation was dire. Consequently, his mental health had deteriorated. He hadn't been sleeping well. His wife and his mother had been the unintended victims of his disparate mood swings. Even the children had been avoiding him when the darkness hit. Sometimes the smallest thing would set him off.

Ignoring his domestic difficulties, when he became aware of the proposal to change the government structure of Huntingdon he felt that he had to fight it. He was unable to cope with the reality of his financial circumstances. So he focused his mind on what he perceived to be the good fight, the fight for good. How would it be if these aldermen were to retain their positions for the rest of their lives? Where is the democracy in that? This new charter was from the king. At this point the king's actions seemed to be reaching further into Oliver's life. It would become a common theme.

It was a week before Oliver received the report of the matter from the Lord Privy Seal, none other than the earl of Manchester, none other than Edward Montagu. He was summoned to appear before the Privy Council. As part punishment he was remanded in custody for six days. He was also blackballed. If he were to attempt to attend any further meetings of the Huntingdon Corporation, he would be shunned. His antics were to come at a huge cost: ostracised from local government. The support of some few other aldermen was not enough to quash the allegation of 'disgraceful and unseemly' conduct. He wasn't in a position to deny it. There were plenty of witnesses. On receiving the news, he retired to his bed; a location he seemed to be frequenting more and more often in these times.

It was a Friday afternoon. The two Cromwell boys Robert (7) and Oliver (5) and their four-year-old sister Bridget were playing fart-in-the-face on the street outside the house when the man arrived. Three-year-old Richard and the baby, one-year-old Henry, were with their mother in the house. The man had come from the direction of the town. The children knew him well. Only Robert was grown-up enough to greet him.

'Can you fart, Dr Simcott?' he asked the man. 'Do your farts smell really terribly?'

'That depends largely on what I have consumed, Robert,' replied the doctor smiling.

'Well, if you can fart now, will you fart in Oliver's face? Bridget and I have no more farts and it's Oliver's turn,' said Robert.

'Please, Doctor! Fart! Fart! Fart! Please, Doctor!' pleaded little Oliver to the doctor's amusement.

'Unfortunately, I don't quite feel up to your game at this moment,' said Dr Simcott. 'Perhaps on another occasion.'

'Fart! Fart! Fart! Fart!' said little Bridget hoping the man would bend over and fart in her brother's face. The man was a big man. So it would be a really big fart.

'Well, Doctor, if you have a fart coming on when you're in the house, will you run out and fart for us then?' asked Robert as he bent over in front of Oliver's face feigning a wind-breaking groan.

'I will do my utmost,' laughed Dr Simcott, leaving the children to their game.

Beth greeted the doctor at the front door. She explained that Oliver had had more hallucinations. She was very worried about him. He was still sleeping very little and he could still not face the fact that the house was not selling, and their debts were continuously mounting. They could simply not continue for much longer like this. Was there nothing that the doctor could do?

'As you know, Beth, your husband's sickness is of the mind, rather than of the body,' said the doctor. 'This area of medicine is not my proficiency. I have the address of a professional who should be able to help. But Oliver will have to go to London. Sir Theodore Mayerne is a distinguished medic in this area.'

'Well, then there's nothing further to discuss. He will go to London to visit this Dr Mayerne.'

'I envisaged that you might say such a thing. But you will need to know that a professional of his standing and experience is not going to be inexpensive.'

'My husband's health is the most important aspect of my life at the moment, Dr Simcott. Money, whatever the amount, will not prevent us from exploring every possibility until he is well enough and has regained his full health.'

'So be it, Beth. I suspect that it is a breakdown of some description that he is experiencing. His reality at the moment is not our reality. I wish you well. Good day to you.'

Dr Simcott left the house, managed to avoid the attention of the little farters outside and disappeared back down the High Street. Beth climbed the stairs and went in to the chamber where Oliver was lying. A wooden framed tester bed was in one corner of the room. It was wedged between the chimney breast and the wall. A woollen canopy covered the horizontal, rectangular frame closest to the ceiling, and closed curtains hung from rods attached to each upright. An oak chest lay on the floor at the foot of the bed in the sparsely furnished room. An earthenware chamber pot sat on top of the wooden chest. The room was lit by one dormer-style lead lattice window that overlooked the street. The farter's voices could be heard in the distance through the closed window.

Beth gently pulled one of the curtains aside. 'Oliver,' she whispered gently. 'Are you awake?' Her husband was in the foetal position facing the wall. He turned his head to face her. His visage was pale, his eyes bloodshot and there were semi-circles under his eyes, inflamed in red. 'It's three of the clock in the afternoon. The doctor has just been here. He has suggested that you see a special doctor in London. A Doctor Mayerne. I think we should follow his advice. What say you?'

'I am so sorry to be causing you and the family so much grief,' replied Oliver. 'Of course. I must go. I will set out for London tomorrow. If there is a remedy for this melancholic temperament then I need to find it. Perhaps this doctor in London will be able to provide treatment.'

It was spring. That optimistic time of year. Oliver's spirits were high. In stark contrast to the previous day. He was practically upbeat. Perhaps this day will bring an end to all of this bleakness. The weather was so mild he had chosen to travel in an open-top carriage. He was preparing the horses on the street outside the house when he noticed a well-dressed man standing on the opposite side of the street looking awkward. The gentleman nodded. Oliver nodded back. The gentleman approached.

'How now, Mr Cromwell,' said the gentleman. 'I believe that all of your property is for sale. I have looked at the land and the buildings and I am interested. Of course the price will determine whether or not the eighty-five acres is worth more consideration. What is the value you have decided upon?'

Oliver was surprised at the man's temerity. This was no way to do business. Being accosted like this.

'My good man. I have no intentions of discussing this issue in the street. And I am for London today, so perhaps we might make an appointment for my return which should be a week from today.'

'I understand. However, I will not be available next week. I also understand that the property has been for sale for some months now and that you are still seeking a purchaser, are you not? I wish to discuss the matter now. If you are serious about this, Mr Cromwell, then I would suggest that you do not look a gift horse in the mouth. My intelligence suggests the value to be two thousand pounds. Is that correct?'

Oliver was caught in a bind. He didn't like being cornered. Not being in control. He didn't like that the man knew so much. And yet, there was an intriguing aspect to the gentleman. But despite his outward misgivings, he knew well that business could indeed be done in the street. This gentleman seemed to be a person of some standing who may well be able to stand over his words. So he decided to pursue the matter.

'What about it? he said.

'I will give you eighteen hundred pounds and not a penny more. And what's more, Mr Cromwell, you may keep the seventeen acres of undulating scrubland on the outskirts of town. That is the best proposition you are likely to receive, and I would encourage you to take it.'

'If this is a serious proposal, then I would suggest we discuss it on my return,' said Oliver now very curious as to how the conversation would go.

'My proposition is made today, Mr Cromwell. It will not be made next week. You must take it or leave it. At this precise moment. Now, do we have an agreement?' said the gentleman as he held out his hand.

So many things went through Oliver's head at that moment. This was the property that his father had inherited from Sir Henry. He himself had inherited it from his father. It had been in the Cromwell family for generations. On one hand he knew that he was the one in the lineage chain who had failed the legacy. On the other hand, he knew that if the property was not sold, the family's circumstances would continue to dis-improve. Caught up in this emotional turmoil, his defences weakened. He reached out and grasped the man's hand.

'Against my better judgement, I will agree to your terms now,' said Oliver. 'I only hope that your confidence with words is matched by the assurance of money in your purse, and that you have an adequate amount of both.'

'You have no need to fear. I can assure you. As it happens we share the same lawyer. I will have him draw up the papers immediately. Could you be out within the month?'

Oliver was still reeling from the magnitude of the conversation. But he held his nerve. 'If all aspects of the indenture are in place, I should be able to accommodate you, sir,' he said, feeling like he had been swindled and was bereft of any power for recourse.

'Then so be it,' said the gentleman. 'Good day, Mr Cromwell. It was a pleasure doing business with you. It was good that you saw sense.'

It didn't strike Oliver at the time but from that precise moment he had ceased being a gentleman. By definition, gentlemen were men of property. Following the local political wrangling he had been stripped of his honour. Now his rank in society was gone. He was without assets, chattels or social standing. As the gentleman walked away, he turned and said, 'I presume you have somewhere to go, Mr Cromwell?'

'Of course,' lied Oliver. He had nowhere to go. But he knew one thing. He knew he must leave Huntingdon, the place of his birth, forever. And soon.

Chapter Eight

Oliver was elated. His trip to London had been a revelation. Literally. He found God. Or more appropriately, God had found him. It was certain. He knew it. While in the city, an epoch-changing event came about in his life that would last until the day he would die. He departed Huntingdon a worthless sinner. He returned as one of the Elect. Spending time away from home focused his mind. He appealed to God for help. On this occasion God answered his prayer. Not with anything material. But with grace. And that was far better. It was the moment for which he had been yearning for so many years. The covenant of life was not revealed to all men. But it was now revealed to Oliver. This, his lowest ebb in life thus far, had presented the opportunity for him to be touched by grace. For the first time ever he could feel the workings of Christ within him. He had not been born with grace, but God had now chosen him as an individual to absorb it.

Exhilarated, he sat with Beth on his return to tell her the news.

'When God calls you to come into Christ, he promises that the virtue of Christ's death shall kill sin in you, and that the virtue of Christ's Resurrection will raise you up to the newness of light!' he blurted out. Beth was somewhat bemused but delighted that her husband was displaying signs of recovery, no matter what shape the recovery took. She hoped that this was not another false dawn. But this time it did seem different.

'Truly, then, this I find: that He gives springs in a dry and barren wilderness, where no water is. My soul is with the congregation of the firstborn, my body rests in hope, and if here I can honour my God either by doing or by suffering, I shall be most glad.' Oliver went on.

'Is this the work of Dr Mayerne? Did he have a part to play in this?' asked Beth, trying to catch up with the precipitous pace of the conversation that Oliver had set.

'In part, my dearest. He encouraged me to seek the Lord. As you know, I was such an unworthy wretch. You know what my manner of life hath been. Oh, I lived in and loved darkness, and hated the light. I was a chief, the chief of sinners. This is true. I hated godliness. Yet God had mercy on me. Oh the riches of His mercy! Blessed be His name for shining on so dark a heart as mine!'

'This is truly a wonderful moment, Oliver. I am so happy that you have seen His light. This new birth is certain to help with our problems. There is one thing you should know. While you were away, a package with some papers arrived from your lawyer, Mr Draycott. I have instructions for you to sign the documents and send them back today,' said Beth, hoping that the positivity accompanying her husband's conversion could in some way prevent the sale of the property to a total stranger. But she was to be disappointed.

'This will be a new dawn for the Cromwell family, Beth. We have to face this adversity together and somehow emerge from it sturdier. I am no longer admired by the gentlemen of this town. We must leave Huntingdon. I have discovered a leasehold property in St Ives. I journeyed by that way from London, and I have signed the lease. We must begin to pack straight away. With God's grace my travails are now behind me. We must have fortitude of mind. In two days we move to St Ives. And the spirit of Christ will now guide us. We must trust in the Lord, now that He has accepted me in His son. St Ives will be a new beginning.'

In 1631, the Cromwell family moved to the docile town of St Ives, five miles from Huntingdon. Another child, Elizabeth (Bettie) had been added to the family before the move. Four years later they had well settled in to their new life. Oliver's mental breakdown was now a distant memory. Since God had chosen him as a member of the Elect, his bouts of anxiety had also reduced significantly. When he wasn't performing some routine task of husbandry, he was mostly spending time in prayer. Along with the money from the sale of the Huntingdon property and the earnings from the rented land, the family just about managed to subsist. A rise on the social scale was simply not an option. This was all about survival. St Ives was a sleepy backwater town. Oliver had no desire to get involved in local government and the king did not seem inclined to call Parliament. So his presence at Westminster was not required.

The printed newssheets from London and other spurious news pamphlets sometimes reached St Ives and Oliver often got his hands on copies. He was always thirsty for news beyond the confines of the town. The polemic newssheets told tales of an authoritarian monarch. The talk in the inns and taverns around the country was all about how Charles differed so diametrically to his father. The established Church, or the Church of the king, was the Church of England. The king's new reforms were being universally resisted. Frequently troubled by what he read, as a Puritan, this king's actions were constantly an affront to Oliver's sensibilities. More and more aspects of popery were being introduced to the Church because of this new king; ornamentation on communion altars, the use of the sign of the cross, paintings, crucifixes, bowings, organs, vestments – all Roman varnish. Instead of 'purifying' religion, the king's reforms seemed to be contaminating it. But for now, Oliver was happy to occupy a discreet role in a tranquil, rural backwoods.

However, it wasn't long before the long arm of the king was to reach out and find Oliver again. It was an issue on which the king and this particular farmer had polar opposite viewpoints. Upon his ascension in 1625, in order to gain money for the Crown, Charles had issued a decree: every freeholder, who had property worth forty pounds a year was invited to attend the coronation ceremony. There, they would have the expensive honour of knighthood thrust upon them. Those who didn't attend had to pay a fine. Oliver hadn't done either.

Oliver had a stick in his hand. He was on no man's clock save the pace of time the seasons and the weather dictated. He was driving a small flock of sheep from one field to another. His eldest son, Robert, now fourteen was coercing the sheep alongside his father. They had formed a pincer movement. It was not generally the occupation of a gentleman to drive sheep. It was certainly the occupation of a yeoman: Oliver's recent diminished status in life. His boots were destroyed with both freshly liquefied and dried animal excrement. Spots of mud of various sizes and qualification were splattered on his well-worn breeches. He had a red flannel around his neck to protect an ongoing inflammation of the throat. He wore no hat. Between them, they managed to coax the sheep into the field. He closed the gate.

Turning around, he recognised the Town Recorder from Huntingdon approaching on the adjoining country lane. He immediately detected a sense of purpose from his visitor. Robert stood alongside his father as if to form some protection from the stranger. There was safety in numbers. This was one of the last people Oliver had ever expected to see on one of his leased lands here in St Ives. Mr Barnard was one of the men he had castigated on the night of his colourful outburst; one of the Huntingdon clique.

'Well now, Mr Barnard. I must admit, you have me at a loss. I can't imagine what possible business you could have with me here. Have you not done with me by now?' asked Oliver.

'You have not paid your knight tax, Mr Cromwell. And I am here to follow it up.'

'Oh the knight tax. Then I take it my day tax debt is fully paid up eh, Barnard? Or has that now been increased to morning, afternoon and evening tax and I still owe more?' Robert laughed nervously at his father's jocundity.

'This is not a trivial matter, Mr Cromwell. You are to be

summoned before the Court of the Exchequer for contempt, should you continue to refuse to pay.' He held out a sealed paper as if to confirm that Oliver's name was on the blacklist. 'You are not entitled to ignore a decree from the king,' added Barnard.

'Ah yes, the king,' said Oliver as sarcastically as he could, with his voice now rising. 'Is this the same king who levies ship money on every county of England without Parliamentary approval, when it should be only coastal towns? Is this the same king who rules by divine right, without any consultation with his parliament? Is this the same king who married a papist? Is this the same king who encourages the evils of popery and invents taxes to pay for it? Is that the king you mean, Mr Barnard?' Robert now stood taller beside his sharp-witted father who had quashed the man's unconvincing position with his noble words.

'I expected no change in you, Cromwell, and I see no change in you. Will you take this summons or does your obstinance allow you to break the laws of England as you see fit?'

'This is not an England I recognise. This king has meddled with the liberties of his subjects for too long. He has wrought havoc over the entire land. How can you remain loyal to such an oppressor? How in the bowels of Christ does your conscience allow you to do this?'

'Charles Stuart is my king. There is no further elucidation required. Now, will you receive this summons, and let me be on my way?'

'Perhaps you do not see the irony in all of this, Barnard. Knighthoods are for gentlemen of property. And as you well know, I do not own any property. So if I might respectfully suggest that you take that summons and insert it into that cow shit yonder. I will not succumb to the idle coercions of this tyrannical administration.'

'I see your coarse vernacular is still as potent as ever it was.'

'You can have your day in court if this is what the king wants.

And I can assure you, I will be only one name on a very long list of names. And I am of the opinion that when that day comes, God will not be on the side of the king. The Lord and Saviour will be on my side. Of that I have little doubt. Good day to you, Mr Barnard.'

Later that afternoon, the father and son made their way back to the rented thatched cottage that sat in a little copse at the edge of the town called the Slepe. On his approach, he recognised his brother-in-law's brown mare tied up to the gate post. This was a welcome sight indeed. Valentine and Margaret and their first-born son, also called Valentine had been regular visitors to the little cottage since Oliver had moved to St Ives. Oliver was now looking forward to relating his encounter with Barnard to Valentine. He was still adamant that he was not going to pay any fine. He stood at the open half-door with Robert alongside him and he looked into the compact room. Valentine was sitting in a winged, upholstered armchair in front of the hearth in the compact little room of the modest domicile. He was stuffing tobacco into the small white bowl of his clay pipe. Beth was fussing around the other children. Valentine junior was the centre of attention for the Cromwell children. It was exciting to have their cousin come to visit. Best behaviour was required. They had guests.

'Have you come to help me with the ploughing?' boomed Oliver from the door.

'Come now. I'll wager you don't need help from this old man, when you have the best young farmer in the county right here, isn't that right, Robert?' The youth turned crimson at the unexpected attention. Oliver's old schoolfriend came to the door and the two men embraced. 'Robert,' said Oliver. 'Go and fetch two pitchers of ale. There's a good lad.' The two men sat on the wooden bench that lay against the whitewashed wall of the house looking out onto the woods. Robert soon emerged from a shed at the side of the house with two pitchers of home-made ale. After a few congenial moments of discussing the necessary banalities, Valentine got down to the real reason for his visit.

'Do you remember meeting a John Winthrope at Hinchingbrooke, Oliver?' Well, Winthrope is now in the New World. He departed England like so many others because of the way the king is destroying the Church. The settlers can worship freely over there now. The land there is bountiful, and God has blessed their harvests every year so far with the perfect elements.'

'Yes, I do remember the gentleman you speak of. He was a lawyer was he not?'

'Yes, that's him. I met him in London recently while he was visiting on business. He has returned to the New World again. He says that the colonies there are thriving. The opportunities for God-fearing folk are myriad. Winthrope talks about large farms of hundreds of acres. Winthrope himself has a farm called the Ten Hills Farm. He speaks of a city on the hill that they intend to create. There, everything will be as of new: no quarrelling over diverse religious convictions, no legacy of opposition politics, and the best of all – no king with whom to directly contend. The settlers are all of the one mind. And further – the fishing and hunting are both abundant. Does it not sound like a utopia of a kind? Imagine – a new England in such a munificent land?'

'From what I can gather from your fervour, Valentine, and knowing you, you must have already spoken to Beth and she is in agreement. I must admit, I have learned of the attainments of the Mayflower society already. *The Weekly Newes* carries stories from the New World and the idea had crossed my mind on numerous occasions.'

'A man like you might thrive in the New World, Oliver. Think of it. You could start again. Owning land is guaranteed. The climate is more agreeable. Your children would have the chance to only intermingle with other children of the Elect. If you have considered this already, and now I have independently raised the subject, is that not how God's will works?'

'A place as far away from Rome where popery can surely never reach is indeed an enticement that is worth serious consideration,' said Oliver. 'But it would be a wrench to my very soul to have to leave my beloved England. And yet, this king will be the death of us all. Why, I have just today encountered one of his henchmen...'

'I know Barnard was here, Oliver,' interrupted Valentine. 'I met him on the road to Huntingdon as he returned.'

'Well, then do you know the foolhardy, nay highhanded errand he was on?'

'I have paid your fine, Oliver.'

Oliver struggled to deal with this disclosure. He wanted to brag to his old friend how he was undaunted by the threats of the king. He wanted to show Valentine just how stouthearted he was when it came to a point of principle. He wanted to prove that no jail term would ever diminish his passion for the ancient liberties that men all over England should still be able to enjoy without trepidation. But Valentine had stolen the moment. And yet, he could never get cross with Valentine.

'I would be grateful if you would justify why you did this,' he said putting down his pitcher of ale and turning his face towards his unsolicited benefactor.

'England has changed since we were boys, Oliver. We all know this. This king has a pitiless quality and his retributions are brutish. The jails are all full, so now he has resorted to cropping the ears of transgressors. Sometimes men are branded on the cheek. I simply could not countenance any of these maltreatments happening to you. So when I encountered Barnard on the road, and he told me of his pursuit, I paid the outstanding amount there and then. I do not expect you to thank me for it. But it is done.'

For the next year Oliver and Beth sought the verdict of God for a decision on where their future lay. They agonised over every event that could potentially have been interpreted as a divine intervention. As the months progressed, a dry summer and an inhospitable winter ensured that the harvest was poor. Money was fast running out. The intercession of the Almighty soon became abundantly well defined. The signs were too strong to ignore. There were no mixed messages. Combined with every horrific new story that Oliver learned about the debasement of the man whose nose he bloodied as a child, the indications that the family should move to the New World were simply overwhelming. God's will must be done. The plans were set in train. On 5 April, 1636 a near penniless Oliver Cromwell, his wife Beth, along with their five children Robert (15), Oliver (13), Bridget (12), Richard (10), Henry (7) and Bettie (6) walked up the gangplank to board the ship, *The James of London*, at Plymouth. The parents were nervous. The children were excited. They were bound for the New World. In two months' time they would step ashore. What new wonders might lie in wait?

Chapter Nine

The ship's departure was delayed for some hours. Beth was standing on the deck taking her final look at England. The children were gone, exploring. So far Oliver was the only one to realise that they weren't going anywhere. He had the letter in his hand. The letter that the ship's captain had given him when he came on board. The letter that had been sent hastily on horseback by Oliver's lawyer in Huntingdon as soon as he received the news. The letter that Mr Draycott hoped would reach Plymouth Harbour on time. The letter that was to change the fortunes of the Cromwell family, and ultimately the destiny of England, forever.

Oliver's relief was incalculable. It wasn't his role to question the actions of the Lord God Almighty. But he was certainly ready to thank Him. This was a special providence. The hellish days were finally over. He had done his time. And now God was rewarding him for his utter devotion since his new birth. He found Beth on the deck near where the gangplank was still affixed to the stationary ship. Below them carried on the hustle and bustle of an industrious sea-port. When she saw him approach, she wiped the tears that had gathered in her eyes and she tried to sound cheerful, 'They haven't raised the gangplank yet. I wonder how long it will be before we set sail?' she said to Oliver as he stood beside her.

'It won't be raised just yet. Some people need to disembark.'

'Is that why the captain summoned you? Do you know who these people are?'

'Beth, I have some news. My Uncle Thomas died yesterday. The captain received this letter for me last night that was delivered to him by hand.'

Beth's heart leapt in her chest. Oliver's Uncle Thomas! Her pupils dilated as Oliver's words swept over her tense body, releasing all the stiffness in her constrained muscles in an instant. Now she knew what Oliver knew. She knew what this meant. The people who would be disembarking would be them. There were some moments in her life that she would treasure until the day she died. Frequently in the coming decades she would regale the story about how close they came to emigrating to the New World. The enormity of it all would fascinate listeners. Oliver, too, would recall the emigration story in years to come. She raised her gaze from the busy harbour below. She faced her husband whose eyes were now smiling back at her. She knew there was no point in condoling with him on his uncle's death. They weren't close relations. 'Then, we are rich, Oliver! We are rich!'

Sir Thomas Steward died without issue. His nephew, Oliver, was his main legatee. The estate he had just inherited consisted of various properties in and around the town of Ely, twenty-five miles from Huntingon. It included ninety acres of glebe lands in the common fields of Ely, eight acres of pasture on the Isle of Ely, with houses, barns and lands. There were tithes and glebe land of the rectory of the cathedral of Ely, the church of St Mary in Ely, the Sextry barn – the second largest barn in all of England according to local tradition. And of course, along with all of the material benefits would come considerable local status as lord of the manor. Cromwell the yeoman was dead. Cromwell the gentleman, reborn.

The new Cromwell home was a large half-timbered, two-storied, medieval black and white house within a stone's throw of Ely cathedral. It lay adjacent to the smaller church of St Mary on the generous esplanade that connected the cathedral with the Cambridge Road, and so on to London. Dwarfed by the breathtaking size of the ancient cathedral, the house itself overlooked a small green that gave the building a certain composed independence. It stood in isolation dominating the pleasant wide-open common area. It was a more substantial property than the two that the family had occupied previously. Most significantly, this time the Cromwells had no debts. Nor would they want for anything ever again. As long as they lived.

Ely was surrounded by fenland: thirteen hundred square miles of water-logged terrain. The low-lying expanse flooded regularly in winter. Fen men grazed their cattle, fished, fowled and grew their crops in the region on land held in common, by long-established right from time immemorial. They, and their families were a society apart. They called all others 'upland men'. A drainage scheme had been recently introduced by the king to improve the land. Charles had concluded that this was a malfunctioning landscape that its inhabitants had failed to manage properly. Adventurers invested money in converting the marshes to arable land. For this they would receive a portion of the newly-drained land, and the king would pocket a tidy profit.

The Cromwell family expanded in 1637 and 1638 when both Mary and Frances respectively were born. Oliver's mother, Elizabeth, now moved in with the family as the space in the new house could accommodate her adequately. They were two years living in the town when Oliver became involved in local activities. The royal plan to steamroll over the ancient rights of the local people was high on his agenda. The draining of the fens was well under way. As the drainage progressed, the adventurers began to erect fences for their parcels of land, where previously there had been none. Was there no end to this king's venality? The discommoded fen men were infuriated. They needed a spokesman. Oliver didn't have to be asked. He immediately rose to the challenge. In time, he would become known locally as the Lord of the Fens.

It was early. Oliver was standing in his kitchen that was located at the rear of the house. He was looking out the window at the serene graveyard that surrounded St Mary's Church, next door. He was trying to plan the morning in his head. The protest had to be a peaceful one. Controlling the wild fen men would be a challenge. They had a reputation for ill-discipline. But if the numbers were small enough, and if he was allowed to, they could make a strong point to the drainer, who was due to erect a fence today.

'Oh there you are, Father,' said Robert emerging from the adjoining parlour. Oliver junior skulked in behind him. 'Won't you reconsider? Can we not come along with you today?'

'Boys. Boys. This is no place for you two. These fen-folk are an unruly and unpredictable faction. I am hoping that they will not be unmanageable. Remain here and help your mother. She will miss you boys around the house. Robert, you leave for boarding school later today. How would it be if something happened to you? This might be a very dangerous situation.'

'I suppose, if I must, then I must. But why are you getting involved, Father? You don't really know these people,' said Robert. His younger brother hadn't really been that optimistic about going anyway, and he let Robert do the talking.

'But I know what's right. The idea is to simply make it plain to the adventurers that the recompense to the common folk in the king's plan is simply not acceptable. They need more land than they are being offered. It is a good thing that God's land is being made functional, so it can be worked. But this must not happen at the expense of those generations of fen men and their families who have toiled on the marshes for centuries.'

'I admire the way you fight for noble causes, Father. I hope that some day, I will make you proud and display the same values as you do,' said Robert.

'Hear. Hear,' said Oliver junior.

'Life has not always been that simple for me, boys. But with God's grace now flowing through my veins, I am determined to make amends for my sins. And it is good that you see the merit in the way God works through me. Now, the fire needs more wood, gentlemen. That is to be your employment for this morning. And I must away!'

Their father grabbed his coat that was hanging on a chair and swept out of the room into the yard at the back of the house. He felt a surge of pride following the conversation with his sons as he strolled around the house and closed the wooden gate behind him. Passing the green, he thanked God for giving him such a reverential family. A small group of about ten local men were waiting at the gates of St Mary's for his arrival. Oliver was pleased that the number was not greater. He could manage this handful of protestors. The Great Level was within walking distance and this is where they were bound.

'How now, Mr Castle,' said Oliver to one of the men. Hugh Castle was a Justice of the Peace in the town. Oliver knew that it was good to have local officialdom represented at what might after all be a confrontation of sorts. He hadn't foreseen that Castle wasn't wearing his official hat this morning. 'Good morrow, Mr Cromwell. It is good of you to take up the cause of the men from the fens. Your presence here today gives them heart. You have stood in the hallowed halls of Westminster, and if God is good, you will stand there again. That is, assuming this king will call Parliament for another session. How long has it been now?'

'Eight years hence when the king last called us. And you and I both know just how reckless he has been with men's lives and livelihoods since. I have every confidence that the common people will be treated fairly from this scheme. But we have to stand up and shout loud!' he said, inflecting his last sentence for optimum effect.

The other men cheered at Oliver's rousing words. He knew he had an audience and he knew the words they wanted to hear. The group made their way down towards the level lands. The Isle of Ely was perched on a slight prominence that was raised above the marshy lowlands. Many of the roads to and from the town were flooded in a wet winter. It was a short walk down

Fore Hill to the Waterside where the fencing was to take place. Crossing over the bridge, Oliver began to realise that the protest was about to escalate substantially. On the far side of the river a large group of fen folk, men and women had assembled. Oliver estimated that there must have been a hundred of them, if not more. Many of them were carrying pitchforks and scythes. It was clear that they weren't about to engage in any pedestrian husbandry. 'Ah, now, Mr Castle,' said Oliver. 'You did not mention that there would be another party joining the assembly.'

'I have no control over what the people may or may not do,' said Castle. 'But I can tell you this: the fen folk are feeling ostracised. Their spirits are in a highly volatile and emotional state. How could anyone reproach them for defending their rights?'

Oliver stood on the apex of the bridge and surveyed the angry mob. He could see that their dander was up. He knew that antagonistic exchanges had been taking place between them for months. He knew they were up for a fight. But above all, he could see the fear in their faces. He could easily empathise with their plight. Here was an ancient fraternity of people who were totally bewildered with what was going on.

As the one with the highest social standing, he immediately felt like he needed to take command. He cleared his throat and he began to address them. 'Greetings to you all,' he began. I am Cromwell. I have been a member of this country's parliament and I expect to be again, whenever the king sees fit to call a parliament. But I am no friend of this king!' He raised his voice to invoke their approval. Some of the listeners cheered.

'However, when we encounter the drainers, we must remember that they are not the king himself. They are simply carrying out the king's treachery. Today your voices will be strong enough. Force will not be required. Blood should not be spilled. Let us not make martyrs of the king's men. Discourse will win the day. I have called on God to assist us with this

74

struggle.' He drew breath and lifted his last sentence in the air, so they were all clear on the point. He threw it at them in a manner that was crafted to animate them. 'And I can tell you now that the Lord God Almighty is on our side! We will right this terrible wrong!'

The entire group cheered their approval, raising their makeshift weapons into the air, shaking them in support. Oliver was exhilarated at the effect his oration had made on the horde. It was his first experience of motivating men. It was to be the first of so many. He strode through the throng and emerged the other side. Emboldened. It was clear that they were to follow him. The mob walked behind their new leader.

Ten minutes later, obscured by a generous hedgerow, they came upon a royal overseer and his men erecting a fence. Oliver emerged around the vegetation first. He strolled boldly over to the man who was clearly in charge. A tactful, yet assertive approach was required. But Oliver's trust in his 'troops' had been completely misplaced. As soon as the rabble saw the new fences they ran wholesale at the perpetrators. The overseer and his men dropped their tools and fled as fast as their legs could carry them. Led by the Justice of the Peace, Mr Castle, the angry mob yelled and bawled insults at the king's men until they gave up the chase. The fen men who were too indolent for the pursuit began to tear down the fence. He didn't quite realise it at the time, but Oliver learned a valuable lesson that day. A fight for a just cause is not won by fine words alone. The protagonists must also be disciplined.

In the following months, Oliver's social conscience and his subsequent representations on behalf of the fen folk did enough to slow the progress of the drainage scheme to a crawl. It was other activity that the king was engaged in that would hinder its progress ultimately. The king's policies of heavy taxation towards the Scots provoked them to a point beyond which they could tolerate. The fact that the tax money that was raised went towards lavish church buildings and the encouragement of Catholic trappings sent them into a spin. The king's directive that his reformed liturgy was to be adopted by Scotland was a step too far. Charles then decided to force his liturgy on the Scots by military action.

The day after the riot on the fens, Oliver assumed his usual morning position at the hearth before tackling the day. The logs that Robert and Oliver junior had cut were neatly stacked in the recess adjacent to the fire. He knew that the boys had also left a pile in the woodshed at the back. It was a good day's work by the Cromwell boys. Robert had left for Felsted School the previous day. Oliver would miss his eldest son around the house until school term was finished. Robert had exceptional academic promise and above all he was God fearing. Oliver thanked the Lord for his children as he beheld the tranquil ecclesiastical scene outside his kitchen window. He hoped that maybe someday Robert would succeed in the world of literary ivory towers where he had failed.

The fire crackled away, and the comforting sounds emanated around the room. The morning sun slipped out from behind the clouds to cast angled shadows of the kitchen furniture on the shiny grey flagstones. Oliver loved these idle moments before the day got properly started. It was then that he heard the commotion in the other room. Voices were raised. Somebody screamed. It sounded like Beth. Although he could not be sure. Oliver turned towards the door. Suddenly Beth flung the door open. The abrupt violence of the moment destroyed the silence in the room. Her face was ashen white. She was clutching both of her arms to her chest. 'There's been an accident!' she screamed. 'It's Robert, Oliver! Our beloved son! He's... been killed!

Chapter Ten

It was a landscape interrupted by grey stone crosses and a listless silence. The soil here contains precious life companions: husbands, wives, lovers, friends, children. Down the sombre rows, reflective feet had trod for centuries. When it was bitterly cold and the skies were an ugly grey, Felsted Church cemetery was a foreboding place. Not for the faint-hearted. Statues in the shadows. Mute through the ages. The mind played tricks in the half-light. Loved ones committed to such an inhospitable place. This is where life and death intertwined.

However impossible the task now seemed, Oliver and Beth now entrusted the body of their first-born child to the soil in this bleak place. Never again would they hear the timbre of his happy young voice. Over the years they had often told him they would always be there for him. But they weren't there for him in the end. The runaway horse had snuffed out his life in one sickening collision. He had been directly in its path. He never stood a chance. It was his first week back at school. They stood there in the cemetery enveloped in a silence of voiceless acceptance. Never again would his eager young eyes sparkle and shine. Never again would they engage in idle chat about cutting wood for the fire. How could he simply be no more? They watched his coffin being lowered into the damp, hostile earth. Their dear, cherished child. The Cromwell family were utterly devastated.

Oliver would never fully get over Robert's death. It took him months to muster up the enthusiasm to step from his grief-stricken retreat back into the routine of life. Nothing would ever be the same. Inevitably, as the time passed, the family of six got closer. The fragility of a life and how it can be so easily taken created an unspoken bond between them. Now reduced to seven, Oliver (16), Bridget (15), Richard (13), Henry (11),

Bettie (10) Mary (2) and Frances (1), eventually a routine was found where they could all move on. Oliver found solace in his other children. They sought the Lord together during their most anguished times. Later, Oliver would reveal that 'this scripture did once save my life when my eldest son died, which went as a dagger to my heart.'

Oliver's reputation as the Lord of the Fens had spread far and wide. As an antagonist of the establishment, he had earned the respect of common men throughout the area. Meanwhile, back in London, having started the war with Scotland, Charles found that keeping an army in the field was an expensive business. On 20 February, 1640, after an eleven-year gap, he finally called Parliament. He needed them to find him money. On hearing the news, Oliver threw his hat into the election ring immediately. He chose a fresh field constituency in which to stand. A place where his name was being spoken about positively. With a reputation as an agitator now carrying a certain prestige, he was duly elected an MP for Cambridge.

The recalling of Parliament was the opportunity that Oliver and his fellow MPs were looking for. After the long gap of not sitting, and the incessant new oppressive tax policies, the representatives of the people could finally address their grievances directly to the king. They also wanted to discuss the possibility of annual parliaments. The new parliament sat on 13 April. Oliver travelled to London full of optimism. The objective of this parliament was that they could finally get the opportunity to get the king to see sense.

Three weeks later the king dissolved Parliament. He had wanted more money. They had wanted to address their grievances. Traditionally, a king and his parliament were generally one united body. Striving for the common good. But these two entities were starting to become very different sides. And both sides were simply too far apart.

The summer of 1640 passed without further incident. The

king was of the opinion that Rex is Lex, the king is the law. But by the autumn, Charles' ongoing war with Scotland had put him in severe financial distress. He had to call Parliament again. Again, Oliver put his name forward and was duly elected as an MP for Cambridge once more.

The months passed and still no common ground could be found between the king and his parliament. Negotiations continually failed. Back in London more often, in-between sessions, Oliver increasingly found himself in the Westminster Abbey library. Founded in 1560, the soothing environment of the characterful bookshelves drew him back every time. He loved the celebration of literature that the room presented: literary observers in neat formation on wooden shelves. The earthen smell of the old room combined with the pungent scent from the hundreds of dusty books on display was simply irresistible. Worn floorboards. Secluded niches. Soundless music. He often got lost in here among the pages of medieval manuscripts. So many books. So much to learn.

On one of these nothing days he strolled idly in to the room. Oliver perused the tantalising leather-bound tomes on the shelves for a few minutes until a book about the Crusades caught his eye. Lifting the volume from the shelf, he found a quiet corner to sit and he began to flick through the pages. Soon a silent ire was activated within him as he read about the horrors of the war in the name of Jesus Christ. Here, were some of the worst popes in history. A succession of Roman pontiffs sending the Crusaders out where they raped and then slaughtered women, looted churches, burned homes, and killed tens of thousands of Jews, Muslims and Arabs to avenge the death of Jesus and to maintain Jerusalem for the West. The carnage was consummate. The evils of popery were irrefutable. It struck Oliver then that he had to do his utmost to prevent this Catholic-loving king from empowering this utterly vile organisation. Deep in thoughts of broadswords, lances, maces and crossbows penetrating innocent flesh, he became aware of a shadow in front of him. He looked up and saw his cousin John Hampden, a fellow MP, his countenance sombre.

'I thought it might be here that you would be,' said Hampden.

'You know me too well, dear cousin. Did you seek me out? Join me, if you will. Tell me why you look so grave.'

Hampden sat on a chair opposite Oliver, reached inside his tunic and spread a pamphlet on the table. The headline read, *Bloody News from Ireland – Or the barbarous cruelty used by Papists in that kingdom.*

Tapping the freshly printed newssheet with his index finger, Hampden sat back in the chair and said, 'The news from Ireland is not good, Oliver. The Catholic clergy have incited a rebellion. Thousands of Protestants have been slaughtered. There are accounts that babies were ripped from their mothers' wombs and then dashed against rocks or impaled on pikes. Men were forced to strip naked and were then roasted over spits in front of their wives. Women and children, the old, the infirm, all mercilessly killed. The numbers of dead are said to be in the hundreds of thousands.'

Oliver was aghast. The malevolence of the Church of Rome was rearing its ugly head right here, right now, in his own time. And so close to home. He tried to process the information that was being given to him. He picked up the pamphlet and stared at the printed words.

'But how is such a thing possible? Why would these clerical savages instigate such outrages? Ireland was at peace. How could they justify killing innocent children? I tell you, John, if I live to be a thousand, I will never understand these murdering papist barbarians. There are some terrible evils in this world. And I cannot think of a worse one than popery. All of my life, I have heard of their barbarism. I cannot believe that it continues to occur today.'

'It astonishes us all who inhabit the civil world, Oliver,

that these papist ecclesiastics profess to act in the name of Our Lord God Almighty and that they can inveigle ordinary men to carry out their dastardly deeds in His name. But you have not heard the worst part yet – there is talk of this papist rabble from Ireland invading England, and who's to say what side the king will be on?'

Oliver stared across the room, his eyes becoming moist at the tragedy of it all. 'Surely the end of days is nigh,' he said. 'What possible impairment did those poor children inflict on their aggressors? Imagine the consequences if a papist army from Ireland were to sack the town of Ely! Imagine if those savages came to the front door of my very home! *My* wife. *My* children These are the very nightmares of my childhood.'

'I have no words of comfort to offer you, Oliver. But I can say this to you: a scheme has been set up to raise an army to quash the Irish Rebellion. I have already invested. When Ireland is eventually conquered – and it *will* be conquered – investors will acquire land there. I reasoned that you might be inclined to become involved.'

'I do not have to think upon it further. I will pledge two-thousand pounds for the succor of Ireland. The bile fomenting in my stomach prevents me from committing any less.'

'That is far too high a figure, Oliver, you don't....'

'I absolutely insist. God works through my soul and it is He I have to thank that I am in a position to contribute satisfactorily to His just and decent cause: the reduction of popery in this world.'

In the next few months two opposing armies began to emerge. Parliament instructed Justices of the Peace all over the country to begin impressment and a militia began to drill and exercise, just in case it was needed to preserve peace and the people's liberties in opposition to the king. On the opposite side, the king controlled those in the military who supported him. He also began to add to his numbers. He departed London for York. He

81

would not return until the time of his death. During this time Oliver began to impress at meetings of the various committees he was on. During the summer of 1642, the country began to prepare itself for war. Could there really be a war? Would there really be a war?

Oliver was a farmer. He had no military experience whatsoever. He knew that his position as a gentleman and an MP meant that he would be given a position of a junior officer in the army. He didn't, however, think that it would happen so soon.

At home in Ely one Saturday morning, Captain Oliver Cromwell was at breakfast. His three boys, Oliver junior (19), Richard (16) and Henry (14) were around the table. They were all so excited about the possibility of there being a war. They were all much too enthused about the prospect of taking on the king's forces for Oliver's liking. 'But, Father,' insisted Henry. 'I can fight just as well as Oliver and Richard can. Why can I not join the army?' Oliver Senior smiled at his spirited son. 'You know you're just too young, Henry. Your mother will need you around the house with your older brothers gone. If indeed a war does come about.'

'Come outside and see my horse handling skills, Father. I am more capable than Richard. And almost as expert as Oliver!'

'When I finish my meal, you can show me how practised you are.'

'Father, you know I will not be joining the fray?' interrupted Richard. Oliver junior kicked him under the table. 'Now is not the time, Richard,' said his older brother.

Their father was puzzled at this interaction and raised his eyebrows at Richard. 'Well, now my boy. You must know by this time that I will not press you into service. But I am curious as to why you would not stand up for the rights of your fellow man.'

'Thank you, Father. You will find my reasoning contained

82

in the Sixth Commandment,' said Richard and he fluttered his hand in a vague gesture of explanation.

Oliver was keen to pursue the conversation with his children when Valentine abruptly appeared at the door. The boys were delighted to see their uncle, and their father, his old friend. When the greetings had subsided, Valentine sat at the top of the table opposite Oliver.

'Well, Oliver. The time has come for our first opportunity to thwart the king's plans,' said Valentine with a sense of resolution. The three boys were suddenly eager to know what their uncle was about. This sounded like something was actually finally happening after all the talk.

'Word has reached us that the king has asked for the plate at Cambridge University to be brought to him at York. Should this happen he will be better able to finance the upcoming conflict. It is estimated that the treasures are worth twenty-thousand pounds!'

Oliver stood up. He was animated. He wasn't exactly sure what his role would be, but he knew he had to prevent this from happening. 'Well, my boys, do you think we should let the king have the valuable spoils from my old alma mater? What say you?'

There was a resounding 'No!'

Beth had been darning one of her husband's socks in the corner. She looked on at all of this bravado. 'But, you're a farmer, Oliver,' she said pointing out what was obvious to everyone in the room. She felt like she had to say something. 'What would you possibly know about warfare?'

'This is true, my dear wife. I have a lot to learn. But I know about the hearts of men. And I know that I will be in good company, as the vast majority of my countrymen have never witnessed combat. There has not been a shot fired in anger in England since Flodden in 1513. I cannot simply stand by and do nothing? What if all men in England were to make that choice?

To do nothing. I have received Christ into my soul, and He will guide me and ensure we will prevail, if that is His will.'

The scene was set. Oliver and Valentine immediately travelled to Cambridge and then on to Huntingdon. Through their personal efforts two companies of volunteers were soon raised. With his money problems now long behind him, Oliver himself provided the finance to arm the men. The following week, it was suspected that a convoy from the king had departed York and were on their way. When he got wind of the king's plans, Oliver gave the order for his men to hide at a point on the Great North Road. They had orders to stop and question all wayfarers. As the day progressed and the word spread, the people in Cambridge started to stream out of the city to where the musketeers were hidden in the hedgerows. Soon Captain James Docwra and his royal troops could be seen on the crest of a hill bearing down on the ambush area. The country was teetering on the verge of Civil War but had not yet plunged into it.

Oliver had learned a valuable lesson when he had tried to control the men from the fens. It remained to be seen how his skills as a commander in a military conflict would play out. As he sat now on his horse behind the hedgerow with a new fresh band of men, he began to enjoy the power. The anticipation of a clash with the king's men excited him. The enemy cavalcade approached. Once more he reminded his men that the cause that placed them in these East Anglian ditches on a Thursday afternoon was the glory and honour of their country.

Suddenly shots were fired and there were cheers from the spectators. The king's man, Docwra, realised that the path was blocked. Since no one had lost any blood in the war just yet, he wasn't going to be responsible for bloodshed. He turned on his heels and led his troops back towards York. No men were killed or injured during the skirmish. Oliver Cromwell had won his first encounter in the English Civil War. The victory would not be his last.

Reluctant to retreat from the area, he waited for Valentine and his men to return from their scouting position to confirm that the royalists would not return. Fortuitously, his brother-in-law had captured two of the king's men. Before Oliver could open the inquisition, Valentine pulled him aside. 'I have already spoken to them. I can't believe that what I am about to tell you is true. But these men have no axe to grind and they swear by the veracity of their statements.'

'Please speak plainly, Valentine,' said Oliver.

'Very well. The rumours are accurate. The king is in league with the Irish papists. He intends to foist them on his own subjects. With him as their leader. Here on English soil. Our worst fear is about to come true.'

On 22 August, 1642, the king raised his standard at Nottingham declaring war on his own parliament. By this action Charles effectively left Parliament running the country. Back at the Cromwell household in Ely, Oliver junior and Henry relished the news. Richard was nonplussed. Oliver junior would get his chance to be a soldier. Himself and Henry endlessly discussed the differences between matchlock and flintlock muskets and the firing range of each. When it came to ordnance, Henry was an advocate of the granado. But they both preferred to be in the cavalry rather than the infantry. The advance guard or 'forlorn hope' were usually made up of foot soldiers and were the first ones into the fray. So, definitely best to be on horseback. Pikes, they deemed were far too big and cumbersome and should only be used by men strong enough to wield one.

Beth watched her two sons discuss the vicissitudes of the various instruments of death. She looked on as Oliver junior pierced the air with the iron fire poker that he pretended was a rapier. 'On guard!' Henry darted out of the way grabbing the breadknife from the kitchen table. The two laughed their way through the mock duel. Beth had lost one son recently. Losing another was inconceivable.

Chapter Eleven

Oliver Cromwell junior charged up the hill on his horse. He was alongside hundreds of his comrades. They were in separate columns. Their orders were to stick together in their own units. The town of yonder Gainsborough was the prize. It was his first taste of battle. He was petrified to his core. A well-aimed musket shot could have smashed his chest open at any minute. He could easily have been killed. Or maimed. Ten minutes earlier, his father, the Captain of the regiment had given an inspiring speech to his men. The words resonated deeply with the listeners. But Oliver junior knew the reality of what awaited him at the top of that hill. He still had to dig deep. He hoped he could remain strong. He could show no weakness. Today he was the Captain's son. He was one of the younger parliamentarian soldiers on the day. He had to rise above any fears he had and trust in the Lord God Almighty. Everywhere he looked he saw the anxious faces of his peers. A few of the seasoned soldiers, who had seen conflict in Europe, were recklessly charging out in front. He couldn't believe how rash they were. For his part, he wanted to make sure that there were bodies in front of him as he went. Dueling with an iron poker in his mother's kitchen was one thing. Being in the frontline of a frenetic cavalry charge was another. The previous day he had gotten his head shaved. Many of the parliamentarian soldiers did the same. There was a sense of inclusion, a bond between them in having a *round head*. In contrast, the royalists sometimes wore their hair long and acquired the name *cavaliers*. Oliver junior didn't want to die. But if it happened, he hoped it would be quick.

When they reached the top of the hill, they formed battle lines. His column was directly in front of one of the royalist cavalry's columns. Directly in front. He didn't have to wait long to see if this was going to be the day he died. When the parliamentarians were within musket shot, the royalists charged. Shots rang through the air. The man directly in front of him was shot clean through the face, his body went limp and he dropped from his charger stone dead. Oliver's father was bringing up the rear. As the royalists began their charge, Oliver senior gave the order for a counter-charge. The father had by now lost sight of the son. Each Cromwell handed their destiny over to the Almighty.

Horses crashed into horses. Bones cracked. The reluctant fell. The committed fell. Men tumbled on to the ground and were trampled underfoot by frightened and flailing beasts. Swords swung swiftly through the afternoon sunlight and sliced heads clean off men's bodies. Lives were annihilated in seconds. Children became fatherless with the press of a trigger, the swish of a stout arm. Mothers lost sons. Wives, husbands. Later the bereaved would receive condolences from the neighbourhood. But that was later. Right now avoiding death depended on the level of your trust in God. Men needed to have honour, courage and resolution. Opponents on both sides, all of whom had all been lovingly nurtured from birth, were smashed to pieces, their bodies ripped apart in a testosterone-fuelled orgy of death. If it weren't for the cries of the manic, the anguish pouring from the throats of the wounded might have been heard. The ferocious hand-to-hand combat continued unabated as each side tried to press home their advantage.

Gradually, after some time, Oliver's men gained a foothold. Soon the royalists found themselves forced into a quagmire. The leader of the king's men was unlucky enough to be stabbed with a frenzied blow under the ribs and he died on the spot. With their principal soldier slain, the royalists began to take flight. To hell with the king. Now it was every man for himself. The parliamentarians immediately began to chase, but the elder Cromwell called them back. It seemed to come naturally to Oliver to realise that a chase would be futile. Oliver junior managed to avoid death thus far today. He was just about to make his way over towards the Captain, when the battle took another turn. The day was not won yet.

With a far superior number of troops than Oliver had at his disposal, the royalist army of the Earl of Newcastle, now arrived on the other side of the town. The timing could not have been worse. They came bearing down on the remaining parliamentarian troops. The farmer from Huntingdon seemed to know instinctively what to do. He showed no signs of panic. He was decisive. Without his direction, the day could easily now be lost.

Barking clear and concise orders, he somehow managed to corral all of his cavalry into one large tight column. They turned and faced the enemy. The royalists couldn't penetrate the density of the unique configuration. Moving steadily, the Roundheads managed to remain in a closed formation. Oliver retreated. He ensured that they would live to fight another day. The numbers of the royalist forces were simply too large to take them on directly in the field. They managed to get away and made it to the safety of Lincoln. Oliver's combat tactics would echo way beyond the battle site. His military aptitude was a revelation to his troops. It was also a revelation to him.

The war progressed apace. With every engagement, Oliver was learning more and more. He looked around him and watched as other parliamentarian commanders chose men of a high social rank for their officers, irrespective of ability. Oliver was not impressed with this method of choice. He knew that above all his officers had to be godly men. If they displayed a flair for battle, even if they were common men, Oliver would make them officers. Fundamentally, each side needed numbers. The country was divided. Communities were fragmented. Families were split. The opposing sides were clear about their positions. How could anyone take up arms against their own king? How could anyone accept a tyrannical king such as this? It wasn't so much the monarchy that was this issue for Oliver. It was the current incumbent. The battle cry from the parliamentarians was 'For king and Parliament!' Just not *this* king.

Oliver went on a recruitment campaign. He went to places where men would frequent. Plain, ordinary, God-fearing men. Men he knew he could trust. He went to the inns of Cambridge, the taverns of Ely, the hostelries of St Ives. It wasn't long before he found himself approaching the Falcon Inn in Huntingdon. This was his home town. The petty squabbles of the past were now irrelevant. He was due to meet with his commanding officer in the market square.

He crossed over the bridge at Godmanchester. He was accompanied by four of his officers. They were all on horseback. He glanced into the River Ouse as he passed. He remembered the day he almost drowned in there. Trotting his horse down the High Street, he inhaled the familiar scenes of his childhood. He smiled and greeted people he recognised as he passed. One or two of the locals turned their backs as the Roundheads approached. Half way along the street, Oliver could see a man standing in their way. The rather plump, round-faced man stood determinedly in the middle of the street. Oliver tugged on the reins of his horse when it became clear to him that the man wasn't going to move. Oliver's immediate bodyguard reached for his pistol. They were used to this. Derision on the street was commonplace by now. It was almost expected. But Oliver sensed that there was something different here.

'Mr Cromwell, we meet again,' said the man. The disdain in his greeting was clear. Oliver knew immediately that the man's sympathies were with the crown. A lot more rotund than he remembered him, Oliver also knew precisely who the man was.

'It must be over thirty years now, my good vicar since you pulled me from the river. Was it not a great providence for me that God saw fit to imbue you with the fortitude to rescue a mere sinner such as I, at the very hazard of your own life. I see the world has been good to you since.'

'There is no law in the land that justifies you taking up arms against your one true king, who has a divine right to govern his people as he sees fit. And deep down in your soul, you must know that I am speaking the truth,' said the vicar.

A small crowd of onlookers had gathered. Oliver was not daunted in the least. 'I have often thought of what you did for me that day,' he said. 'And I still praise Almighty God for your heroic deeds, Vicar. I was clearly not meant to die. And while your present demeanor reveals that you might not want my thanks, I bestow it upon you again – a thousand times.'

'Unfortunately, Mr Cromwell, it is your actions as an adult that repulse me. When I see how you revile and attack the monarchy of this country, I wish today that I had allowed you to drown. By your abhorrent actions you endanger the king's life and the lives of his loyal subjects. The king of your country. Of *my* country! You and your fellow rebels are already responsible for the deaths of many.'

'*Not* the monarchy!' said Oliver raising his hand. 'But this king. This king does not deserve my respect. He has divided his subjects. He has proven that absolute monarchy is grossly flawed and can so easily be abused. Constitutional monarchy would be *my* preference. And further, Charles Stuart is a Catholic-loving king. I will not pretend that it doesn't disappoint me to hear you say such things. It was God's will that I lived. There are things over which we have no power. As you well know. Now, I will thank you to allow us to pass. Kindly stand aside and let us be about our business.'

The vicar stood aside. But not before he had the last word. 'You will regret the day you took up arms against the king, Mr Cromwell. Because nothing on this earth will make your poisoned cause an honorable one. The king will prevail! Hail glorious King Charles.'

The former orchard thief of Huntingdon emerged into the old familiar market square and tied his horse to a post. The officers that accompanied him sought his permission and then disappeared into the Falcon Inn. He was early. He glanced over at the little Huntingdon Grammar School building and the memories came flooding back. In his mind's eye he could see his sisters and Valentine running home along the street after school. He thought about the times he and Valentine had stolen apples from fruit stalls in this very marketplace. He was part of the fabric of this town. Sensations of nostalgia rose within him. He connected so easily with his past among these familiar, welcoming buildings. Such a feeling was not possible anywhere else on earth.

He sat on the wall of All Saints and he watched the local men pass him and enter the inn. The intelligence had obviously spread that he and his superior officer would be there to address them today. The words he would speak to them began to formulate in his head. If the common men had come along to listen, well, Oliver would not disappoint with his passion. The eight pence a day for infantry and the two shillings a day for the cavalry were bound to help with the recruiting process. For the first time in a long time he felt that his work in the world was meaningful. He had an outward confidence now that he had only shown glimpses of before. The death and destruction that came along with warfare did not seem to impinge on his conscience, like it might have done with other men. The alternative – to succumb to oppression was simply not an option.

His reflections were interrupted by the arrival of a small party of parliamentarian troops. The commander of the Eastern Association forces was at their head. He dismounted and approached Oliver.

'Captain Cromwell,' he nodded. 'If my memory serves me well, I do believe that the last time we conversed was in this very location. I'm not sure if you remember it?'

'The conversation is impressed on my own memory, sir. I do believe you relieved me of a tidy sum of one hundred pounds that night. Those days were the days before my re-birth. You will not find me engaging in such idle pursuits any longer.'

'Ah, then you disappoint me. I was hoping to have a similar experience when our work was completed here.'

'Then you must remain disappointed.'

Oliver knew that the Earl of Manchester, Edward Montagu, wanted to take him down a peg or two. So far in this conflict where Oliver had shown guile, his superior officer had shown indecision. Where Oliver was resilient, Manchester was tentative. Oliver wasn't fully convinced of Manchester's commitment to Parliament's cause. And that gave him an edge.

'Before we go in, Captain,' said Manchester. 'I would like to discuss your method for choosing officers. Why do you insist on commissioning men of poor parentage and not men of estate to make decisions of enormous magnitude on the battlefield? Do you have any idea how much of an insult this is to the men of nobility? You will destroy Parliament's chances of progressing with this war with your puerile approaches. These lower classes should not be elevated to positions that are clearly above them!'

Oliver was ready for the question. He looked confidently into Manchester's eyes 'I had rather have a plain, russet-coated Captain, that knows what he fights for, and loves what he knows, than that which you call a gentleman and is nothing else,' he said as assertively as he could.

Manchester took note of the flash of self-assurance from his captain. 'Very well. I just hope you know what you are doing.'

Oliver was happy that he had stood up to a Montagu. If there was a winner of the battle of wits, it was definitely him. The two men turned towards the inn. There was an army to be raised. As they approached the door, Manchester changed the subject.

'I was quite shocked when I heard that you had died yesterday, Captain Cromwell,' Manchester grinned. 'For some time, the rumour was circulating around my camp this morning that you had died in action.'

'I hope to be around for a long time to come, sir,' said Oliver. 'How do rumours like this begin? The ramblings of idle men with nothing better to do in between battles, I'll wager. And there is plenty of time for that.'

'Yes indeed. Your name is not so unique after all. I had to look at the casualty list myself. It turned out that it was another Oliver Cromwell who has gone to his reward. A much younger man. A distant kinsman perhaps?'

Oliver stopped in his tracks. Manchester's words hit him like a hammer blow.

Chapter Twelve

Very few appreciated the huge task ahead of the official gravediggers. The soil was dense and claggy. The graves had to be dug deep enough. But maybe not quite six feet deep. There were tens of half-naked bodies to be buried. The locals had already scavenged whatever they could get from the dead. Anything that wasn't ripped to shreds or bloodstained beyond saving had already been taken. Boots were the prized plunder. Or a concealed dagger that the victorious regiments missed in the weapon and goods retrieval process. There were material benefits to be had from being early on the scene.

With the number of dead to be buried, it might take a couple of weeks to clear the entire battlefield. This was the day after the battle and the local living were still foraging through the effects of the visiting dead. Nobody paid any attention to the man who had recently dismounted from his horse and was also searching among the bodies. It was pretty much a free-for-all. The body looters didn't realise that the man's life would never be the same again, that his entire familial landscape was turned completely upside down; that one of these bodies was his second-born child and that he had already lost his first-born.

Oliver was distraught. Telling Beth the news of the death of her second son was the worst thing he had ever had to do in his life. Watching the appalling information display in her eyes was an image that he would never forget. She had still not managed to accept the death of her first child. Now there were two. Two sons. Two fine, strapping, handsome sons. Both taken away by horrific circumstance. The Lord giveth and the Lord taketh away.

Oliver walked among the lifeless bodies and their detached parts searching for what might be left of Oliver junior. Steeled, he hoped that if he found the body, that it would not be badly disfigured or mutilated. He saw random isolated limbs, parts of arms and decapitated heads that were placed next to torsos, some of which might not even belong together. After a few minutes he found his son. Praise God, he was in one piece. Up to this moment, Oliver had been strong. He had to show Beth and the children that he was able to take the blows God delivered to him. But, now, in this inhospitable place, looking at his motionless boy among dead strangers, he sunk to his knees. For all the absence of movement, it was still the same child. He reached down to Oliver's flared nostrils hoping to detect a breath or a tremor. Nothing. The emotion within erupted. He pulled his precious son to his chest and he sobbed. At least now he would have a decent burial.

It was Beth that Oliver felt most sorry for. He had the war to focus his mind. Back home in Ely both Beth and Elizabeth had to pick up the pieces of their lives with two of the Cromwell boys now gone. The children were their world. Richard was now the eldest boy. His older brother's death made him even more determined not to get involved in the war. Conversely, young Henry just wanted to exact revenge on those bastard Cavaliers. He secretly hoped that the war would still be waging when he became old enough to fight.

After many small battles, skirmishes and sieges, the first major battle of the war was when the Roundheads met the Cavaliers at Edgehill. Both sides claimed victory. Oliver arrived late into the fray and only took part in a late counter-attack against the royalist army. But he saw enough of the battle to realise that when a cavalry charge was made, the trick was to ensure that they could be rallied again. He watched the cavalry of the royalist Prince Rupert charge and then scatter and fly about like headless chickens. It was now two years since Charles had raised his standard at Nottingham. Because of his many victories thus far in the field, Oliver had risen through the ranks and had recently been appointed a Lieutenant General.

His superiors recognised that God must have chosen Oliver as someone on whom to bestow happy providences. He was now with the main body of the parliamentarian army on Marston Moor. A stretch of moor between the village of Tockwith and Long Marston in Yorkshire. It was a wet summer's day.

Oliver had his Bible tucked inside his tunic. Everywhere he looked there was a sea of soldiers. They were lounging about, idly chatting and generally trying to while away the time. He picked his way through buff-coated men with bandoliers around their necks, swords by their sides. They all showed him the respect that his rank warranted as he walked. He could see the church tower of nearby Knaresborough off in the distance. Since the Scots had now joined with the parliamentarians there was a vast army of about twenty-eight thousand men just outside Long Marston. The royalist army, under the control of the dashing Cavalier Prince Rupert were within sight. Rupert had an army of about eighteen thousand. It was 1 July, 1644.

After about a half hour's walk, Oliver reached the church. Stepping inside the front door, he immediately noticed the steps of the tower. He made his way upwards until he came to a landing. A door was ajar, so he pushed it open. The room was sparse. A wooden table sat in its centre. Two chairs were placed opposite each other at the table. The west-facing stained-glass window on the bare stone wall splashed different coloured diamond-shapes on the stone floor. Oliver swung one of the chairs around, placed his Bible on it and sank to his knees.

It was two hours later when he finally stood up. If there was going to be a battle, God had to be consulted. Invoked. Entreated. He felt refreshed. He felt buoyant.

Oliver walked to one of the windows. Although the latch was unwilling to cooperate at first, he managed to coax the window open. From his lofty position he could see for miles. There was going to be a battle. Perhaps tomorrow. He gazed out at the vast numbers of willing participants and he marvelled at the world he now inhabited. A world of war. Far away from the fens of Cambridgeshire. Further away from the little farmstead at Huntingdon.

He surveyed the immense mass of men. He and his fellow officers will use these bodies as they will. Their minds have been manipulated. They will obey orders. They have embraced the life of blood and sword. In the name of freedom they will kill. They will not question if it is right or wrong. Their loyalty and their hearts have already been won. He turned his head to see the royalist camp. Their points of view might be different, but their dedication was the same. He bore the king's soldiery no ill will. He respected them. And now after two hours of prayer, Oliver was convinced that God would bless his endeavours tomorrow.

The next morning Oliver was awake early. He spent a lot of the morning in silent prayer. A council of war was to take place at noon. The parliamentarian commanders, Leven, Montagu, Fairfax and Oliver would attend. A strategy needed to be planned. On his way through the camp to Lord Fairfax's tent where the conference would be held, Oliver was stopped by a young parliamentarian soldier. It was his nephew, young Valentine Walton. The two men embraced. They spoke about Valentine's father, Oliver's friend. They spoke about Valentine's mother, Oliver's sister. They spoke about Oliver's two sons, Robert and Oliver, both of whom would surely have been there had fate not intervened. They spoke of memories that they shared in Huntingdon, St Ives and Ely. They didn't speak about the upcoming battle. They reminisced so much that Oliver was nearly late for the council of war.

The Roundhead commanders were all agreed. They would attack. Manchester and Leven would form the centre. Fairfax would be on the right, with Oliver on the left. The Roundheads had twenty-five field guns. Far more than the Cavaliers. The two armies faced each other across the moor. There was a road with a ditch in between them. The parliamentarians had the higher ground. Their front line stretched for a mile and a half. All day long each side sized each other up. Nobody made any moves. At about 7pm Prince Rupert decided that a battle would not take place now because it was too late. He retired to his tent for his supper.

But the parliamentarians had other ideas. As the weather got worse and thunder claps brought heavy rain, they decided to attack. Oliver's men were first to mobilise. Charging steadily towards the enemy, by sticking together, they managed to rout the royalist right. The close cohesion also meant that they could charge a second time. And a third, if necessary. Meanwhile, over on the parliamentarian right, Fairfax was struggling with his attack due to the rough terrain.

Oliver was in the thick of the battle. He wasn't sure exactly how it happened but as he pressed his men forward his rear was left exposed. A Cavalier sword suddenly came from nowhere and struck Oliver in the neck, just above the shoulder. It was a heavy blow and there was blood. Many would speculate later that had the strike been more true it would have completely changed the course of history. The royalist attacker managed to get away. Oliver pulled his horse up. He needed to check the damage. He had seen men with legs and arms torn off still attempting to fight for some seconds after impact. The blood would not stop pouring from the wound. Reluctantly, Oliver had to retire from the battlefield, albeit temporarily. He made his way to the village of Tockwith. There, he had his wound hastily dressed. After twenty minutes, he returned to the fight.

The confrontation was fierce. Parliament's superior numbers meant that they just about had the advantage. It was at that stage that Oliver received word that Fairfax was struggling. He immediately rallied his men and circumnavigated the royalist rearguard in the centre to assist Fairfax on the right. He now approached Fairfax from where the royalist attack on the left had started. In no time, he had broken the royalist resistance and saved Fairfax from defeat. It was his crowning glory thus far in the war. The Huntingdon farmer had prevailed over his enemies again. It was the biggest battle ever to be fought on English soil. Forty-four thousand men in total. It was clear to Oliver that the time spent in the church tower the previous evening was time very well spent.

About 9.30pm, the Cavaliers were all but a spent force. The rain had not stopped. The blood mixed with the mud. The fighting hadn't quite finished when, completely by chance, he encountered his nephew again. Valentine Walton junior was on horseback. His regiment were being instructed to rally when Oliver passed by.

'How now, Uncle!' cried Valentine in Oliver's direction.

Above the now dwindling battle noise, Oliver heard the greeting and glanced over his shoulder. He beheld his sister's child. His young face was bathed in sweat. He expertly held his reins in one hand and his rapier in the other. He looked like he was ready for battle again. Faith was his armour. God was his shield. Oliver saw the excitement in his eyes. He looked strong in the saddle. Heroic almost. He was the epitome of why this war was being waged. Valentine represented the future of England. It was to improve the lives of young Englishmen everywhere that they were fighting the king.

'We have them on the run, Uncle!' shouted Valentine.

'Yes, Nephew! The scoundrels are retreating!' replied Oliver. 'The day will be ours!'

'This is my third horse! The other two were shot from under me!' yelled Valentine trying to impress his uncle with his gallantry.

Oliver was impressed. He would have told him so if the cannon shot hadn't hit Valentine in the leg just at that precise moment. The force of the shot upended both horse and rider. The horse fell backwards, his insides spilled open, splashing mud in all directions. It landed on top of the young man. Oliver was horrified. He dismounted in a flash and ran over to his stricken nephew. Valentine was grimacing. His leg was still under the horse. The horse was dead. Oliver immediately ordered some of his men to raise the horse from Valentine's limb. This was done with some difficulty. At first Oliver thought Valentine was gone. His right leg was completely shattered. After some minutes the boy eventually began to speak.

'One thing lays upon my spirit, Uncle,' said Valentine as Oliver knelt over him.

'What is it, my boy?'

'Obviously God does not suffer me to be the executioner of my enemies any longer.'

'You have no need to make such a judgement. When your wound has been treated, you will return to doing God's work. You'll see,' lied Oliver as he tried to take in the shocking abruptness of the incident. He was used to war. He was used to death. But this was his sister's boy. His best friend's child. His children's cousin.

Just then a shout went up. The Roundheads were crying victory. The Cavaliers were now all on the run.

'Uncle! Uncle! Get my comrades to move, so that I might see the rogues run,' said Valentine.

Oliver instructed the soldiers in the immediate vicinity to part. They were on an elevated spot on the moor. Down the hill the enemy were now scattered. Valentine could see the royalists running in all directions. It was clear that the battle was over.

Five minutes later Valentine Walton junior died on the battlefield of Marston Moor. He was one of about four and a half thousand men to die that evening. Four and a half thousand devasted families. Oliver blamed the king.

Chapter Thirteen

The wooden seats in the House of Commons were not really that comfortable. Oliver shifted on the smooth, flat wooden surface, waiting for his turn to speak. He had held his tongue too long. Manchester, aka Montagu, was the focus of his irritation. He was going to blow Manchester right out of the water and there wasn't a thing his military leader could do about it.

Oliver's reputation as both an MP and a successful soldier was now a formidable one. He had proven himself to be more committed to the cause than his superior officer. As a proficient reader of men, he also knew that his peers regarded him more highly than they regarded his former dice partner who once bought Hinchingbrooke from the Cromwell family. Following Marston Moor, Manchester had failed abysmally to press home the parliamentarian advantage. The army simply went separate ways after the battle. The militia had been drawn from various areas around the country and the regiments merely went back to their area of origin after the battle.

Oliver was convinced that the war against the king simply had to be won. Parliament had to take the initiative. In order to beat him, the king would have to be captured. The debate they were having was about the war. Ten minutes earlier, Manchester had already spoken up against taking any further action. The Speaker of the House gesticulated towards Oliver. He stood up. He was ready. He was so ready. It was retribution time.

'It is the likes of my Lord Manchester, Mr Speaker, that is the problem, not the solution.' begun Oliver. Heads turned towards him at the temerity of his words. Manchester glared at his subordinate, bewildered.

'He has a profound inability to grasp fully the true import of our victory in the field. Only by beating the king will we achieve the much-desired religious settlement and liberty

101

from tyranny. We must continue the war. We have the eternal military advantages of strength and surprise. What if the king succeeds in obtaining aid from the queen's country of origin, France? Or worse still, what if he receives support from Ireland? We already know that he has sought support from these popish ruffians. My Lord Manchester, you have failed to exploit our victory at Marston Moor. The king's army struts around the country with impunity. There are reports that the royalists have now taken the strategic stronghold of Donnington Castle! The king is not yet beaten. By a long way. We must put a speedy end to this cataclysmic conflict. We must find the king and take him captive. Without their leader, the royalists will wilt.'

Manchester couldn't help himself. He rose from his seat and he faced Oliver. 'You have overstepped your responsibility, Lieutenant General Cromwell! You know nothing of these things. What would a country farmer know about issues that will settle our nation? Your naivete in military and political matters astounds me as I'm sure it does other honourable gentlemen in this chamber. Have you not considered that if we beat the king ninety-nine times, he would still be king and his posterity, and we his subjects still. But if he beat us just once we should be hanged and our posterity undone?'

Manchester sat down, happy with his rejoinder. There was a roar of applause from his House of Lords' supporters. Oliver thought that Manchester looked quite smug. Excellent. It was a good argument. But Oliver was ready for it. Manchester had no idea what was coming. 'My Lord, if this be so, then why did we take up arms against the king in the first place?' More applause. This time the cheering was louder. It was clear that there was a significant majority on Oliver's side.

But rather than focus on the pettiness of the conflict between them any further, Oliver stepped it up a level. He had done his homework. He was well prepared for this moment. He knew that simply making officers from members of the aristocracy was a flawed military strategy. This is what Parliament had done from the start of the war simply because it was tradition. These men were not professional soldiers. Nor was he. He had no intention of simply making his row with Manchester the issue of the day. He had far more important things to propose.

'I would like to bring forth the idea that this parliament bring in a law that requires sitting members of either the House of Commons or the House of Lords to resign from the army.' There were gasps.

'And professional soldiers with experience abroad will fill these vacancies,' continued Oliver. 'Of course, I myself will also have to resign. But some things are more important than individuals.'

Oliver's suggestion caused consternation. The members couldn't agree. So there was a vote. During the voting, Manchester went around the chamber trying to persuade his peers that they should not vote for Oliver's proposal. Their commissions would be gone. Their army pay would be no longer. The businesses in which they had invested needed the war to continue so they could reap the rewards. Manchester had seen opportunities and had invested in businesses that provided weapons. It suited him to prolong the war. But it was futile. The result was clear. Parliament agreed with Oliver's proposal. It made perfect sense. All members of both houses had forty days to resign their army commissions. In one unexpected fell swoop, Oliver had brought Manchester down. Manchester watched the events unfold. He watched his power fade away. His investments would now be in trouble. His army pay gone. His underling had finally defeated him.

But even at that, Oliver wasn't quite finished.

After the vote was decided he declared. 'I would like to now propose that we newly model the army. That we establish a full-time professional soldiery. Ready to fight anywhere on this island. They must not be tied to a single geographic area or a single garrison, to where they are bound to return following a conflict. I also propose that no army officer should ever have a seat in the House of Commons or the House of Lords. I also hold that this new army be a different entity to Parliament and that it does not engage in politics.'

Oliver was starting to emerge from the shadows of obscurity. The upper echelons of Parliament had already been aware of his prowess in battle and now there was a significant politician emerging from deep within this feisty officer who had yet to taste defeat of any sort in this war.

In a matter of months the New Model army was ready. All of Oliver's proposals had been taken on board. All of the MPs and Lords resigned their commissions. With the exception of one – Oliver Cromwell. Oliver didn't seek an extension to his resignation date, but he got one anyway. Parliament were not that keen to relieve Oliver of his stripes quite yet. So they made an exception, just to see where this would take them. Oliver seemed to have God's ear. He was on quite a roll.

It was 14 June, 1645. The medieval village of Naseby was set in the rolling hills of the Northamptonshire uplands. It was here that the two opposing armies eventually found themselves in close proximity to each other again. The royalists were being pursued by the Roundheads. The king had decided that instead of retreating they would turn and face their enemies. Oliver was pumped. This might well be the day that all of this war ends. If the Lord God Almighty sees fit, then by nightfall, the king will be decisively beaten and he himself will be in the hands of Parliament. Then negotiations for a peaceful settlement can begin. And with the king in a position of weakness, surely a positive future for the three kingdoms was within their grasp. It was a foggy morning.

Each man that stood on the battlefield that day was about to face terrible horrors. Some of his comrades would die agonising deaths. Bodies would be blown up all around them. More than anything they wanted to make it back home to their wives, their mothers, their children. The last thing they wanted to do was to make their families bereft of a breadwinner. Or make them grieve their loss. Soon blood will seep like sewage on the battle ground. However principled the quest, the nightmare was about to begin. Men will screech fervently for the cause. Men will screech excruciatingly in pain. The wrong move at the wrong time in the wrong place could mean certain death. Who lived, who died, who was disfigured for life was in the lap of their God.

When the battle of Naseby was all over, about a thousand royalists and one hundred and fifty Roundheads lay dead. It was Parliament's day again. And again Oliver's men performed heroics. The king and his commander, Prince Rupert, had managed to escape. But the royalist army was decimated. Surely now it was only a matter of time before a resolution would be brought to the war.

After the battle, now second in command of the entire army, Oliver was summoned by his chief commander. Sir Thomas Fairfax was tall, debonair and had an attractive countenance. He had dark features and was known to his men as Black Tom. Oliver dismounted from his horse and the two men gripped each other's hands.

'Truly England and the church of God had a great favour from the Lord, in this great victory given us,' said Oliver. 'I could not, riding out alone about my business, but smile out to God in praises, in assurance of victory because God would, by things that are not, bring to naught things that are.'

'Aye, Oliver. This is indeed true,' said Fairfax. 'A famous victory indeed. Our children's children will celebrate Naseby and posterity will thank us for this momentous day.'

'We study the glory of God, and the honour and liberty of Parliament, for which we unanimously fight, without seeking our own interests. I profess I could never satisfy myself on the justness of this war, but from the authority of the Parliament to maintain itself in its rights; and in this cause, I hope to prove myself an honest man and single-hearted.'

'After today, you have proved yourself more than worthy. Now we must press our advantage. I need you to see this.' Fairfax handed Oliver a bundle of papers.

'What is this, my Lord?' asked Oliver.

'They were found among the king's possessions when we took the baggage train. There are details contained therein, which implicate the king in his dealings with the Irish. To date, our men in Ireland have managed to prevent an Irish army entering this war. But judging by these documents, we have no time to lose.'

'Yes, what you say is true. The monarchy must be preserved in all of this, but we simply must prevent an Irish army from supporting the king here in England. These papists simply must not prevail. The world has witnessed their savagery for too long.'

Following Naseby, Parliament's momentum was not halted. Mopping up various other garrisons around the country was carried out with ruthless expedience. Oliver was again to excel, particularly at Basing House, where the Marquis of Winchester's home was not only a royalist stronghold, but a nest of papists.

In May 1646, Oliver found himself within a day's ride of Ely. He decided to take a well-earned break from the hostilities. It was some months since he had seen Beth and the children. It was a fine spring day as he made his way across the fens towards the town. The colossal tower of Ely cathedral drew him closer as if he were one of the multitudes of pilgrims hearing its call. He could discern the changes in the landscape. He was minded of the fen people and he wondered what the war had done to their lives. The devastation. The desolation. He passed old gnarled trees, isolated by an absence of vegetation, that stood as stilted sentinels on the sodden landscape. Reaching the outskirts of the town, the gradient began to rise. He smiled to himself as he imagined the surprise on Beth's face when she would see him.

He rounded the corner into Saint Mary Street and now the white, half-timbered house was in view. He beheld the familiar, unfamiliar house for a while. It was because of this property that he wasn't now forging a new life in the New World. There was no question about it, but it was God's verdict that he remained in England. God had proven by assisting him on the battlefield that it was Oliver's destiny to engage in this war.

He directed his weary horse through the gate at the side of the house, which took him around to the rear yard. He was looking forward to a nice meal, some home comforts and a comfortable bed for a change. But most of all he wanted to feel the hot breath of his lover, his life partner on his face. His fingers tingled with anticipation as he tied the horse up. There was that familiar sensation in his loins. The sensation that had been absent from his life for so long. He wondered to himself if this was the real reason for making the effort to get home for a few days. He convinced himself it wasn't.

He turned to face the House. Beth was standing at the kitchen door. She was beaming. She looked thinner. She was clearly restraining her tears. Oliver thought she looked absolutely radiant. Standing there in the evening light. She presented a picture of a life companion who had coped admirably in this world of utter chaos. Oliver knew that he needn't have worried about the children. Beth's self-assurance conveyed a story of domestic accomplishment. Not only had she coped during this time of upheaval, in her husband's eyes, he knew that Beth will have excelled. That was the kind of woman she was. And he thanked God for it.

She ran to Oliver and he pulled her close. Beth took Oliver's face in her hands. 'Truly my life is but half in your absence,' she said smiling into his eyes. 'You are dearer to me than any other creature,' replied Oliver as he drew her close to him again. The enfolding of their bodies so close, after such an absence, had the inevitable effect of mutual arousal. They both knew it. It didn't need to be said. They would wait until the household had retired. The foreplay had already begun. And it would go on for hours.

It was very early the next morning when the soldiers knocked on the door. They must have done so with some trepidation. To disturb the second-in-command of the parliamentarian army at home would have to warrant significant justification. Oliver knew this too. Ever alert, he had heard the horses approach. He instinctively knew that something was afoot. He answered the door in his nightclothes. The young officer braced himself as the door swung open.

'Captain Ireton,' said Oliver recognising the officer and smiling to allay his fears.

'Good morrow, Lieutenant-General sir. I bear war tidings. Commander Fairfax has ordered me to inform you of these developments immediately.'

'Well, boy. Pray tell me, what is this most important dispatch?'

'The king is in custody, sir. The war, the war is over.'

Chapter Fourteen

Hampton Court Palace, London. Charles Stuart was calm. Serene even. He was sitting at the end of a long table. He cast some venison slices from the large platter in front of him towards two spaniels sitting at the hearth. The dogs squabbled over the food. Some of his royal courtiers stood close by. Royalist officers occupied the chairs in his immediate vicinity. Roundhead officers were seated at the opposite end of the table. There was a symbolic gap between both sets of negotiators. There was a material gap between their viewpoints.

Oliver watched the king's every move. He listened to his every word. Here, now in the cold light of day, despite the beastly actions of the king in starting and pursuing this war, Oliver was overawed being in the presence of royalty. Charles exuded dignity. Oliver was reluctantly impressed. He was fascinated by the king's capacity to command attention. Oliver had never witnessed such supreme poise. Such utmost reverence for one person. There was a breathtaking confidence about the king that belied his present position. It was a confidence that had been imbued in him since he was an infant. It was this same haughtiness that made him slap Oliver on the face all those years ago, when the king was just three years old. It was soon clear that Charles did not outwardly acknowledge that it was he who was the captive. He spoke and acted as if it were he who were in control. And nobody was going to argue.

Nobody spoke when the king was speaking. Nobody interrupted him. Both sides, friend and foe respected his physical embodiment of the monarchy. Oliver had not uttered a word. He felt unnoticed among the negotiating assemblage. Parliament had long agreed that Oliver need not resign his post. He had earned his place on the negotiation team. For now, he was perfectly happy to observe. For the moment, Charles was some distance away and Oliver was happy to remain anonymous. It was clear that this initial meeting was getting nowhere. Charles had difficulty with everything that the parliamentarians presented.

The king suddenly announced that he was tired. They would have to return to the discussions another day. He needed to retire. They must surely understand that this was a tiresome business. He stood up. Everyone else in the room followed suit. 'Sit!' said Charles assertively, gesturing towards his captors. 'I shall depart momentarily.'

Oliver and his comrades obeyed the command immediately. The king walked towards them. As Charles approached, Oliver got a better view of the man who he felt was responsible for wreaking such havoc on England. The other parliamentarian officers kept their eyes down, so as not to make eye contact with their monarch. Oliver didn't. He was strangely beguiled by the king. He wanted to try to rationalise this human being who swaggered towards him as the man who had caused so much bloodshed. The elegance. The sophistication. The refinement. The violence. The murder. Charles was only a couple of feet away now. Oliver caught a whiff of the king's fragrance. It was a scent that he had never experienced before. It was a world away from Oliver's humble origins; it was the smell of absolute power.

'Is Cromwell here?' asked Charles suddenly. 'Your Majesty,' said Oliver rising from his seat. He bowed his head towards his sovereign ruler.

'Indeed,' said Charles. 'I guessed it might be this one. Your reputation has preceded you into this room, has it not, Lieutenant-General? Your prowess in battle was established in foreign lands, I am informed. Am I to understand that my information is accurate?'

'I am guided by Almighty God in all of my actions and it is Him I am beholding to, for whatever advancements in this life that might befall me. It is also down to Him and Him alone that I have never departed from the shores of my beloved England.'

'Ah, the retort of the quintessential Puritan. Perennially cowed and consumed by the Almighty. You're not as tall as I had imagined,' patronised the king.

'I am taller on Mondays, Your Majesty. Today is Saturday, the day in the week that I am at my smallest,' replied Oliver making light of the moment.

'Very amusing indeed,' said Charles feigning a smile. Staunch enemies perhaps, but the two men seemed to be making a connection. 'Perhaps you can tell me, why is it that you Puritans hate Catholics so much, Commander Cromwell. My wife is a Catholic. Do you hate her, although you have never met her?' asked the king. A silence descended over the assembly. Charles was wily. He was used to being direct.

'With the greatest of respect, the Godly, those who have been personally chosen by God are what you term Puritans, Your Majesty. I am perfectly happy to acknowledge that Puritans do not indeed hate all Catholics. Most pointedly this would include the queen.'

'I am expecting that the momentary spark in your eye will facilitate a more broad explanation than an outright denial of what appears a resounding truth to me. I had hoped that you would be more explicit than many I have asked the same question of heretofore.'

Oliver stood his ground and stared straight into the eyes of his king. He was relishing the opportunity to expound his views. 'It is the Roman clergy who have chiefly made use of fire and sword. Not the laity. As for the people, the flocks, as they are known by in Rome, what thoughts they have in matters of religion in their own breasts I cannot reach, nor would I ever desire to. The poor creatures that the Roman Church call the laity are deluded and deceived by a horrid organisation with a loathsome legacy. Even in these times, in Ireland, the Catholic clergy – and no others – have instigated a despicable rebellion by preaching from the pulpits that the only good protestant is a dead protestant. I would meddle not with any man's conscience. I am an advocate of liberty of conscience. So, I do not hate Catholics, I simply abhor the hierarchy of that church who poison the people with their false abominable and antichristian doctrine and practices. And this, they have done for centuries.'

'If that be so, then perhaps we might consider toleration for Catholics as part of these negotiations. What say you?' said Charles putting it up to Oliver to add substance to his remarks.

'For my part, I would have no objections to discussing this issue. The practice of Catholicism is outside of the laws of England, as they currently stand. If it was my decision, I would allow the conversation to take place and let the cards fall wherever they may,' replied Oliver.

The negotiations went on for months. In the early days of the talks Oliver became more and more absorbed by Charles. On one particular day he witnessed the king interact with his own children. It brought a tear to Oliver's eye to observe Charles' tenderness towards his family. But as the time passed it was clear that Charles was simply being intransigent. It also became equally clear that holding the king prisoner was a perilous thing to do. This was the head of state. They moved their royal captive around to thwart any would-be escape plan by the royalists. They really needed to come to an agreement soon. But the more compromises Parliament made, the more the king demanded further. At the same time as he was in peace talks with Parliament, Charles was covertly encouraging uprisings in England and Wales and an invasion from Scotland. Oliver eventually began to see Charles for what he had always imagined he really was: duplicitous and deceitful. He was disappointed with himself that he had allowed himself to fall under the king's spell.

But Parliament gradually became divided. Many moderate MPs wanted to give Charles back all of his royal powers. The

Puritan MPs were in the minority. Despite the fact that they had banned the celebration of Christmas in 1647, due to the Christian overtones and the drunkenness and debauchery that went along with it, the key thing was that they had the army firmly on their side. The Puritans wanted to restore Charles to the monarchy, but with reduced powers. They also wanted to be able to practise their religion, without being oppressed. Oliver knew that God had ended the war. He also figured that God would play a part in bringing the king around to an agreement. Parliament just had to grind the king down and make him see sense.

There was quite a shock then when news came through of the king's escape. With the help of a royalist escape party, in the dead of night, Charles slipped out of his parliamentarian shackles at Hampton Court to freedom.

What would happen next? Where would the king surface? What were his intentions? Despite Oliver's grave misgivings about Charles, he never once considered that the king would start up the war again. Did the parliamentarian negotiators not appeal to his human side during the negotiations? Did Charles not display his compassionate side? Did they not all agree that war among themselves and the horrors it brought were anathema to self-respecting Englishmen everywhere? Did the king not concede that the level of bloodshed was needless and preventable? Did they not all decide that dialogue was the way forward?

They didn't have to wait long for the answers. Immediately upon his escape, with the aid of some dissident Scots, that 'man of blood' Charles Stuart marshalled his troops for battle again. So began the second English Civil War. This additional conflict was almost too much for Oliver to bear. He could simply not fathom how Charles could engage in the wanton destruction of another war. Vicious battles were fought at Colchester and Preston; thousands more men were killed. The vast majority of them on the royalist side. The king lost the second civil war after five months and eventually he surrendered himself into Parliament's hands again.

There were growing calls to now once and for all put him on trial. The army led the charge. In Parliament's eyes Charles had committed treason by declaring war on his own subjects – not once but twice. Like many MPs, Oliver was now convinced that there was no point in pursuing a negotiated settlement. The king was just too obstinate. The royalists were just barbarous wretches happy to do Charles' bidding.

December 6, 1648, was a cold morning in London. Oliver was miles away in the north and so, he figured he could never be blamed for what was about to happen. But he was well aware of the unfolding events. He had played a significant part in their planning. The regular militia who usually guarded Parliament arrived as usual to take up their positions in the Palace Yard of Westminster Hall, on the approach to the House of Commons. But their positions were already taken up by Colonel Thomas Pride's regiment, who had arrived much earlier on Oliver's instructions. The two army factions almost came to blows, until Oliver's emissary, Major-General Philip Skippon, persuaded the regular militia to stand down.

When the time was right, Colonel Pride then gave the order. The army entered the House of Commons. Any MP who was not in favour of putting the king on trial was forcibly ejected from the chamber. It was decided. The king would be tried for treason. The charges were clear: he 'traitorously and maliciously plotted to enslave the English nation with the wicked design to subvert the ancient and fundamental laws and liberties of the nation and in their place to introduce an arbitrary and tyrannical government for his own self-interests.'

Five weeks later, the immense Westminster Hall was packed. Onlookers were crammed into every corner of the place. People gazed upwards at the massive hammer-beam oak roof. The complex wooden construction supported about 200 tons of lead above. The roof was commissioned by Richard II in 1393. It was an ancient and hallowed building. Oliver sat among his fellow MPs waiting for the arrival of the accused. He scanned the prying spectators in the public gallery. The occasion was momentous. Unprecedented. Surely now Charles knew that by refusing every deal that had been put to him, he had put his own life in danger. Surely now the king could see that there was no point in resisting the power of Parliament. Surely now Charles would see the folly of his ways, he would display contrition and return some stability to a bleeding nation.

Charles entered the room. To Oliver, he had not lost any of his arrogance. The king took his seat. Standing to the right of the king, the Solicitor General, John Cook, began to read the charges. Charles tapped the floor with his silver-tipped cane to interrupt the proceedings. The Solicitor General ignored the tapping. Charles raised the cane and slapped Cook hard on the shoulder with it. Much like he had slapped Oliver all those years ago. The ornate silver tip flew off the cane and landed between the two men. Perhaps for the first time in his life, no one rushed to pick the tip up for the king. He leaned down and retrieved it for himself.

The room fell silent when the charges were read, and the king was asked how he would plead. Without standing he said, 'I would know by what power I am called hither. I would know by what authority, I mean lawful authority. There are many unlawful authorities in the world, thieves and robbers by the highway. Remember I am your king, your lawful king, and what sins you bring upon your heads, and the judgement of God upon this land; think well upon it. I say. I have a trust committed to me by God, by old and lawful descent; and I will not betray it to answer to a new unlawful authority; therefore resolve me that and you shall hear more of me.'

By this stage Oliver was no longer surprised at Charles'

inflexibility. He had expected as much. Charles must have known by refusing to recognise the court there could only be one outcome. The trial lasted seven days. Witnesses were called and still the king refused to plead. On the final day of the trial Charles asked for a meeting with both houses, Commons and Lords. The meeting was refused.

The verdict was guilty. The sentence was death. The king who was then, in the theory of the law, already dead for legal purposes, demanded a last word. He was refused it. The guards began to take the prisoner away. The king sought to speak. Again, he was refused the chance. On leaving, he cried pitifully, 'I am not suffered for to speak: except what justice other people will have!' As he was taken out, the cries of 'Execution!' and 'Justice!' filled Westminster Hall.

On 30 January, 1649, Oliver stood outside the banqueting house at Whitehall. He was accompanied by thousands of spectators. He had a vague memory of punching Charles on the nose as a child. He had lived with the acclaim of the punch all of his life. A couple of days earlier, along with fifty-eight other MPs, including one Valentine Walton he had signed the king's death warrant. He was absolutely convinced that Charles was a tyrant. For Charles' part, he wore two shirts on the day, so he would not be seen to be shivering in the cold January morning. Literally defiant to the death. His last day on earth.

The axe fell. The cut was clean. The king's head dropped. The crowd groaned. The English monarchy would never be the same again.

Chapter Fifteen

The daffodils in St James's Park lifted their heads as if they were each trying to compete for the sun. Robins and blue tits flitted around, ready to scrounge. The early spring leaves filtered the bright evening sunlight transforming the ground into a luminous patchwork. The neat copses around which the park paths led were dappled with sunlight and shadow in equal measure. A giant pelican basked on the rocks at the edge of the lake. Beyond the park the world seemed to be moving very fast. There was a serenity here that eased Oliver's mind. Sometimes he just needed to embrace the solitude that the park offered. It reminded him of his fields in far off Ely. It was so convenient having this amenity so close to parliament buildings. The park was often populated by other Members of Parliament as they too, sought seclusion or a discreet location for circumspect conversations beyond the halls of politics.

Oliver found a free park bench alongside a thick beech hedge, overlooking the lake. He hoped he wouldn't be disturbed by a fellow isolation-seeker. He took the risk and sank onto the warm wood. Immediately, his soul settled in to his surroundings. He took his hat off. The early evening sun warmed his face as he leaned his head back to relax. He pushed his hair back from his high forehead to complete the unwinding process. He liked the way the shadows fell gently on the alluring environment. He began to yearn for the fens. He could see them now in his head, the expansive, flat Cambridgeshire wetlands, bathed in spring sunshine. A simple life. Far from the insanity of war. The corruption of politics.

Voices.

Men were talking. On the other side of the hedge. It would be impolite to listen as the conversation was clearly audible. Irritated that he felt compelled to leave, he got up to go. Just at that moment, he thought he recognised one of the voices. When he heard one of the men say the word 'Cromwell', he made the impulsive decision to sit back on the bench. He glanced furtively around to see if anyone had noticed that he might be deliberately eavesdropping. A family stood on the opposite side of the lake feeding the ducks. Two ladies were fully engaged in a conversation on the bridge close by. Nobody was paying any heed to the middle-aged man dressed in black, holding his hat in his hands. He leaned backwards slightly to hear more distinctly. The hedge was dense with copper-coloured leaves, so the talkers would have no idea that they were being heard.

'You must see. Ireland has proven to be the death knell of so many English generals in the past.' said one of the men. 'It would bring him down. His gallop would be well and truly halted. He may even die there. The Irish have a fearsome reputation.'

'But what if he succeeds in Ireland?' replied the other man. His character would be even more enhanced. His renown would be celebrated throughout the land. Where all others have failed, he will have conquered.'

'I think the risk is well calculated. Cromwell believes that his victories have been down to God. Well, God's patience has to run out some time. Ireland is the place where English authority goes to die. It has been this way for centuries. No Englishman has ever reduced the country to obedience. Surely it is inevitable. History is on our side. I tell you that if he goes, Cromwell will come back like a lost sheep. Vanquished. The Irish will carry the king's son, the young Charles on a sea of victory back to the throne. Cromwell will regain his place among the anonymous.'

'I agree that his wings need to be clipped. He's merely the son of a farmer, or is it a brewer? He has no refinement. No breeding. How has he risen so high, so quickly?'

'He is nothing but an insolent farmer, who has been extremely fortunate in his military endeavours. But Ireland will finish him. Who knows, he may even end up on one of their famous human spittles being roasted alive.'

Oliver had heard enough. He chose not to confront the men. It was enough for him to know that one of them was the earl of Manchester. He knew the voice only too well. The other was one of Manchester's cronies. He got up and walked away.

Because of his unrivalled success in the field, Oliver was asked to consider commanding the Irish expedition. Ireland was by far the most likely direction from where a royalist intervention might be expected. The rebellion that had occurred there in 1641 meant that two-thirds of that country was now in confederate/royalist hands. The Confederation of Kilkenny had been drawn up in the year the rebellion broke out and now the Catholics of Ireland had formed an alliance with the royalists. Many were even Protestants. All confederation factions supported the crown and were against Parliament. As far as Oliver was concerned many honest Englishmen, including himself had invested money in the Irish wars in return for Irish land. Without the suppression of Ireland, their investments would never mature.

But Oliver wasn't sure that he wanted to leave England. He worried that if he were to be absent from the country that a royalist uprising might easily occur again on home soil. Upon the death of the king, the monarchy had been abolished. The Commonwealth had been born. It was true that Parliament had asked him to go to Ireland. But in Oliver's mind, there were many other generals who could take on the Irish mission. And now he was aware that there were some MPs who wanted him to take on Ireland so that they could see him taken down a peg. These are the things that were going on in his head as he approached his London home on King Street, Westminster.

Oliver turned the key in the front door. He hesitated before stepping inside. The aroma of a lady's perfume hung in the air. His senses were heightened. He pushed the door open. She stood by the long sash window at the opposite end of the

119

room. The window shutters were closed. The fading evening light penetrated through the cracks in the shutters. Long flecks of light discreetly lit the crack-shaped spaces in the otherwise darkened room. What he couldn't see of her shape, he imagined. Without any hesitation he strode purposefully across towards her. The sound of his sturdy, firm-heeled, silver buckled shoes filled the room. He knew exactly what to do. He moved as close to her as possible so he could fully inhale her fragrance, her sex. As the scent settled tantalisingly in his nostrils, his member rose in anticipation. The moment was intoxicating. He knew how it would end. She knew how it would end.

She wore only a loose white linen shift. No undergarments. The low-cut neckline had frills that added to the sensuality of the moment. Their noses touched. He could see her clearly now as his eyes adjusted to the half-light. Her eyes were like blue sapphires. Her skin was so fair, like alabaster. Her cheekbones were high and delicately drawn. Her mouth was accented by two deep dimples. No words passed between them. They spoke only with their eyes. He pressed his groin into hers and she gasped. Already firm, he began to throb from her response. He leaned down and gently bit her bottom lip, tugging it slightly and as erotically as possible. She smiled a delicious smile. He longed to be inside her. But not yet.

He reached down and ran his fingers lightly up her right thigh. She stiffened. He did the same with her left thigh. She parted her legs so he could run his fingers wherever he dared. He gently lifted her shift exposing her lower regions fully. He placed both of his hands on her buttocks. He sunk his nails into her, and she winced with pleasure. She deftly opened the buttons on his breeches, and they dropped to the floor. He placed his hands on her cheeks, touching her lips with his index finger. She placed her hands on his erect manhood. He felt the pleasure of a woman's stimulating touch searing through him. He threw his head back as she slid her other hand under his tight testicles. He licked her lips with his tongue as she began to move her right hand lightly up and down. Then he lifted her hair from her neck and began to kiss behind her ear. Now it was her turn to throw her head back.

He reached down and pulled her shift right over her head. She was now fully naked. She pulled him closer and rubbed his stiffness between her own legs. He frowned with pleasure. He prodded her as she moaned in expectation guiding his every thrust. She suddenly let go of him and turned around to face the window. She bent forward, parted her legs and offered herself to him. Not yet.

He pulled her hips towards him and he slid under her, still teasing. He rocked back and forth, his shaft tight to her underbelly. But he did not enter. She wanted him so badly now, but she also wanted to heighten the gratification. She reached forward and pulled the window shutter slightly ajar. The window sill was elevated by about three feet above the street outside. Folk went about their business along the pavement as dusk was falling. He slid slowly into her as she watched the pedestrian traffic pass the window just a few feet away. He could see the people too as he began to slowly thrust in and out. A couple. A man. A flower-seller. Another couple. A group of soldiers.

He quickened his pace as she pushed back to meet his movements. It would only take a side-glance from a passer-by to discover the lovers. But nobody looked. His thighs slapped against her buttocks. She loved the sound they made. He reached around and placed his middle finger at her opening. He began to rub. She nearly screamed in ecstasy. Immediately outside the window an old man stopped and held on to the railings. He was resting. Just feet away. They could both see him. He was oblivious. She tightened up. The man outside took his hat off. He wiped his brow. She watched him look up the street aimlessly. One turn of the head. And they would be discovered. She knew she had to let go now. She opened the shutter wider. Just one turn of the head. It was so thrilling. It has to be now! It just has to be now! The thoughts of everything that was happening gripped her. It all came together in an electrifying moment of euphoria. She climaxed in a frenzy of rapture. As soon as he sensed that she had reached her peak, Oliver ejaculated inside her, pulling her as close as he could for optimum penetration. She shuddered with the involuntary aftershocks that her body made. She slammed the shutter closed. But too hard with the excitement. The old man looked towards the window. It was just too late. The show was over. Later that evening the two lovers lay in their bed. They were in a tender embrace. One that transcended passion. Extenuated intimacy. Beth stroked Oliver's chest and said. 'I know you are to depart soon. And Ireland will be your destination. I shall miss you. I know your country needs you. And your family needs you. And I know you will choose your path wisely. You continuously do.'

'I have not fully decided yet, my dearest, there are so many considerations to cogitate. I hear now that many of the royalists have flown to Ireland and they have joined with that contemptable Catholic clergy. I must declare I have less patience with those Cavaliers who are now in league with the Catholic hierarchy. There are many generals that could go, and each one could do Parliament a great service.'

'Your delaying on the matter is causing concern, Oliver. I have heard this. And you know it well. There are those in the city who are taking wagers on what you will decide. Whether or not you will go or stay. I think you should inform Parliament of your decision once and for all.'

'And what does the great lady herself say? Should I go or should I stay?'

'I profess that I am convinced that God has decided you shall indeed go.'

'Well, I shall rather be overrun with a Cavalierish interest than a Scotch interest, I had rather be overrun with a Scotch interest than an Irish interest, and I think of all, this is the most dangerous. All the world knows of their barbarism. Then let us go, if God go. But there is one thing I need above all else, before I step shipboard.'

'What is it?'

'Money. I will not go to a foreign land, where the natives are hostile, and the terrain is unpredictable without the necessary resources. Money will buy weapons. Money will buy food. Money will pay soldiers. I have already estimated that Parliament must raise at least one hundred and twenty thousand pounds. And perhaps even more. If they can promise me that, I will have every opportunity to suppress the Irish.'

On 20 June, 1649, the House of Commons formally constituted Oliver Commander-in-Chief and Lord Lieutenant of Ireland. At five o'clock in the afternoon of 11 July, he embarked on his coach en route to Ireland. Above the coach was a white standard to indicate peace. The coach was drawn by six white Flemish mares. His lifeguard of eighty men surrounded the coach. This was precious cargo. The event was publicised throughout the country in all of the newsbooks. It was a further two weeks before the fleet of ships would actually depart. Oliver waited patiently for the money to arrive at Milford Haven before he would take his leave.

Eventually the war funds did come. It was now Oliver's responsibility to ensure that the adventurers who had contributed to the Irish wars would benefit with land. It was his job to make certain that no military threat to the new Commonwealth came from Ireland. Now he would finally see this legendary country for himself. This country of Catholics. Soon he would land in Dublin. On Irish soil. Oliver was well aware that he might never again return to the country of his birth. He was heading into the unknown. He had never been on a boat before. The sea was choppy.

Meanwhile, in Ireland, the populace had no idea what was about to descend on them. The enemy was coming. It had money. It had weapons. It had experience of war. It had Oliver Cromwell. It had God. The Hammer of Thor was about to fall directly on Ireland. The Irish earth was about to be scorched. The name Oliver Cromwell was about to be seared deep into the Irish psyche. And there was absolutely nothing anyone could do about it.

Chapter Sixteen

The taut ropes that made up the rig of the three-master galleon creaked with the motion of the water as the vessel bobbed about just a mile offshore of Dublin's Ringsend. Oliver stood on the stern side of the square quarter gallery, his stomach retching with every movement the waves chose to make. It had been a hellish journey for him personally. He had practically vomited his way across the entire Irish Sea. He had thanked God on numerous occasions that he hadn't travelled to the New World on one of these. The armada of thirty-five Commonwealth sailing ships were making their final approach through the calmer waters of Dublin Bay. It would be less than an hour now before the lead vessel would make landfall. The moment couldn't come quickly enough for Oliver. He longed to feel *terraferma* beneath his feet again.

While on shipboard, Oliver had received the welcome news that the parliamentarian forces in Dublin under Colonel Michael Jones had routed Lord Ormond's royalist army at Rathmines, striking a huge blow for the Commonwealth. Up to now, the London administration had not been in a position to properly support their fragmented parliamentarian army in Ireland. But that was about to change. From his vantage point, Oliver could see the wide expanse of the Dublin and Wicklow Mountains. At the mouth of the Liffey, the lofty stone walls of the city of Dublin lay in wait, off in the distance, upriver. A pleasant patchwork of various-coloured crops and vegetation stretched from the city walls southwards towards the Rathfarnham uplands and eastwards across towards Bray Head.

'Your carriage awaits, Lord Lieutenant,' said the Mayor of Dublin to Oliver when he finally set his feet on the stone steps that had been smoothed by countless feet and countless tides over the centuries. A group of aldermen had been sent by

Colonel Jones to greet Oliver. He was now the highest ranking individual in both civil and military affairs in Ireland, according to the English Commonwealth. Oliver stood on the harbour, breathed deeply and took in his surroundings. He wasn't exactly sure what he had been expecting, but there was nothing sinister in the air just yet. Not quite yet. 'This is indeed a country worth fighting for,' he said to the mayor. He stepped into the open-topped carriage. The body guard took up their positions. The driver flicked the reins. The entourage pulled away.

The road from Ringsend ran alongside the River Liffey. It was populated along the way by clusters of folk who had come out to see the renowned Oliver Cromwell. His reputation easily preceded him across the Irish sea. The carriage entered the city through Saint Mary's Gate. Inside the city walls, tens of people lined the streets. There was cheering and waving. Oliver stuck out his chest as the carriage passed. The Protestants of Dublin had evicted all the Catholics from the city. This was friendly territory. Oliver absorbed the city. Dublin reminded him of any English town. Except there was a doleful ambiance to this particular urban landscape. Once elegant half-timbered houses lined the narrow streets. Many of them now clearly run-down. Narrow laneways opened up at various intervals. The lanes disappeared down dark recesses where only the brave or the familiar ventured. Too many half-dressed urchins could be seen wandering aimlessly. The streets were drab. The buildings had a sombre character. It was clear that almost ten years of war had taken whatever gloss had once been on the city and turned it into a harsh, unwelcoming environment. Oliver was used to the desolation that war can bring. But there seem to be an extra dimension here. A desperate hopelessness.

Children ran alongside the carriages. The throng began to thicken. The old limestone walls of Trinity College loomed up in the distance. Soon, the convoy halted in College Green. Oliver watched as the inhabitants of the city began to flock around his entourage, pushing and shoving. Trying to get the best view of him that they could. To them, here was their liberator. Here was their hero. If anybody could bring peace to Ireland, it was Oliver Cromwell.

Oliver stood up in the carriage to address the crowd. As they surged closer he could see their emaciated bodies. He could tell that they had been through extremely challenging times. He was touched by the unspoken stories of woe that were etched into their gaunt faces. He thought of the newspaper reports he had read, about how the Catholics had massacred hundreds of thousands of these poor, innocent people. He thought of the marauding armies that had traversed the country here looting and pillaging as they went. He thought of the king and how far his poison had reached. He thought of the Pope and his evil servants of death and destruction on this very island. Lurking in the dark corners. He thought of how the ecclesiastical vermin had whipped their flocks up into a killing frenzy from the pulpits. He thought of God, and how the Almighty had chosen to work through him so that this blight on the world can be thwarted. The high moral ground was his. Now he must do God's work in Ireland, where the Catholic clergy thrive with impunity. He cleared his throat.

'As God has brought me hither safely, I hope to, by Divine Providence, restore you to your just liberties and properties. (Cheering.) You have been much trodden down by those unblessed papist-royalist combinations and the injuries of war. My mission is for the propagation of Christ's gospel and the establishing of truth and peace. I hope to restore this bleeding nation of Ireland to its former happiness and tranquility. All persons whose hearts' affections are real for the carrying on of this great work, against the barbarous and bloodthirsty Irish will receive such rewards and gratuities and will find favour and protection from the parliament of England. (Cheering.)

'Whereas I am informed that, upon the marching out of the

armies heretofore, a liberty has been taken by the soldiers to rob, and pillage, and too often to exercise cruelties upon the country people. Being resolved by the grace of God, diligently and strictly to restrain such wickedness, for the future, I do hereby warn all soldiers and officers under my command, henceforth, to forbear all such evil practices, and not to do any wrong or violence towards country people or persons whatsoever, unless they actually be in arms or office with the enemy; and not to meddle with the goods of such, without special order.

'And I further declare that it shall be free and lawful to, and for all manner of persons living in the country, as well as gentlemen and soldiers, as farmers and other people, such as are in arms or office with the enemy excepted, to make their repair and bring any provisions unto the army, while marching or at camp, or under any garrison under my command. I hereby assure all such, that they shall not be molested or troubled in their persons or goods but shall have the benefit of a free market and receive ready money for goods, or commodities they shall so bring or sell.'

'We will live and die with you!' came the response from the cheering people of Dublin, who looked to Oliver to be at the end of their tether.

In the following days, Oliver kept busy by making his preparations for the campaign. Dublin was safe, for now. He heeded all of the advice that Col Michael Jones had given him. Parliament had been in control of the town of Drogheda up to 11 July, the gateway to the north. The royalists managed to take it from them on that day. As Drogheda was a garrison of equal significance to Dublin, it was the perfect strategic location to start the campaign. His army now consisted of about twelve thousand men.

Elsewhere, Oliver had done his homework assiduously. He knew that Drogheda had been besieged by a Catholic army during the awful peak of the Irish Rebellion just eight years earlier. He knew that the siege had lasted five long months and that the Catholics eventually had to walk away and admit defeat. He had heard that the place was virtually impenetrable. He dreaded to think what horrors the people of the town could have expected if the Catholics had breached the walls. He knew that the population had been reduced to eating cats and dogs since the supplies had run so low. And that the siege was only raised when a supply ship from Dublin managed to evade the Catholic blockades and rescued the town.

It was a dreary, wet and windy day in late August when the militia assembled three miles north of Dublin. Oliver made the decision to send the field pieces by ship along the coast to Drogheda. The plan was to backfire as the ships were delayed when the weather dis-improved.

It was a two-day march to the garrison town. Oliver wandered around the men as they passed steadily through North County Dublin and Meath. It was his personal connection with his troops that made them go that extra mile for him in battle. He wanted to engage with them. He wanted them to know that this cause was even more noble than battles they had fought on English soil. He wanted them to see the honour in their quest. He told them that God would be on their side in whatever was to come.

But Oliver had inherited some renegades from Dublin. A small proportion of his men had been in Ireland for some time and had never fought under him directly. It came to his attention that two of these men had stolen some chickens from an old lady at a cottage along the journey. Oliver prided himself on his discipline. Without that, no battles could ever be won. This was a clear breach of his orders. He ordered the entire army to halt. He had the two perpetrators hanged in front of the rest, to show that he would not tolerate ill-discipline. The people of Ireland were to be left unmolested. The English army had money to buy supplies. Stealing food was not acceptable.

It was a humid September evening when Oliver arrived before the walls of Drogheda. The main army held back as he and his immediate officers trotted to the edge of Sunnyside Hill to observe the extent of the town. It was as pleasant a place as he had ever seen. The River Boyne split the walled town in half, each side occupying a high hill. The ancient river ran through the valley between them. From his vantage point he could easily see into the northern part of the town, where the gradient was more gentle.

He was happy to witness innumerable inhabitants evacuating the place through the gates on both sides of the river. Oliver figured that they expected a similarly long siege to the one that had occurred eight years previously. So, of course it made sense for them to leave. He guessed that everybody on the royalist side was expecting a long siege. He had learned that the town was stocked full of supplies for the occupying royalist soldiers. Five months' supply. That made sense to him. Non-combatant inhabitants would be a drain on supplies. Too many mouths to feed. Superfluous people had been ordered to leave by Ormond, who, Oliver was aware, had also installed the best men he could find to defend Drogheda.

But fundamentally Oliver knew that such a prospect was unconscionable. He disliked sieges. He was a much better battlefield commander. Besides, this was a big country. The royalists had to be crushed expediently. And this was only one garrison town. The success of Parliament continuing in power depended on success at Drogheda. Killing the king would be all for naught if the royalists were to win in Ireland. There was no time for long, arduous sieges. And there were always the adventurers' investments. Money for land.

Eventually after a week, the artillery arrived. Oliver summoned the town to surrender. He received no reply. According to military convention, by refusing to surrender, the royalists laid their lives on the line. Any attacking commander could legitimately kill the defenders, if the attackers gained entry to the town after such a refusal. The royalists knew it. The parliamentarians knew it. This attacker's prerogative had not been exercised during the Civil War in England thus far. But this was not England. This was Ireland.

Oliver gave the order to batter a hole in the walls of St Mary's churchyard with the large field pieces. After two days of battery, the breach was deemed assault-able. No fortress was impenetrable to Oliver Cromwell and his God.

Oliver was in his tent surrounded by his infantry officers. 'Gentlemen,' he said. 'It all comes down to this moment. I need a regiment to volunteer to assault the breach. But before anyone speaks, let me say this: God is watching our every move. He will be with us at the breach. He will be with us in the town. I guarantee you this. If we can break into the churchyard, we should be able to hold it and allow the reserves in. Who among you will take on this great mantle? Who among you will go down in history as the man who struck the first blow against the royalists in Ireland for the Commonwealth of England?'

Colonel James Castle, who had fought with Oliver both at Marston Moor and Naseby, stepped forward. 'I will gladly put the responsibility for this great work upon my own men,' he said with a passion that impressed Oliver to his core. This was just the man he could trust. 'Well then, there is nothing more to be decided,' said Oliver. 'Colonel James Castle, may God be with you and your men in this honourable assignment. Remember, these rabble are the barbarous wretches who reignited the war in England when it was over. Like their precious king, these villains have blood on their hands. Some of those who defend this town today are also are the same Catholic rebels who have imbued their hands in so much innocent blood in the Irish Rebellion this short time past. They are all in league with each other. Conceive the horrors that they have all committed together. Infuse them in your souls and let this guide you in your actions. Be valiant! Be bold!'

In less than half an hour Colonel James Castle was dead. Shot through the head at the breach. Many of his men met the same fate. The assault had failed. Oliver chose Colonel Hewson's men to make a second assault. This simply must not fail. So much depended on this crusade. Hewson's men attacked the breach. But they were beaten back. The second attack had failed.

Oliver was incensed. Castle was dead. One of his bravest men. The royalists might have had valour, but there was one thing for sure, they didn't have God. But Oliver had God. There was only one thing for it. He called Colonel Henry Ireton into his tent.

'I shall lead the third assault myself,' said Oliver. 'Prepare the men. We will win the day for Parliament if it's the last thing I do on this earth this very day.'

'But, sir, the entire campaign depends on you. We cannot afford to lose you. Surely, you must choose another commander. Allow me to go. My men are already fired up. They have anger in their stomachs. They will not falter.'

'My mind is made up. I will lead this assault. If I know my men, they will take heart from it. Now, do as I say. I must affix my armour and prepare for battle. Pray for me so that I may walk worthy in the Lord and all that he has called me unto.'

At 5pm that day, Oliver led a third assault himself. They thundered down into the verdant Dove stream valley and up towards the breach in the walls. They sang psalms as they tore into their enemies at the breach. He had made the right decision. He carried his men through the gap in the wall and in one fell swoop the royalist defenders all capitulated.

Oliver had no way of knowing it then, but what was about to happen in the next few hours would contaminate his reputation for centuries. And yet, it was very clear in his own mind. The whole of Ireland must hear about this. He must show these barbaric Irish Catholics and their English royalist affiliates that further resistance in Ireland is futile. What happens here today will save the further effusion of blood in the long run. He ordered his men to kill all of the defenders that they found in arms in the town, which was his right according to the rules of engagement. The carnage continued throughout the night. It was retribution time. Finally, Oliver could do something to avenge the deaths of thousands of innocents at the hands of despotic popes, bishops and priests throughout history.

The following morning three thousand soldiers lay dead on the streets of Drogheda. Including five priests. Three thousand families freshly bereft of a father, a son. The anguish was incalculable, the appalling business of warfare now routine. One street in particular literally ran red with torrents of blood. It was henceforth known as Bloody Street. At Drogheda, God preferred to champion the cause of the attackers. He deserted the ill-fated defenders. Just as Oliver believed He would. It was a far cry from the pleasant wheat fields of Huntingdon. Or the soft wetlands of Ely. It was war. And Oliver was still winning.

Chapter Seventeen

Wexford. Oliver sat on the Trespan Rocks overlooking the pretty little walled town. It was very conveniently located at the mouth of the River Barrow. Access to the sea and England beyond could be a great boon. This place would have made the perfect winter quarters. It was October. He was perched beneath a spreading oak. Wet, tousled, rust-coloured leaves lay thick on the ground all around him. A foraging squirrel picked through the vegetation for acorns directly below the rocks. An industrious robin darted hither and yon. His lobster-tailed pot helmet, complete with face-cage sat idle beside him. His mortuary-hilt sword still attached to its sword belt, lay discarded nearby. He had cut his hand on brambles as he climbed up. But he didn't notice either the blood or the sharp prick of the thorn. He was preoccupied.

Below him clouds of white smoke rose gently from some of the buildings in the town. Fires had been freshly set. Hundreds of bodies were floating in the water. A ship lay capsized in the harbour. From this distance he could have sworn that one or two of the bodies were female. Corpses of sliced-open soldiers littered the narrow streets. He could hear the pitiful wailing of women and the cries of children cut through the afternoon air. Fifteen hundred defenders lay dead. This was a war. It was either kill or be killed. He had always tried to protect the innocent, but some women had clearly drowned in boats that sank as they fled the town.

Oliver's conscience was pricked. Accidents of this nature were inevitable during fighting. But he had to remain steadfast. His adrenaline levels were gradually reducing. Reflecting on his life on these rocks, he suddenly became pensive and began to think of Beth back home in London. He wanted to be back on the farm in Ely. Everything was so much simpler then. Maybe after the war. It can't go on forever. He was a good husband. Wasn't he a good husband? It's just that God had called upon him to carry out this work. He wondered what his favourite daughter, Bettie, might be getting up to right now. He hoped young Henry was in good health and that he was turning into a fine soldier. And his eldest, Richard. What was to become of him at all? How had things got this far? How was it that Oliver found himself in a foreign country? At war? The family man. The gentleman farmer. Always away from home. Is this really what God had planned for him?

Oliver hadn't meant another killing spree to take place at Wexford. That town was a nest of piracy. Responsible for the killing of so many protestants. He hadn't given the order for it. But it happened nonetheless. It turned out that the massacre at Drogheda had not prevented further resistance from the Catholic/royalist army, despite his hopes.

He had been negotiating terms with the governor. Several written communications had passed between them. The mayor of the town had even sent out ale and whiskey to the besieging army for Oliver and his officers to enjoy while the dialogue continued. Relations had been cordial. But while Oliver was writing a reply to the governor in his tent, a cry suddenly went up that one of the town gates had been opened. Whether by accident or treachery, Oliver never did find out how this happened. Fresh from cutting down the Drogheda garrison, the Roundhead army simply repeated the same activity. They killed every armed defender they encountered as they swept through the streets and lanes of Wexford. Some townsmen had taken up arms to defend the town. They were summarily slain as they were clearly in office with the enemy, and therefore could expect no mercy. So many more dead. So many more families bereaved.

It had been several years since Oliver last had a panic attack. Like all of the other ones, this one came out of the blue. He had been anxious all day. But he had just put that down to the apprehension of the siege. Now he suddenly felt cut off from his family. From his country. What was he doing here anyway? None of these people really knew him. Suddenly it was all closing in around him. All of this death. He thought he was going to die. How could he stop it? There was nothing he could do to stop it. He was alone. Isolated. The vast Irish sea was between himself and Beth. He was overwhelmed by the magnitude of everything. The task at hand. What made him think he could conquer Ireland? Nobody had ever conquered Ireland. It was all too much. And there was nobody there to help him through this attack of the mind.

He put his head in his hands and he started rocking back and forth. Be calm. He had to try to be calm. What could possibly happen? There is no danger now. Nothing bad will happen. What was it that Beth used to get him to do? Plant his feet firmly into the ground and concentrate on his breathing. That was it! He pressed his two feet into the rock and focused on his breath. Long deep breaths. This has happened before. Nothing bad happened that time. And it won't happen this time. It's a condition. A medical condition. It will pass.

'I crave your pardon, sir, but the men are waiting for your orders,' said Colonel Jones as he emerged from a copse, flanked by two other soldiers.

The interruption helped with the recovery process. Oliver couldn't respond just yet but his fear of exposing his vulnerability began to rise within him. The new fear quashed the old fear. He could feel the anxiety abate and he knew that he had managed to control it. He was disappointed that this had happened again after such a long gap. He immediately accepted that this was now part of his life. Clearly this can happen any place any time. When he is least expecting it. Maybe on this occasion it was the trauma of the massacre of the defenders of Wexford that brought it on. Was it triggered by the fact that he lost control of his troops? Or was it the fact that he was looking across the sea and home seemed so far away. A full minute passed before Oliver's composure returned and he felt like he could respond to the question.

'Apologies, sir. But the town has been laid to waste. It might not be so suitable for our winter quarters, as you had initially hoped,' said Colonel Jones failing to sense what was happening and instead concluding that the Lord Lieutenant was pondering his next move.

'I had rather wished that the men had not been so overzealous,' said Oliver assertively as the moment had now passed. 'This place had many fine advantages for wintering, but it will not be conducive now to our winter repose. And yet, the season is young still, we will move on. We will find a more fitting location. How many men did we lose?' There was no hint whatever that he had just emerged from a panic attack.

'Not more than thirty, sir.'

'May God have mercy on their souls. In His righteous justice we have brought a just judgement on the defenders of this town by an unexpected providence. This caused them to become prey to the soldiers, who in their piracies had made prey of so many families and now with their blood to answer the cruelties, which they have exercised upon the lives of so many poor innocent Protestants. It is to be wished that an honest people would come and plant here. We pray God may have all the glory of this day.'

'Yes, sir. It is of course as you say it. We also found this in the town,' replied Jones. He brandished a newspaper.

'What of it?' asked Oliver.

'The royalist newspapers have begun to print their lies and calumny against us already, sir. This newspaper is *The Man in the Moon*, a poisoned publication if ever there was one. They have accused us of appalling deeds at Drogheda.'

'This is a war, Colonel Jones!' said Oliver tersely. Terrible things happen in a war. God will judge them all on the last day.

Appalling? What has been reported?'

'You will find it hard to believe what depths the royalists have sunk to in order to blacken our names, sir.'

'Read it to me.'

'Very well,' said Jones, as he lifted the paper to read it.

'The parliamentarians have taken Drogheda. Their barbarous cruelty in that abhorrent act, not to be paralleled by any of the former massacres of the Irish, sparing neither women nor children, but putting them all to the sword. 3,000 indeed they killed, but 2,000 were women and children and divers aged persons that were not able to support themselves, much less unable to resist them, the towne thus gained with the loss of 5,000 of their own... shall I continue, sir?'

'No, I have heard enough. Paper will never refuse ink. The truth is on our side, Jones. Nobody on this earth will ever be able to give us an instance, since my coming into Ireland, of one man, not in arms, massacred, destroyed or banished. We lost sixty-four men at Drogheda. And no innocents in that town whatever were deliberately harmed. Catholic or Protestant. How could they be? They have committed no crimes. My orders are clear. This is a new low even for the royalists. But while we all are aware of this newspaper's abject dishonesty, perhaps some good might come of their lies. This report might strike fear into the remaining defenders of the king's cause in this country. Their further resistance might be now reduced. And then we might bring the hellish darkness of these times to a swift conclusion and have peace restored with the help of God.'

They wintered at Youghal. Town after town fell to Oliver's hands as he marched through Ireland. The news of the Drogheda and Wexford massacres raced before him everywhere he went. Death and destruction from illness and warfare were pervasive. In two months after Wexford, Colonel Michael Jones was dead. He succumbed to country sickness. Oliver himself had various legacy ailments that returned to afflict him. Now in his fiftieth year, he also began to feel new age-related infirmities as the months passed. Despite the difficult odds, Oliver kept notching up the victories. With each success, more troops and more money came from England to support the army. The newspapers in London were soon promulgating the news that Oliver might actually slay the Irish dragon. Could he really actually conquer Ireland? Or would he fail yet, and the earl of Manchester and his cronies have the last laugh? Victor or vanquished? Only time would tell.

Nothing was inevitable. Oliver had not yet come up against an O'Neill of Tyrone. And that was about to change. The O'Neill dynasty was famous throughout Ireland. Throughout Europe. Many of the O'Neill family had engaged in wars on the continent. They had a reputation for bravery and guile in equal measures. And if these attributes are combined with experience, then the mix is indeed a formidable one.

May 1650, Clonmel. Of the twenty-nine garrisons that Oliver had encountered in Ireland to date, just two had not surrendered ultimately: Drogheda and Wexford. But Clonmel had a secret weapon; his name was Hugh Dubh O'Neill. Unlike Oliver, he was a professional soldier. He had served in the Irish regiment of the Spanish army in Flanders during the Eighty Years' War against the United Provinces of the Netherlands.

Nestled between the Comeragh Mountains and the Slievenamon peak in the heartland of Ireland, the walled town of Clonmel had orders from Ormond to thwart Oliver's relentless progress through the country. So far, Oliver had lost far more men to illness than he did to sieges. Ormond had been too fearful to meet him on the battlefield. The more royalist garrisons Oliver took, the more men he had to use up by transforming them into parliamentarian garrisons. Oliver was well aware that everything was still on a knife edge. One significant reverse where the parliamentarian army lost significant numbers, everything could easily change. Oliver was about to find out that an O'Neill from Tyrone was his superior in siege warfare. For the first time in his life he was about to experience God's fluctuating loyalty. This was not something he was used to.

Oliver followed the same process he had followed since his arrival in Ireland. Taking towns by storm. He summoned the governor to surrender. O'Neill resolutely refused. The battering of the walls began. Oliver watched the big guns do their work all during the day. When the breach in the walls was wide enough, he would send his men to storm the breach. But it was late. And the chances of a successful storm would be higher if it was daylight. Oliver decided to wait and storm the breach the next day. This was a huge mistake.

During the night, under the cover of darkness, O'Neill, his elite Ulster forces and every available hand within the town fashioned a funnel of stones, timber and mud. Anybody entering the breach would have nowhere to go, as the funnel was cut off on all sides. Behind the makeshift funnel walls he placed tens of musketeers, chain-shot cannons and pike men at the ready. A cul-de-sac of death. All O'Neill had to do now was wait.

The next day dawned. Oliver had no knowledge whatsoever about the night's activity. He assembled his troops for the assault. He commanded them to storm the breach. By doing this, he sent a thousand of them to their deaths. They ran straight through the gap in the walls. The men at the front reached the impenetrable wall at the end of the funnel. They cried 'Halt! Halt!' But the men at the rear misinterpreted the call and they piled in on top of their comrades. Soon there was a thousand Roundhead troops trapped in O'Neill's snare. O'Neill was watching from one of the curtain wall towers. His men looked to him for the signal. He raised his hand. He looked to the skies to his God. He lowered his hand. He shouted 'Fire!'

The attackers were annihilated. Pummelled to death on all sides. They could not even see their killers, never mind fight back. Chain-shot ripped into their soft bodies at close range.

Pikes came through the holes in the makeshift walls and slashed into terrified soldiers. Musket balls punctured heads, torsos, groins and legs in an orgy of killing. Blood splattered, limbs fell, heads exploded. Men shrieked for mercy in their agonising last throes of death. They could expect none. They got none. In less than thirty minutes, a thousand of Oliver's best soldiers were dead.

Oliver was devastated. He had never seen his men so utterly routed. And yet, he was still convinced that God would wield his almighty power and change the course of this siege. He rallied his troops. He ordered his infantry to attack the breach once again. They refused. Point blank refused. Oliver was shaken. Is this the end? Is this where it all goes wrong? It was his cavalry commanders who came to his rescue. They immediately volunteered to lead a second assault. It was far too dangerous for Oliver himself to lead an assault into this breach.

The cavalry dismounted. They faced the breach. About a thousand of them. Oliver used the deaths of their fallen comrades as motivation to stir them into action. They have an immediate opportunity to avenge these deaths and turn this potential loss into a victory. He was depending on them. God was depending on them. The future of England was depending on them. 'Go forth and send those murdering royalist bastards into the oblivion of hell!' were his parting words as they ran towards the walls singing loudly.

They attacked the breach. They poured into the funnel. O'Neill couldn't believe his luck. Oliver fell for his trap – a second time! O'Neill dropped his arm. He shouted 'Fire!' Carnage ensued. Within an hour a thousand more Roundhead troops lay dead in bits on the ground of Clonmel.

It was early the next day when the mayor of the town presented himself in Oliver's tent, catching Oliver totally off guard. The mayor had a smug air about him. He was ready to negotiate terms. To surrender. Oliver enthusiastically signed the terms. They were very generous terms, as the mayor clearly had the upper hand.

'And now, Mr Mayor,' said a very relieved Oliver. 'Now let us meet this O'Neill of yours. I must meet this man face to face. Our army will benefit greatly with him as a captive.'

'Alas, Lord Lieutenant, there are no soldiers left in the town. They all departed during the night, including O'Neill,' said the mayor with a wry smile.

'Then why did you not say so, before I signed your terms, you knave?' demanded Oliver.

'Because you didn't ask me, my Lord,' said the mayor.

Despite the clear defeat, Clonmel was Oliver's. Another victory, albeit a hollow one. Ireland was Oliver's. Manchester would eat humble pie. Again. Soon afterwards Oliver boarded a ship bound for home. Never to return. Over the years the royalist lies about the massacre of innocent women and children would somehow mutate into truth. But for now, Oliver's problems in Ireland were over. Yet because of him, Ireland's problems were only beginning. The bloodshed would effectively last for centuries. And only her rivers ran free.

Chapter Eighteen

It was two in the morning. Commander-in-chief of the parliamentarian army Sir Thomas Fairfax sat in Oliver's Drawing Room back home in King Street. He looked tired. He had made his decision. He was resolute. There was nothing Oliver could do about it. Dressed in his nightshirt, Oliver was pacing back and forth at the opposite end of the room. He was trying to digest the information that he had just been given. Ten minutes earlier he had been asleep. Until the knock came on the door.

'Resign?' asked Oliver again. 'Are you absolutely determined to follow this course of action, Your Excellency?'

'Yes, Oliver,' I have to follow my heart in this matter,' said Fairfax.

'But we have come so far. How can you possibly forsake our cause at this testing confluence of events? The army needs you. England needs you. Englishmen of the future will be eternally indebted to you if you see this business through.'

'I cannot go to war against the Scots. I will not go to war against the Scots.'

'But there is so much to be done yet, Your Excellency,' replied Oliver. 'The Commonwealth is not yet proven to be a success as an instrument of government. There are many MPs who remain corrupt. And now that Scotland has declared the young Charles II king, there is a new menace to be defeated.'

'My mind is made up,' said Fairfax. 'I will continue to fight for peace in the House of Commons. But no longer on the battlefield.'

'But, Your Excellency! Just think what would happen if the Scots were to defeat us in battle and carry the young Charles to London to install him on the throne? All will have been for naught. We *must* capitalise on the fruits of our victories until there is peace on these islands!'

'I have no appetite to engage in war with our neighbours, Oliver. There has been enough devastation already wrought throughout this land.'

'But in all probability there will be a war against the Scots now. We will have to defend ourselves. God hath given us this glorious prospect of a peaceful resolution. And only us!'

'Human probabilities are not sufficient grounds to make war against a neighbouring nation,' said Fairfax. He stood up, motioning to leave the room.

'That there will be a war between us I feel is unavoidable,' said Oliver. 'And I think we should take the offensive and quash the Scots in their own country. That is my judgement. We do not want them coming here. We should go to Scotland, and it should be our desire to avoid blood in this business at the first. But who will lead us, now that you're resigning?'

'All of England knows that the men live and die by you, Oliver. The acquaintance you have with them is matchless. You are now in charge of the entire army. Parliament will confirm your position directly. May God remain with you.'

Fairfax put his hand on Oliver's shoulder. The two men smiled at each other. Oliver knew there was no point in arguing further. Fairfax left the room. Oliver heard the front door close. He sank into his favourite walnut Wainscot chair and he gripped the handles tight. The room was quiet. A burned-out log shifted in the embers of the evening fire. Some sparks spilled onto the black slate hearth and dissipated into nothing. Oliver tried to take it all in. Will he never get back to the farm in Ely? He looked to the ceiling. Was this his destiny? To become the most senior general in the parliamentarian army? So soon? After just eight years a soldier? Is this the path that God was guiding him on?

It was less than a month since he had returned from Ireland. The large crowds that had come out to see him on his journey to London all along the way were all jubilant. The parliamentarian newspapers bestowed a myriad of tributes on the man who had finally tamed the Irish beast. The threat of a Catholic Irish army coming to wreak havoc on English soil was finally over. The adventurers who had pledged money to the conquest of Ireland in return for land could now reap their rewards. Including Oliver. And most importantly for him, on behalf of the rest of the right-thinking world, he had exacted revenge on the blackguard Catholic firebrands who had destroyed the perfect peace that had existed in Ireland not nine years since.

Sure enough, Parliament validated Oliver's new position as overall commander of the entire army within days of his conversation with Fairfax. He was given the title General of the Forces of the Commonwealth of England, or Lord General for short. He left for Scotland. His plan was to discuss the issues with the Scots, thereby hopefully bringing a peaceful resolution. Mostly, he wanted to avoid a war, if he could possibly help it. A third civil war? How could he countenance a third war?

But the Scots were a canny lot. The men Oliver had brought from London were starving within weeks of crossing the border into Scotland. The Scots had laid waste to any crops surrounding the city and had retreated to Edinburgh. By 2 September, Oliver's army was trapped at Dunbar, just south of the city along the coast, cleverly cut off by the Scots.

The Scottish army soon smelled blood and so they left the city and surrounded the English on a high escarpment called Doon Hill. After Clonmel, some of Oliver's troops began to have serious doubts about his military ability when the reality of their weak position dawned on them. It was only a matter of time now. Surely they would be wiped out. With twenty-two thousand men, the Scots had by far the superior position and they clearly had the upper hand. Some of Oliver's officers advised him to withdraw by sea. Oliver was having none of it. The English army, with only eleven thousand men waited for the Scottish onslaught.

The night of 2 September, 1650, brought driving rain to the

little hamlet of Dunbar. The invading English army to a man thought that they would be routed the next day. They cowered on the open ground, cold, wet and starving as the rain pelted into their faces. They were soaked through. The torrent fell through the night and did not abate. This was as dire a situation as any that the parliamentarians had ever been in.

But Oliver Cromwell had a plan. All during the early part of the night, he went through his regiments on his horse by torchlight telling them his strategy. Oliver had long since worked out the one thing that the Scots had completely overlooked. This English army were battle-hardened and experienced men, who adored their leader with an unrivalled passion. The Scots were not experienced. The Scots camped on their seemingly impregnable heights, had started their ascent the previous evening to begin the massacre of the trapped English invaders the next day. To take Oliver Cromwell captive would be a seismic achievement. But they came no closer that night. Everything would wait until the morning. Nothing could go wrong now.

At 3am Oliver assembled his men. A 4am he stood up in his stirrups, commanded the attention of his soldiers, and shouted, 'Take heart men. For God has heard us. He will appear for us. He will deliver them into our hands. Now let God arise, and his enemies shall be scattered!'

The battle of Dunbar was Oliver's most astonishing victory. He had completely turned an ignominious defeat into a glorious victory. In just over an hour, three thousand inexperienced Scots lay dead. Ten thousand more were captured. Within days, Parliament decreed that a Dunbar medal should be struck with Oliver's effigy on one side. The medal was to be given to all of the men who took part. The English army took over Edinburgh. Scottish resistance was not fully broken yet. One battle does not a war make. But this was a very significant victory indeed.

Not long after the battle, Oliver trotted his horse through the streets of Edinburgh. For the time being at least, the threat of the Scots was gone. The English army were in control of the city. He soon arrived at the house of the Countess of Moray at Canongate, where his lodgings had been arranged. He entered the forecourt of the house through two high gateposts with sharp pyramidal finials. The main part of the house had a gable on to the street. On the first-floor level was a large balcony, supported by bold stone corbels. On one side a semi-octagonal turnpike tower gave the opulent building a European aspect.

Jean Duret, Oliver's manservant, ran from the front door to greet his master. The young Frenchman had arrived only a couple of hours beforehand to prepare the place for the Lord General. As Oliver dismounted from his horse, he suddenly became dizzy. Now disoriented, his foot remained stuck in the stirrup and he crashed humiliatingly onto the cobbles in a heap. Two of the soldiers who had accompanied Oliver immediately moved to help him up. Jean had further to run but sprung to his master's help.

'No! It is only my pride that is hurt,' said Oliver. 'I would only want my Duret to help me in any case,' he snapped at the two men.

The soldiers stayed back. Jean reached down and offered Oliver his hands so he could pull him up. But Oliver was still dizzy. He lay on the ground. The courtyard around him was now swimming around in his head. The grey sky merged into the roof of the house, which in turn merged into Jean's head and shoulders, standing above him. There was a hazy kaleidoscope of circles in front of his eyes. He closed them tightly. But the dizziness did not abate. He felt nauseous.

'How is it I help you, Lord General? Tell it to me!' asked Jean in his broken English. He could see that Oliver's pallor was greyish now that he had come close. Drops of sweat had appeared all over his face. Jean knew this was more than just a clumsy fall from the horse. Oliver opened his eyes again and this time he could make out definite shapes. He knew that he had eaten very badly over the last few weeks. He wondered if this was the reason for the dizziness. He also knew that he had to at least try to get up off the ground, as there were so many people depending on him. If the word got out that Oliver was not well, he was well aware of the impact this could have. Both on his friends and his enemies. His men had nicknamed him Ironsides. This was a name he simply had to live up to. His pride somehow managed to overtake his present inability.

Oliver found his feet. With the help of his valet he walked towards the door. Once Jean had closed the door and the two were inside, Oliver slumped onto the nearest chair. 'You must find a physician, Jean. I have some variety of illness. I have been bilious for some days now. I will remain here until you return. Off with you now and be as swift as you might.'

Oliver was somehow bundled into bed. When the doctor arrived he put the condition down to the torments of a stone and the fluctuating weakness of a fever. He was ordered to stay in bed for the foreseeable future. The days passed. Oliver did not improve. Fits started to engulf his body. He thought he was going to die. The only thing that kept his spirits up was the knowledge that the Lord's work was not yet complete. Surely, God would not take him from this world just yet. Things still hung in the balance. Days turned into weeks. Weeks into months.

While ill, Oliver would only take food from Duret's hands. Nobody else was permitted near him. Unfortunately, word had gotten out that the Lord General was unwell. The royalist newspapers had a field day asserting that it was the Scottish climate that had brought him down. Meanwhile, Jean Duret waited on his master, hand and foot for weeks. Eventually Oliver rallied. Soon, with every passing day he managed to improve. At first, sitting up in bed was as much as he could do. But eventually, he was sitting by the bedroom window. By the time Oliver was back up and walking around again he began to notice a change in his valet.

Jean himself then fell sick, out of the exhaustion of nursing his master back to health. He took to his bed. Oliver switched roles and now began to visit Jean assiduously. There was a special bond between a valet and his master. But unlike his Lord General, who was used to adverse conditions, Jean's constitution was much weaker. He did not recover. In his dying breath he commended his mother, sister and kindred in France to his master's care. Oliver was happy to oblige. Some weeks later when Jean's mother arrived, Oliver had gone to the trouble of learning some French phrases to convey the message of how grateful he was to this woman's son.

Meanwhile, as Oliver was recuperating, the Scots had done a deal with the young Charles II. A year had almost passed with Oliver in Edinburgh. During this time the Scottish campaign had not been prosecuted any further. As Oliver had suspected, the Scottish plan was to make their way to London with the young prince and have him take back the throne. This was the king's idea. What's more, they now had a head start on Oliver. They crossed the border and slowly made their way south. Oliver couldn't catch up with the Scots and so he sent a communication to London and asked them to muster what soldiers they could and head the Scottish army off.

By 5 August, the Scots had crossed into England with the 'king' at their head ready to hoist the royalist flag again. Oliver began the chase. His men averaged twenty miles' marching a day. By 27 August, the king was at Worcester. Oliver was gaining quickly. With the awful memory of his tyrannical father on their minds, fewer men attached themselves to the king's cause. Far more men joined Parliament as the two armies moved through the country. There was going to be a showdown. Oliver's army had now grown to thirty thousand men. The Scots had less than half that number. Oliver was not unaware that the anniversary of Dunbar was approaching. He was determined that the upcoming battle would be the final one in all of these civil wars.

Oliver waited until 3 September to make the first assault on the Scottish royalists. The battle lasted most of the day. It ebbed and flowed, despite the numerical supremacy of the parliamentarian army. But for the final time in these civil wars Oliver again won the day. The battle of Worcester was won by Parliament. September 3 was now Oliver's lucky day. The king escaped to France, at first by hiding in an oak tree at Boscobel House, from where he made his way to Brighton.

It was now clear that there was no one left to fight. Parliament had won the war. They were in control. No more men would die. No more families would be bereaved. The madness was finally over. Oliver would never take to the field again. On his way back to London, he dreamed of getting back to his fields in Ely. Normality. Imagine. Just to walk through the marketplace on a bustling fair day. To contemplate life lying on the lush banks of the River Ouse. Maybe now. Maybe he could get back home now. However, his celestial master had a very different plan. His upward trajectory in life had barely even begun. One thing was for sure; he was never going back to Ely.

Chapter Nineteen

The small flotilla of two shallops and a large barge approached the wooden jetty of Hampton Court Palace. Elizabeth and Beth were seated in the second one, behind the vessel that was carrying Oliver and his servants. The three boats were decorated with gilded carvings of various emblems and motifs of the new republic, the most prominent of which was the arms of the Commonwealth. These were the very vessels that would have carried Charles Stuart and his royal courtiers on their journey down the Thames from Hampton Court to Westminster and back. Charles would not be needing them anymore. Nor was there any royal use for Hampton Court Palace itself. It had just lain idle since the king's execution. Parliament decided that their supreme military hero should now dwell in an establishment that was better suited to his burgeoning reputation. He was also gifted a townhouse and several other properties as well as the appropriate financial recompence. After all, it was to Oliver that Parliament were compelled to defer for the power that they now wielded. Without his astonishing list of military victories they would be totally impotent. After Worcester the conquering hero had been greeted with hysterical glee on his return to London with cannon fire and colourful garlands. Rockets, Serpents, Raining fire, Stars, Petards, Dragons, Fire-drakes, Gyronels, and Fire-wheels splashed their colourful sparks through the dark night air to hail the invincible and gallant Ironsides.

Now eighty-six years old, Elizabeth had seen the world totally transformed from the one that she once knew. She had lived through the reigns of three monarchs. And one parliament. Because of the seismic changes she had witnessed in recent years, she had almost become immune to the spectacular progress her son had made in his life: Hampton Court Palace. They had reached their destination. There was an air of complete unreality to this morning's events. As she waited to disembark, she watched Oliver being assisted up onto the wooden pier by some servants. Her only son was not as sprightly as he had once been.

The vast ornamental Privy Garden stretched from the banks of the river to the enormous redbrick Tudor palace in the distance. A perfectly symmetrical configuration of gravel paths crisscrossed through the orderly, luxuriant green lawns. Classical marble statues caught the rays of the mid-morning sun. Luxuriant arrangements of perfectly circular and perfectly square flowerbeds were strategically placed for optimum visual effect from the river. Birds bathed in three-tiered fountains that gushed water upwards. The water fell in cascades of sparkling liquescent charm. A squirrel stopped and quietly listened to the bubbling waters. The smell of freshly-cut grass filled up the visitors' senses. It was clear that the landscape had been recently prepared for the new palace occupants.

How was it possible that this could be their new home? Her thoughts drifted to her husband, Robert. How he had toiled on that old Huntingdon farm in cold and heat, season after season to put food on the table. Now here they were, about to step across the regal threshold of their new home, the opulence of which was simply breathtaking: from another world. Valentine and Margaret were passengers in the third boat. Each of the two boats were being rowed by two oarsmen who were employed by the new Commonwealth. Bargemen controlled the barge. The arms of the republic were embroidered on the livery that the men wore. Lower orders. At their command.

It was then that she remembered the monkey. She tried hard to think of Caesar's name, but it was too long ago and too far away. Nothing came. It may have been over fifty years since the primate had snatched Oliver from his cradle and climbed onto the roof of Hinchingbrooke, but she could recall the events in her mind now as if they had only happened yesterday. The amount of times over the years that she thought of how things would have been so different for her family had the monkey simply released his grip at the wrong time. As she always does, she got that old familiar dart of pain in her heart when she thought of little Joanie and her petite face as she went to God. Joanie kept rehearsing that rhyme as her young life ebbed away, so she could impress God when she met him in heaven. Elizabeth fought back the tears. As she always had to do.

And now it was clear that England's destiny would also have been very different had Caesar dropped Oliver all those years ago. Such are the vicissitudes of life. All pre-determined by the Almighty. It was also God who made the curate dash back to the river when he heard Valentine's screams years later. It was clearly due to the same divine power that Oliver was spared on the battlefield. How fortunate she was that God had chosen Oliver as England's redeemer.

Even Elizabeth could feel the sense of anticipation in the city. Everything was anew. The official newspapers were full of promise: anticipation, optimism. The inhabitants of London could talk about nothing else. The possibilities of Parliament's reign, now without a war to contend with, were endless. Now that the country was finally at peace, the people's government could focus on reform. Parliament could properly undo so many of the policies that Charles had implemented. Elizabeth was excited for Oliver because he had played such a major role in this new England, whatever it would turn out to be. She was so pleased that she had lived long enough to see all these events transpire.

Oliver stood on the jetty waiting for the rest of the party to join him. He surveyed the palace, remembering the last time he was here. It was when he had met the king for the first time. He had been in awe of both the king and his palatial surroundings. Now it was all his, for the benefit of his own little family. Valentine sidled up beside him and the two men stood in silence. They both grasped the magnitude of the moment in unison.

'No one rises so high as he who knows not whither he is going,' said Oliver wistfully.

'These are the strangest of times,' said Valentine. 'You have come to be honoured and esteemed by Heaven to establish this republic by divine service. When good old King Henry built this palace, he could not have foreseen that a mere commoner from Huntingdon would one day be its primary occupant,' said Valentine.

'No indeed. Only God could have known such things. We must always thank Him for such mercies. And now, thanks to Him we can look forward to a new England. Parliament must now embrace this occasion. The world needs to see that this mighty country can stride forward, without a monarch, or a one-person rule, as the centuries have dictated thus far.'

'Forgive me for asking this, Oliver, but do you think such a thing possible?' asked Valentine.

'There are those who remain to be convinced that the country can be ruled by parliamentary jurisdiction alone. Factions can develop among factions, as we have already seen. I am one of those yet to be convinced. But I am hopeful that disunities will not break out among parliamentary sections,' answered Oliver.

'There are corrupt men everywhere, Oliver. But this is the parliament for whom you have laid down your life these past years. These are the men to whom we have all pledged our undying allegiance. When Colonel Pride purged the House of Commons in 1649, this is the Rump parliament that has remained. Through you, this parliament ousted a malevolent king. They have been our taskmasters and our paymasters. They deserve our patience, do they not?' said Valentine.

'While I have been away from London all this time preserving their power, and while I am not intimately acquainted with each of these men, I am still confident that if we put our trust in the Lord, He will see to it that this parliament will prevail. But the long-term solution to a lasting settlement must surely be a formal claim of legitimate authority, and Parliament are now that authority,' said Oliver.

'Very well. I hope you are right,' said Valentine.

Oliver turned to his wife and mother and gesticulated towards the palace. 'This does not become us. I am not fit to dwell in such an establishment. I will refuse Parliament's gift of accommodation and we will take up our lodgings in the Cockpit in the city, where they have offered us a townhouse. Both Beth and Elizabeth knew that Oliver was right. The palace just seemed far too far fetched for their wants in life. This was simply too much opulence to his puritanical mind.

Over the coming months Oliver took a well-deserved rest and did not get directly involved with politics too much. He had developed a unique renown, unrivalled in England. But rather than exploit his new-found reputation, he receded into the background. It was parliament's job to run the country. He was still only the Lord General of the army. And yet, the significance of his role was not lost on anybody. Least of all Parliament.

Meanwhile back in the hallowed halls of Westminster, Parliament began to focus on policies that surprised Oliver. They set up a fleet of ships and went to war with the Dutch, effectively establishing the English navy. The Dutch were fellow Protestants. This did not go down well universally. Oliver showed no real interest in the Dutch war, which was fought at sea. Soon it was clear that the Rump parliament were going to achieve little in the way of reform. The more Oliver came to Westminster, the more he saw things that he disliked. There was very little focus on religious toleration or the remodelling of the legal system, both of which were close to Oliver's heart. But even worse: Parliament were reneging on so many of the terms with the royalists that Oliver had negotiated on the battlefield. Including, and especially the ones that he had negotiated in Ireland.

Soon, there was talk of a dissolution of parliament among many observers. A parliament needed to be in control, but the present incumbents might need to be replaced. Perhaps new elections should be held. This parliament seemed more focused on their self-perpetuation than engaging in the policies that would settle the nation; more interested in self-aggrandisement than the reorganisation of the country.

Dissatisfaction with the Rump became pervasive, especially among the army. It wasn't long before many thought a solution simply had to be found. But what? There was no higher authority. Parliament now held the ultimate power in the entire country. They answered to nobody. Oliver gradually became more and more disillusioned as the months progressed. Is this what he had fought for all those years? A corrupt parliament? The material benefit of scoundrels? It took him a while to admit it to himself, but ultimately he could no longer ignore the facts. The men he had pledged his life to in battle were now men who had lost their way in life. They had become unscrupulous and dishonest. Power clearly corrupts.

20 April, 1653. It was morning. Oliver's lavishly decorated townhouse withdrawing room was full of army officers. The pungent smell of body odour filled the room. Frescos with biblical scenes were displayed on the white walls, bordered with elaborate gold-plaster surrounds. Oliver was still dressed in his white nightgown and grey worsted stockings. Sometimes he liked to mix informality with formality. The previous evening in the House of Commons chamber there had been a bill presented that would effectively prolong Parliament's sitting for years. Oliver had assembled a group of officers to his house to discuss the bill. Parliament had agreed to defer its passing pending further discussions. Something had to be done.

The discussion was heated. The army officers had lost patience with Parliament. There was a knock on the door: a messenger from Westminster. The chamber of the House of

Commons was packed, the bill was to be discussed immediately. Oliver refused to believe it. Parliament would surely not stoop so low. Col Henry Ingoldsby volunteered to go down to the House of Commons and see for himself what was happening. Meanwhile, while the discussion continued, a second and a third messenger came from the House of Commons. It was true! The passage of the Act was nearly through. 'I do not believe that persons of such quality could do it!' Oliver yelled as he grabbed only his black coat and dashed out on the street with the rest of the officers. He didn't even put on his shoes.

The effect on Oliver was immediate. The last time he was so incensed was when he stormed Drogheda. This was the same parliament for whom so many of his men had died; the same parliament who conspired together to try and then execute the king. Oliver could clearly see that Parliament would lose whatever support it had gained from a somewhat disorientated populace if this bill were to be passed. So much for their honour, so much for their offer of compromise, so much for their honesty as individuals, so much for their corporate identity. They had broken their word. They were clearly prepared to use any means, fair or foul to perpetuate their existence. These men never fought for their freedom. It was Oliver and his men who had battled through the fires of hell for England. Not this band of absolute cowards!

Oliver's blood was up. Stopping only to order up a regiment of soldiers, he ran through Whitehall in a passion. At around 11.15am he burst into the House of Commons chamber. He took his seat. Sure enough, the messengers were right. After several minutes, he got up to speak. His first words were calm. But he was battling with the passion that was just beneath the surface. Soon he was walking up and down the chamber, kicking the ground with his shoeless feet and shouting. He pointed at this man and that as he strode about.

'Fucking whoremasters and drunkards! You are scandalous

to the profession of the Gospel! You are fucking corrupt and unjust! Perhaps you think this is not parliamentary language? I confess it is not, neither are you to expect any such from me! It is not fit that you should sit as a parliament any longer! You have sat long enough unless you have done more good!'

The assembled MPs were stunned. This was their army general. The man they trusted so highly. How could he have the temerity to talk to the highest power in the land like this? Sir Peter Wentworth led the charge of protestors. 'Your language and your abuse will do you no good! We are the power in England now. There is no higher authority. Leave this chamber at once or we will throw you out! Then we will see fit how to deal with this outburst in due course!'

This was the last straw for Oliver. 'Come, come,' he riposted savagely. ' I will put an end to your prating. You are no Parliament. I say you are no Parliament! I will put an end to your sitting!' He turned to one of his officers and he shouted, 'Call them in!'

Suddenly in rushed six files of musketeers. Oliver pointed at the Speaker, 'Fetch him down,' he said forcefully. The soldiers pulled the Speaker down. The same Speaker to whom Oliver had written all of his battle reports to years earlier. Oliver went and stood in front of the Speaker's table. The mace, which was the symbol of the Speaker's authority was lying there. 'What shall we do with this bauble?' he said contemptuously. 'Here, take it away!'

As the MPs were being forced out of the chamber, still in a rage, Oliver bellowed at them, 'It is you who have forced me to do this! For I have sought the Lord, night and day, that he would rather slay me than put me upon the doing of this work!' It was then that he caught sight of Manchester. Edward Montagu's devious activities had just come to an abrupt end. Oliver smiled sneeringly at the corpulent MP as he passed close by. 'Perhaps now you can return to playing at dice my Lord Manchester,' he said. 'You are good for not much more, it turns out.'

It was then that he saw the bill that was to be passed on the Speaker's desk. He whipped it up, folded it in half and stuck it in the pocket of his old black coat.

The man in the grey worsted stockings and wearing no shoes was the last to leave the chamber that morning. This was not the way things were meant to be. He had not planned to do this when he left the house in such a rage. But he *had* done it. Even if it was only the product of impulse, rather than reflection. And now, whether he liked it or not, by default he had dissolved parliament with no authority whatsoever. By this action he had disbanded the entity everybody thought was the supreme power in the land. But everybody was wrong. The supreme power in the land was actually the shoeless Oliver Cromwell.

Chapter Twenty

For April, the weather was mild. Oliver and Beth were sitting on a sheltered terrace to the rear of their townhouse in the Cockpit. She liked for them both to spend as much time outdoors now, as the elements would permit. The terrace overlooked the large garden. Stone steps descended towards a substantial globular pond in the centre that was its focal point. The pond was encircled by a large coarse formation of hand-cut, curved limestone segments. The elaborately planted garden stretched down to a high wall and was enclosed by an enormous Griselinia hedge. Aromatic fragrances from a profusion of reds, yellows and blues were sent airborne with every soft breeze.

'The newsbooks are all of a similar opinion, Oliver,' said Beth smiling at her husband, closing and placing the latest official publication on her lap. 'You have put an end to an accursed assembly of rogues. Your popularity in many quarters for your stance on this has soared, many quarters from which you might previously have expected only criticism.'

'I only did as God directed me to do. It was their preposterous haste to perpetuate themselves that created the prevailing atmosphere. This was beyond my design and beyond my previous thoughts. In that heated moment, I concluded that there was no other way to get rid of the odious Rump. I flourished my sword in the face of all England. It was never my intention that violence should raise its hideous head in the House of Commons. But now it is done. And we will move on,' replied Oliver.

'It is clear that the end of the Rump has been hailed with a general satisfaction,' said Beth. 'One of the newsbooks I have just read even reports that your deeds were declared in The Hague as a 'glorious action'. If I know my beloved, I can sense that you have the semblance of a strategy for the future of the country. Am I correct?' she asked.

'I have given this matter a lot of thought,' said Oliver. 'And I must act with all speed. I will assemble a Decemvirate of ten officers, all of whom I can trust implicitly. They will be persons of approved fidelity and honesty. The constitutional resettlement of the country will be in their hands. I will lead this new assembly and we will get a full governing authority of this country in place once more. This is the opportunity we fought for.'

Within days Oliver had selected the ten people to form a Council of Officers. The idea they came up with was that they themselves would choose the next parliament. One hundred and forty God-fearing civilians would be chosen from all over England, Ireland and Scotland. There would be no elections. They would be personally chosen. The premise was that if they were hand-picked there would be much more of a chance that they would succeed. The new parliament would have all legislative and executive functions and the Council of Officers would remain only as long as they were required. Although public opinion was that some sort of monarchial rule, the tried and trusted method of governance, was the preferred choice, there was no appetite to invite the Stuarts back. If the country were to look for one man to assume the monarchy, it was clear to the electorate exactly who that man would be. But one thing was abundantly clear – that man was not looking in the same direction at all.

The following day was Sunday. After a private service in the palace, Oliver and Beth had travelled around the city by horse in an enclosed rig in the afternoon. They liked to ride about the city on Sundays to experience aspects of a normal civilian life. They were on Fleet Street, when approaching Fetter Lane at the lower end of the street, Oliver could hear a strong voice resonate over the routine urban hubbub. He knew by the speaker's pitch, it was a preacher.

'Oliver gave two knocks on the roof of the carriage, which was the signal for the driver to halt. Oliver leaned out of the carriage window and beheld the preacher. The man was tall and gaunt. His cheeks were shaven, but he had a short pointed grey beard that was perfectly trimmed. He wore a simple white collar and a dark brown cape that was cut in a plain style. His voice was rising and falling. His hands graphically confirmed the points that his mouth was making:

'God is the highest good of the reasonable creature,' regaled the preacher to no one in particular. 'The enjoyment of Him is the only happiness with which our souls can be satisfied. To go to heaven, fully to enjoy God, is infinitely better than the most pleasant accommodations here. Better than fathers and mothers, husbands, wives, or children, or the company of any, or all earthly friends. These are but shadows; but the enjoyment of God is the substance. These are but scattered beams; but God is the sun. These are but streams; but God is the fountain. These are but drops, but God is the ocean!'

Oliver was transfixed. These were wise words, and ones with which he could readily identify. He watched as the preacher's audience of three apathetic listeners drifted away. He stepped down from the carriage and walked towards the preacher. 'My good man. How do you fare?' asked Oliver purposely interrupting the man's flow with intention.

'Faint not poor soul in God still trust. Fear not the things thy suffer most,' said the man snipping at Oliver.

'For whom he loves he doth chastise, and then all tears wipe from their eyes,' replied Oliver catching the man's undivided attention with the appropriate response. 'I would be glad to know to whom I have the pleasure of speaking,' continued Oliver.

The man was momentarily confused. He had expected to be verbally mistreated as had often happened before. There were many who did not agree with his zeal, his views, his message. But Oliver was not one of them. 'My name is Unless-Jesus-Christ-Had-Died-For-Thee-Thou-Hadst-Been-Damned Barebone,' said the man, as he had enunciated on thousands of occasions previously, not recognising the most powerful man in the country. 'But I am known more simply as Praise-God.'

'Well Praise-God Barebone. That is a name indeed. I am merely Cromwell. And you are a lion among men. That is plain for all to see.'

Praise-God was stunned. His cheeks began to flush. He looked at the stocky, grey-haired, copper-nosed man in front of him and he could see immediately that this might well in fact be Oliver Cromwell. 'My Lord,' he said bowing his head. 'I did not mean any offence. I am often accosted on the streets by naysayers, and I must beg for your forgiveness.'

Oliver laughed. 'Pray tell, whatever possesses you to display contrition? Your words are like sweet music to my ears. There is nothing you have yet said that offends. It is the entire opposite. You must come with me. And we must talk. Is there anywhere else you need to be on this day?'

'No, my Lord,' replied Praise-God now almost shaking nervously. 'If you lead the way, I will most gladly follow Your Excellency to the ends of the earth.'

For the rest of that day Praise-God Barebone said all of the right things. Oliver took him to his townhouse and the two men talked religion and politics late into the night. 'You must overnight here and leave on the morrow,' said Oliver as the clock in his parlour struck one. 'If Your Excellency will permit, my wife will be quite distressed should I not return on this night,' said Praise-God reluctantly.

'Very well,' but know this, Praise-God Barebone. It is godly men like you that I seek to be members of the next parliament of England. You are the very model of piety and devotion. You are not unworthy of this elevation that I now ask of you. It was the design of the Almighty that we should meet each other on this day. I would be honoured should you agree to join this new assembly.'

'It would be a privilege to work with you, my Lord, if you think that I might have something to contribute,' said Praise-God.

'I am convinced of it. Then there is nothing more to be said. Except that you will not be working with me. I have no intention of being on the Council of Officers or the parliament. I am not a statesman. I expect to play an anonymous role in any future government.'

The Barebones parliament as it came to be known, after the nominee from the City of London, began life on 4 July, 1653. Once again, all over the country there was a fresh wave of optimism that finally, with these specially selected men, the future of England was bright again. The possibilities were endless. And yet, there were still pervasive undercurrents throughout the land that a one-person rule was the only way that England would be at peace. History had shown that. England had never been ruled by a parliament in peacetime. But Oliver was determined that a parliament would work.

On the day that the new parliament were inaugurated, Oliver strode into the chamber to address them. He had no formal role to do so as there was no precedent for the mantle that he now bore. But these were unprecedented times. His hopes were high. He would champion this gathering and from these saints great things would surely emanate. Oliver scanned the room and looked at all of the expectant faces. The future of the country was in these men's hands. A governing authority of civilians. This was their apocalyptic moment. He rose to his feet and he started speaking:

'Surely this is a great occasion indeed! God doth manifest it to be a day of the power of Christ. You are as like the forming of God as ever people were. You must therefore own your call since never before has there been so many people called together by God. It is true that God's purpose in the past has often been hidden from us, is it not all the more wonderful that this remarkable solution should be reached? You are at the edge of promises and prophesies.'

Oliver then read aloud an Instrument of Government which in effect devolved his own power over the assembly, even though it was not officially even his to devolve.

Everything was now in place. Oliver could surely retire and let the new parliament get on with running the country. It was the summer and the brightness in the days could almost be discerned in the potential glow of the coming years. He had given his all to England. What else could God want of him now? He returned to his home at the Cockpit and he began to take an interest in the garden.

On 12 December the mace, that ultimate symbol of the authority, was delivered to Oliver. This parliament was over. The assembly that was named after the preacher of Fetter Lane, London, lasted just five short months. It was a total disaster. Within weeks they fell out amongst themselves. They were united on nothing, divided on everything. It was very clear from the start that the experiment to settle the nation wasn't working. Newsbooks began to promulgate the notion of a one-person rule. Public opinion agreed. It soon became clear that there was only one person for the job. But it could not be a king. The army would not tolerate another king. And by implication the title was essentially a permanent one, when a temporary solution was preferable to the obvious candidate. Might it be a Protector? Oliver played a majorly passive role in what was to happen next.

Oliver and his family were at home in the withdrawing room. It was a cold December evening. They were being entertained. Oliver loved music. A middle-aged man sat sweating at an organ as he entertained the familial assembly with a liturgical concerto. The manic notes filled the room and echoed down the halls of the house. Colonel John Lambert could hear the frenzied music as he was being escorted reluctantly towards the doors of the room. The servant had protested that the Lord General was otherwise preoccupied. But Lambert, one of the members of the Council of Officers, was on a mission. He was a long-standing colleague of Oliver's and he had guessed that Oliver was expecting him. Any day now. Even the dogs on the street knew it.

Lambert opened the door. The organ player continued to hammer away on the organ. It was Beth who saw the intruder first. She kicked Oliver's leg to extricate him from the trance he was in from the frantic melody. Oliver saw Lambert. He banged his cane on the floor and the organist raised his head and suddenly stopped playing. The final notes hung in the air in one elongated and abrupt tone and eventually dissipated. Lambert's ears began to ring as the cacophony died.

'I have been expecting you, Colonel,' said Oliver before Lambert could make any apology or excuse.

'My Lord General, I am come to discuss a new Instrument of Government with you. And I am aware that you feel a general reluctance towards it, but this is a heavy load, and it is clear that you are the only one that God has chosen to carry it,' said Lambert.

'My dear Colonel. With many tears I would rather take a shepherd's staff than the Protectorship, since nothing is more contrary to me than a show of greatness. But I see it necessary at this time to keep the nation from falling into extreme disorder, and from becoming open to the common enemy, and therefore I will step in between the living and the dead, in that interval, till God should direct us further.'

'The title of Lord Protector has been governed by its temporary connotation,' replied Lambert. 'Up to now it has been used with the regent for infant monarchs, an office which inevitably always resulted in the sovereign's majority. A Lord

Protector is a title that is much less permanent than that of a king. Therefore, we will pray that God will reveal his plan of permanency in due course. You are to be formally offered the title of Lord Protector of England, Ireland and Scotland at one of the clock on Friday next.'

The tears welled up in Elizabeth's eyes. This time she remembered the monkey's name. It was Caesar.

Chapter Twenty-One

As she sat there on the stairs, a mouse darted across Beth's peripheral vision and disappeared into the shadows. Mice? Here? Yes, it was a mouse. Couldn't be anything else. The building had been empty, for a while now. She knew the ways of mice. There was no fear. She smiled. It was a wistful smile. Sitting here now, it was impossible for Beth not to recall the compact, whitewashed thatched cottage in the little wooded copse at St Ives, where there had been mice aplenty. She remembered standing there on that first miserably wet day, peering through the half-door, accepting her fate, wondering what had become of them. What would become of them. The cottage had smelled of damp. The tiny windows gave the open-plan kitchen/living area a squalid character. Broken furniture added to the cheerless mood. But as soon as she had a fire lit in the hearth, the little cabin began to reveal its homeliness. It was she who had transformed it from a house to a home.

Perched on the dramatic, imperial marble staircase in the entrance foyer of Whitehall Palace, the view Beth had of her new entrance gallery was so spectacular it was utterly preposterous. The proportions were astounding; the space munificent. The first flight of stairs divided into a half-landing, which then divided into two symmetrical flights, both rising with an equal number of steps turning to the next floor on each side. The upper flights narrowed as an architectural trick to lengthen perspective in order to increase the impression of size. Beth estimated that the lower flight was wide enough for twenty horse-drawn carriages to ascend at the same time. Alabaster statues of Wisdom and Justice were set in a massive gothic alcove between two huge granite columns overlooking the half-landing. Fidelity and Equity were in a slightly narrower niche higher up again. Mercury and Mars stood as silent sentinels at the foot of the colossal staircase. One of them on each side. The murmur of monarchs seeped from the gold leaf-covered walls.

Beth stood up, strode back down the stairs running her hands along the smooth gilt bronze bannister and admired the balustrades of white marble, which were populated by an array of cheerful, chubby-cheeked cherubs. She had things to do. It was true that she now had a staff of hundreds; stewards, ladies in waiting, coachmen, grooms, domestic servants, chaplains, gardeners, footmen, nurses, courtiers, sub-servants, the list was endless. But Beth wanted to make her own mark on Whitehall. She had assembled an army of wardrobe-keepers, braziers, upholsterers, silkmen, turners and linen-drapers. There would be a lot of red velvet, damask, silk curtains and rich canopies now in the palace after she was finished. Following a period with no occupants, there was a new order at Whitehall. The old would have to go. The rodent trespassers no longer had the place to themselves.

Oliver and Beth soon took to spending weekdays at Whitehall and weekends at Hampton Court. Their lives had taken the most astounding twist. Ambassadors were to be hosted. Official engagements were to be held. Sumptuousness abounded. Lavishness proliferated. It was a far cry from brewing ale in a hut on a country farm worth three hundred pounds annually. A yearly sum of sixty-four thousand pounds was now set aside for the expenses of the Protectoral family.

It was at one o'clock on Friday, 16 December, 1653, just four days after the dissolution of the Barebones parliament that Oliver had sat down in front of the Lord Mayor in Westminster Hall, where the king's trial had been held. He was presented with the Great Seal, the sword of state and the cap of maintenance, the ancient symbols of royal authority. Still somewhat railing against his weighty destiny, Oliver simply wore a plain black suit and a black riding coat, embroidered with gold lace. His hat was adorned with a broad golden hatband. He wanted none of this to smack of royalty. His investiture as Lord Protector was complete by a quarter past four in the afternoon.

Oliver was still determined to rule with a parliament and a Council of State. He may be sleeping in his bedroom and using his royal lavatory, but Oliver was no King Charles; the monarch who only called parliament when he needed money. The Instrument of Government he had agreed to dictated this also. Having experienced the disappointing failure of both the Rump and the Barebones parliaments, he spent the first few months of the Protectorate drawing up a list of 84 bills to present to Parliament for ratification. Elections were to be held. There would be 400 members. This was the first time Scotland and Ireland were to be represented at a Westminster parliament. By July, the parliament had been chosen but they did not sit until the beginning of September. Oliver decided that 3 September – his lucky day – was to be the date of their first sitting. But when it was pointed out to him that 3 September was in fact a Sunday, he had no choice but to hold it over for another day. On the Monday, he rose again in the chamber to imbue a new parliament with a resolve to succeed where others had failed:

'Gentlemen, you are met here on the greatest occasion that I believe England ever saw, having upon your shoulders the interest of great nations, with the territories belonging to them. And, truly I believe I may say it without hyperbole, you have upon your shoulders the interests of all the Christian peoples in the world.'

It was at this stage that the new Secretary of State John Thurloe became close to Oliver. Thurloe had been a lawyer in a previous life and Oliver made him his Head of Intelligence. Thurloe then proceeded to set up a widespread network of spies in England and on the continent. If there was any whisper of a royalist uprising anywhere, John Thurloe should know about it before it gained any traction. The two men had a lot in common. Including a love of all things equine.

A few days after the inauguration of the latest parliament, Thurloe and Oliver were both engaging with their visitor the Count of Oldenburg in one of the Whitehall Palace courtyards. Using the roofs of the outbuildings for symmetry, the September sun cast distinctly straight dark shadows over the rough cobbled yard. Servants milled about, making sure not to make eye contact with either the Secretary, the Protector or the Count, who were deep in conversation. Oliver loved horses. The Count knew of this famous fondness and he wanted to present his host with six grey Friesians. On hearing that they were just outside, Oliver couldn't help himself and asked to see them. Equally besotted with the idea, Thurloe accompanied the two men outside.

After some time the informal conversation ended naturally. The Count climbed into his waiting carriage and was whisked away to his lodgings. As soon as the Count was out of sight, Oliver looked at Thurloe. There was more than a hint of devilment in his eyes. 'Well, Secretary of State, shall we test out these fine animals?' he suggested audaciously.

'I see no good reason why we should not. Do you mean exactly at this moment?' replied Thurloe.

'That is precisely what I mean. It is merely fifteen minutes to Hyde Park,' said Oliver. 'We won't be missed for an hour.'

Oliver snapped his fingers. The non-seeing, all-listening footmen immediately sprang into action. In ten minutes, two of the horses were in harness and attached to a coach. The Protector took the reins and the Secretary of State hopped in beside his leader. Off they trotted through the streets in the direction of Hyde Park. They soon reached the gates. Later it would be reported in the newspapers that preachers were asking folk to pray for 'an ill-advised coachman who had undertaken to manage three kingdoms.' It may have been the case that since the horses had been cooped up on shipboard and the fact that they now saw these vast swathes of green grass on which to gallop, that they took off at speed. Whatever the reason, that's exactly what happened.

Almost immediately Oliver lost a grip of the reins. The horses thundered through the wide-open spaces of the park. The passengers were violently flung about as the animals made no clear distinction between path, flowerbed or grass. It was all fair game. Suddenly Oliver was thrown from the coach. But as his foot lifted up he somehow managed to get it tangled in the reins. He was now being dragged along the ground at the mercy of the gleeful horses. Thurloe was hanging on for dear life. The horses gaily ignored the plight of their two passengers and kept galloping at pace. Walkers in the park stopped in their tracks to see the bizarre scene. Wild horses were dragging the Lord Protector along the grass by the foot, while the Secretary of State was lying prostrate in the accompanying coach, valiantly trying to release him. Suddenly Oliver's Protectoral shoe came off and he was somehow free. But Oliver's terrifying misfortune wasn't quite over just yet. Seeing his Protector freed, Thurloe leaped from the coach and as he landed the pistol in his pocket went off and the bullet went screaming in Oliver's direction. Yet again, God decided that this was not Oliver's time to die. The bullet just missed him by inches. The newspapers had a field day. Oliver had once again survived a life-threatening circumstance. It had become a common theme.

It was mystifying how Oliver had survived. Apart from some bruises, cuts, and a bad swelling on the head he was allowed by his physicians to get on with the running of the country. By early November he was mobile again. But the running of the country was not all that Oliver had to contend with in September, 1654. His mother, Elizabeth, was not at all well. The average life-expectancy was forty. Even Oliver was now in his old age. His mother, however, was something special. Elizabeth Cromwell had reached her ninetieth year. As she lay on her bed, she was well aware of her circumstances; she was dying. Her body had failed her. But her mind was still alert to the end.

It was evening. The medics had called the family to Elizabeth's bed chamber. She wasn't expected to last the night. But Elizabeth was far from sad. Not for the first time, she studied the lavishly-coloured fresco on the ceiling above her head. She loved the image. It was of the Good Shepherd, a beardless youth in pastoral scenes collecting sheep. It was her safe place now. In her mind, she was one of the flock. She had striven all her life to follow Jesus. She was almost excited at the prospect of finally meeting her Saviour. And as well, all those years ago, she had made a promise to little Joanie that she would join her in heaven. She never forgot that promise. And today was the day: heaven. Her young son Henry was there. Her husband Robert was there. Her grandchildren, Robert and Oliver were both there. She was relishing the family reunion.

'What was the rhyme, Oliver? Do you recollect the rhyme?' she managed to say opening her eyes and seeking her son out in the room.

'Yes, Mother, I remember the rhyme. You taught me it well when I was a boy. But you will not be needing it this day,' replied Oliver. 'The Lord can wait. He has waited this long.'

'Recite it for me, Son.' said Elizabeth.

The Lord Protector felt the tears rise. He contorted his face to prevent them from manifesting. But it didn't work. The moist tear ducts joined forces with his crackly vocal chords, and both contrived to prevent his oration. But he fought them both. And he won. He began:

To market, to market, to buy a fat hen,
Home again, home again, jiggety-jig.
To market, to market, to buy a fat hog,
Home again, home again, jiggety-jog.
To market, to market to buy a plum cake,
Home again, home again, market is late.

'Yes, Oliver. I am ready to say it. Before I depart I need you to know that my pride for you knows no bounds. Joanie is waiting for me now. I cannot wait to see her beautiful countenance again. Your father and your sons are waiting too. The chimpanzee was influenced by the Lord at Hinchingbrooke so many years ago now. And since that day, the Lord caused His face to shine upon you and comfort you in your adversities and enable you to do great things for the glory of the Most High God, and to be a relief unto his people. My dear son, I leave my heart with thee. A good night.'

Oliver dealt with the grief he felt about losing his mother the only way he knew how. He simply threw himself into his role and focused on dealing with his parliament over the 84 bills that needed passing. But there was a problem. There was always a problem. These men had been elected representing their counties and not their boroughs as previously and so the ruling classes were overly represented. They were having difficulty embracing this new regime; embracing Oliver's proposals. Very quickly the new parliament became two groups, radicals and moderates. But Oliver was prepared to compromise, provided that four fundamentals contained within the Instrument of Government were not conceded – a single-person rule plus a parliament, wholesale liberty of conscience when it came to religion, regular elections of parliaments and joint control of the army. By Christmas, none of the 84 bills had been passed.

On 22 January, 1655, Oliver made his way to the House of Commons, a familiar enough journey now, except these days he was always accompanied by his lifeguard of several men. Wild horses aside, hostility could come from any direction at any time. He took his seat on the throne, which was usually only occupied with a visiting royal seat upon it and he waited for his moment to rise. When he did rise, he said this:

'There be some trees that will not grow under the shadow of other trees. There be some that choose to thrive under the shadow of other trees. I will tell you what has thriven. Instead of the peace and settlement, instead of mercy and truth being brought together, righteousness and peace kissing each other, by reconciling the honest people of these nations, and settling the woeful distempers that are upon us, weeds and nettles, briars and thorns have thriven under your shadow, dissettlement and division, discontent and dissatisfaction together with real dangers to the whole.'

Then Oliver dissolved his very own Protectorate parliament. This was the third parliament that had been in place since the king was executed. It was the third parliament that did not work. What on earth was he going to do now?

Whatever it was, it would have to wait. Because all over England the royalists were getting ready to revolt. War was on the way. Again.

Chapter Twenty-Two

Colonel John Penruddock didn't anticipate being beheaded. But nonetheless, that's exactly what happened.

In the royalist officer's mind this artificial government, this bogus Protector was a charade. Protector? What's a Protector? Kings and queens ruled this land. Nothing, or nobody else ever has, or ever will. The Stuarts were the rightful heirs to the throne of these kingdoms. Penruddock had kept in touch with the young Prince Charles, who was biding his time in France, waiting for the opportunity to secure his triumphant return. John Penruddock was the man who would orchestrate that return.

The plan was a good one. Charles had sent his orders to Penruddock. All over the country there was to be a series of coordinated risings particularly in Nottinghamshire, Cheshire and the royalist heartland in the West Country. Men who were loyal to the Stuarts were to take up arms. They were to seize as many parliamentarian enclaves as possible and facilitate Charles' landing at Dover. This would galvanise universal royalist support in towns and villages everywhere. Then these pretenders would be ousted from power. The young prince would be restored to the throne, his legal birthright. And England would regain its status quo.

The date was set. March 11, 1655. Penruddock surveyed his small band of Cavaliers of about a hundred men. They had been travelling all day and were now outside the town of Salisbury. He sat on his horse and he considered their faces. Their numbers were small, but their hearts were big. And they had right on their side. Contained within Salisbury jail were several hundred royalist prisoners. Penruddock and his men waited until the early hours of the morning. They needed to have the element of surprise. At about 1am they entered the town. He gave orders to put a guard at the door of every inn, to prevent opposition from lodging parliamentarians. Next, he instructed his men to commandeer all of the horses that they could find. Then they dragged the High Sherriff Colonel John Dove from his bed and decided to keep him as a hostage. Even if he was still in his night clothes.

When they left Salisbury they left with 400 men. Penruddock was hopeful that by the time he met with the other uprisers there would be 5,000 rebels for Parliament to contend with. Just before leaving Salisbury, Penruddock proclaimed Charles II the rightful king to the throne. A small number of inhabitants who had dared to venture out into the streets looked bemused. With 400 men in only this small part of England, the threat was becoming real. When they understood what was happening, surely royalists everywhere would rise up. Was the Protectorate about to fall?

Meanwhile, back in London, spies had informed the Protector's secretary, John Thurloe, of the royalist plot and at that moment in Whitehall Palace, Thurloe was revealing this information to Oliver.

After sending a party of cavalry to chase Penruddock, Thurloe tried to break the news gently to his Protector. Oliver was in his private chamber at Whitehall Palace. He was sitting in his French walnut throne chair, the back splat bearing a heavily carved Commonwealth dragon flanked by matching urns and shells with acanthus leaf foliate carving throughout. The acanthus leaf foliate also ran down and across the sweeping arms, apron, legs and stretchers, the seat was also lined with similar intricate silk needlework embroidery and stuffed with natural horse hair and burlap.

Oliver had by now embraced the trappings to which he had ascended and was fast becoming accustomed. Having reached the highest station in England, a position where no non-royal had ever reached, he had finally accepted his calling in life. It was clear in his mind that God had tested him as a youth, come to him as a young adult, and elevated him to greatness as an old man. Because it was his destiny. And now God was challenging him again.

'Your Highness,' said Thurloe. 'The Cavalier party have been designing and preparing to put this nation to blood again. They are organising a national uprising. Pockets of the country are set to rebel. The young Charles Stuart has given his blessing to this treasonous act. But they will not succeed.'

'Have the royalists not shed enough blood in this land?' said Oliver. 'I could sometimes wish that they would be in the parliamentary chamber to hear what we have to say before they occupy themselves with their despicable transactions. Then they would see that we are for the permanent settling of this nation and above all, liberty of conscience when it comes to all religions. Do I take it, John, that the Commonwealth have already prepared for this uprising? And that I have no role to play?'

'Yes, Your Excellency,' replied Thurloe. 'Parliament have even called back some troops from Ireland to assist. And we have strengthened the guard around the palace.'

'The rebels will see. So far are they mistaken who dream that the affections of this people are towards the House of Stuart,' said Oliver.

Meanwhile, Penruddock had arrived at the rendezvous point with his 400 men. It was only a matter of time before the support would arrive from Newcastle, Shrewsbury, Portsmouth and Plymouth. And so he waited. And he waited. But nobody came. Penruddock was not to know it at the time, but none of the other uprisings had taken place. Not one.

Despite this he decided to press on. He arrived in nearby Blandford with the sheriff still as a hostage. There he proclaimed Charles II king but there was no local support forthcoming. Penruddock and his men, now numbering less than 200, due to so many desertions, stopped in the small Devon town of South Molton. It was here that they made their last stand. Weary and disaffected, they were no match for the professional troopers. Within a few hours Penruddock and his men were defeated and in custody. The sheriff was released.

Penruddock's uprising was over. During his trial he foolishly argued that he could not be tried for treason because the government had no legal standing. He even suggested that he would not have rebelled if Oliver had been king. Despite pleas for clemency, to deter others from engaging in such futile acts, the audacious Cavalier Colonel John Penruddock was beheaded on 16 May, 1655. And along with him died the last vestiges of mass royalist resistance that would take place during Oliver's lifetime.

Following the failure of the uprising, Oliver then simply got on with the business of administration. To prevent further uprisings he installed eleven Major Generals in eleven different geographical locations around the country to run local government. Unpopular taxes were introduced. The Protectorate had begun to develop a financial crisis. And so Oliver had to call another parliament. Royalists were barred from standing and even from voting. There were echoes of Charles I in this move – calling Parliament to raise money and the irony was not lost on the Protector. But Oliver would not rule the country on his own. Resentment against the high-taxing military rule of the Major Generals ensured that many opponents of the government were returned. This did not auger well for harmony between the Protector and his parliament. The results were vetted by the Council of State. Out of approximately 400 MPs returned, 93 were judged 'ungodly' and were prevented from taking their seats at Westminster.

As the months passed, Oliver became less and less of a commoner and more and more of a king. In the early days the majority of the populace had objected to this unprecedented system of government, the Protectorate. But as there was no possibility of any alternative administration system, people simply got on with their lives.

One Wednesday morning Oliver was in his meeting rooms at Whitehall. There was the usual knock on the oak panelled door. Every day Thurloe went through the Lord Protector's upcoming audiences with him. It was Thurloe. 'May I enter?'

'Of course, John. How do you fare this day?' asked Oliver.

'I am well, thank you, Your Excellency. This morning the Countess of Dysart has an audience with Your Excellency. Shall I ask her to enter?'

Something stirred in Oliver at the sound of the lady's name. Something long forgotten, but yet easily remembered. He knew that Elizabeth Murray, the Countess of Dysart, was a very attractive young woman. He had met her during his stay in Scotland when he was well. There was a connection between them. There was even more than a connection. There was a chemistry. She was a very self-assured young woman. Thirty years his junior. Oliver liked that. He remembered her fragrance particularly well. She smelled of Jasmine. His immediate instinct was to tell Thurloe to admit the lady and that Thurloe was dismissed. The desire to just have this woman on her own in the room with him was overpowering. He couldn't fight it. He didn't fight it. Now that he was the Lord Protector, he knew that there were ladies out there who looked at him differently. He also knew that God was watching his every move closely. But once the feeling of lust had started, it was not going to go away quickly.

The Countess of Dysart swept into the room. She was wearing a dark red gown with hanging sleeves lined in white satin to match her bodice and undersleeves. Her petticoat was pinned to a cartwheel farthingale. She was carrying white leather gloves and a garishly-coloured folding fan. She smelled of Jasmine. Thurloe left and the closing of the door latch echoed through the room. Her young bosoms made the most noise now in the Protector's head.

'Countess,' said Oliver, watching her move confidently towards him. He wanted this woman to come as close as possible to him.

'Your Highness,' said the Countess exuding all of her female charms in her self-assured stride across the polished orange and green chequer-patterned tiled floor.

'It is such a pleasure to see you again, Countess. It has been some years since we were last acquainted,' said Oliver trying to retain his composure.

She was even more stunning than he had remembered. It was at that point that he caught a whiff of her perfume. He gasped lightly. Oliver tried to fight it, but this was a very sensual moment. He wanted to prolong it for as long as possible. The Countess moved closer than protocol allowed. She held out her hand for the Protector to kiss. As Oliver took her hand a surge of familiar craving went through his entire body. His fingers tingled with an urge as he became enraptured in her bewitching aroma. Age had not dulled his energetic libido.

'I am glad that we are alone,' announced the Countess boldly. His mind raced. She curtsied. He stole a look at the cleavage that she had purposely fashioned earlier in the day while dressing. It was just suggestive enough to imply that just beneath her garments lay a world of carnal delights. For her part, she would always use her breasts to her advantage.

Oliver held on to her hand for too long. All the while she did not draw it away. He felt his loins stir. They had not stirred in a couple of years now, since Beth and he had started to pretend that they no longer needed love-making in their busy lives. Over time Oliver had developed an inability to satisfy Beth. The unexpressed pact was mutually understood. Satisfying himself was a sin. He tried hard to abstain. But he didn't always succeed. He was mesmerised by this nubile form in front of him.

He wanted her so badly. He wanted to take her right there on the throne. But he knew he could not. God was watching. He had to banish these thoughts from his mind. But at least, he would enjoy the game.

'I am here on a task,' said the Countess. 'I have just returned from Europe and I seek your assistance. I have borne witness to a horrific event. And when you hear of it, I know you will demand restitution.'

The sound of her voice. The passion with which she spoke. The look in her eye. The confidence. The erudition. Everything he was experiencing right now made him want her more. To feel her soft, supple skin close to his.

'You have my attention. You may proceed,' said Oliver, finally letting go of her magnificently soft hand.

'The Roman Catholic Duke of Savoy has committed a massacre of a number of his Protestant subjects in a place known by Piedmont. All of Europe has been shocked to its core. Those who have not died have been driven from land to which they are entitled. The Duke has been influenced by a devilish crew of priests and Jesuits. Such cruelties and inhumanities as have never been heard of before. The suffering of women and children was immense. I have initiated a public collection on behalf of those who remain. I hope that you will pledge some money to this worthy cause.'

Already highly-charged, Oliver's eyes at once became moist. It was the old familiar story. Atrocities carried out by Catholics. He couldn't help himself. He began to weep. The emotion was a combination of the frustration contained in the inability to consummate his desires and the tragedy of what he was hearing.

'The sickening atrocities of these wretched Catholic clergy will be avenged in the next world,' said Oliver. I am constantly outraged by their horrifying actions and the hideous details therein contained. I will contribute to your public collection, Countess, and I will pledge two thousand pounds. This is a matter that is very close to my heart.'

'This is an eminently righteous cause,' said the Countess. The Catholic clergy threaten poor and helpless people everywhere if they are not of the same faith. The Piedmontese will be forever grateful to Your Highness for his generosity at this time.' As she said these words, she touched him on the knee and squeezed. She knew the effect that she had on him.

There was a knock on the door just at that moment. Thurloe entered the room. His countenance was sombre. Oliver knew immediately that something was afoot. He reluctantly concluded his farewells to the Countess and Oliver watched her depart just as confidently as she had arrived.

'I must raise a grave matter with you, if you are in agreement?' said Thurloe immediately changing the mood in the room.

'You may proceed,' said Oliver, sitting back in his throne and raising his eyebrows in expectation.

'My spies throughout the country have uncovered some disturbing news. Since the royalist uprising has not been successful, the Cavaliers have chosen another means to bring this government down,' said Thurloe.

'What possible action could they take now that would make us obeisant to their foolish cause since they have no army and no means to raise one?' asked Oliver.

'They plan to assassinate you, Your Highness.'

Chapter Twenty-Three

Miles Sindercome was very determined to kill Oliver Cromwell. Miles had a rendezvous on London Bridge. All the houses on the bridge were two storey, timber-built, but with brick chimneys, and weather-boarded. An array of haberdashers, glovers, cutlers, bowyers and fletchers had shops at bridge level. The overcrowded bridge itself was home to over 500 inhabitants. It was effectively a small village spanning the width of the river. Most of the shops had a cellar below, either one within the stonework of the pier or a hanging cellar suspended from one of nineteen hammer beams. The bridge also had nineteen piers with pointed, oval-shaped stone starlings around each one to protect the stonework from the scouring current of the Thames below.

It was a Saturday morning. The bridge itself was heavily populated with passers-by. Miles nursed his pistol in his pocket as he passed a plethora of baskets and barrels of goods. Always good to have a gun. Never know when you'd need it. Rash Londoners haggled for bargains with canny hawkers, who invariably came out on top, while making out that they didn't. Miles was searching for the red-painted fletcher's shopfront. He had been told it would stand out. And sure enough, he couldn't miss it. There it was. Following the instructions that he had been given, he stepped inside. Ignoring the fletcher in the corner of the shadowy room who was surrounded by completed and half-completed arrows, and the raw materials for more, he pushed the door at the end of the shop. He had been told it would be unlocked. It was.

Given both that he was at bridge level and what Miles understood about gravity, it seemed somewhat unsettling to be confronted by a set of dark wooden steps going downwards. It was clear from the light below that the stairway descended to a turn and then descended again. How was that possible? At the bottom of the stairs Miles stepped into a room, the size of which surprised him. It was about 20 feet square. A pile of leather quivers lay in the centre of the floor. Sacks of what clearly looked like feathers were piled up against one of the walls. On the opposite side of the room there was a man hunkered down taking a shit through a large hole in the floorboards that revealed the hostile tidal waters of the Thames, a hundred feet below. Miles' instinct was to hold on to the nearest wall just in case the hanging cellar fell from the bridge at that exact moment. The man howled with laughter.

'That won't do thee any good! Anyhow, this cellar ain't goin' nowhere. You'll get used to it,' said the man pulling up his breeches. 'Just a few planks between us and certain death eh? Sinderbuck is it?'

'It's Sindercome,' said Miles, still holding on to the wall. He may have been good with a rifle, but he wasn't good with heights.

'Well, whatever it is you can let go of the walls now,' said the man.

John Toope was one of Oliver's lifeguards. There were about eighty men in this role in total. And there had been at least that number since he was first elevated to the position of Lord Lieutenant of Ireland. While many of them had different opinions they all swore an oath to protect the Protector. John took the oath too. But John was a liar. He was also a traitor. Sindercome and Toope had something in common. They both wanted Oliver dead and the king returned.

'Where's the gun?' asked Miles. 'Is it a French flintlock, like I asked for?'

Toope pointed towards a brown leather quiver that Miles noticed now was placed separately to the pile. 'In there. You wanted a fork rest as well? Well, that costs extra.'

'The price was agreed,' said Miles totally expecting his

185

turncoat colleague to pull some sort of stunt like this.

'Well, Mister Sinderbuck, the price has fucking changed. And you 'ave no choice now, 'ave ya?'

Now steadier on his feet, Miles took his hand from the wall. He picked up the quiver and pulled out the arquebus that was encased in straw. It was clearly a new model – French – with a crossbow style trigger. He might get two shots away in a twenty-second period. It was perfect. Just what he'd asked for. The fork rest was alongside it.

'How much extra for the fork rest?' asked Miles.

'Two shillings, and that's a bargain,' said Toope. 'But the most valuable thing I 'ave is information. You want to know 'is movements dontcha? Well, I can tell you 'is movements. Every Frid'y, he leaves Whitehall and goes to 'ampton court. Every Frid'y. About eight.'

'Does he go along King Street?' asked Miles.

''Ee certainly do. Just make sure you don't miss 'im. A lot of people want 'im dead. Includin' me. So don't fucking miss 'im!'

Miles rummaged in his pocket, found some coins and handed them to Toope. He turned and made to go back up the stairs. 'Aim for one of 'is warts. Or 'is 'uge copper fucking nose!' laughed Toope. 'That should do it,' he added. 'And if you ever turn me in, I'll rip your 'ead from its fucking shoulders. You got that?'

Miles nodded and climbed the stairs eager to get back to whatever *terraferma* the high bridge could offer. The plan was in place. He had already rented the empty house in King Street for the last few weeks. But he hadn't been there much. Best to keep away so as not to arouse any suspicion. On his way back over the bridge he decided that he would do it this Friday. Why should he wait any more time? Cromwell needed to die. The Stuarts needed to be back on the throne. He was about to become a national hero. But he was nervous.

Six days later, Miles was ready. Well, he felt that he was. As he approached the front door of the rented house he suddenly had a revelation. After he would kill Cromwell there was only one way to escape out of the house. That was through the front door. No back escape route. The wall was too high. How did he not think of this before? Killing protectors was a multi-layered business. He abandoned the plan. Two weeks later, he had rented another house, this time near Westminster Abbey. He used the alias John Fish to complete the transaction.

It was eight o'clock. Miles was sweating. The pressure was palpable. This was an enormous undertaking. The Protectoral carriage would appear around the corner any moment. But Miles was now suddenly irritated with the amount of people who had gathered on the street for a glimpse of their head of state as he left the city for the weekend. The stress became too much to bear. Too many people around. He might get caught too easily. A wayward shot. He might hit the wrong person. He lost his bottle and abandoned the plan.

The next day he returned to the fletcher's shop and organised a meeting with Toope. This would have to be a group effort. The fletcher's name was William Boyes. Miles got into a conversation with Boyes, who had been the go-between with Toope and himself. Now, Boyes wanted to get involved. He was no lover of Cromwell's. Boyes then introduced John Cecil into the group. Cecil, Boyes, Sindercome and Toope became the assassination team. They proceeded to concoct the murder attempt together. Cromwell was a dead man. It was only a matter of time.

Hyde Park. Toope's information was kosher. Sure enough the Protectoral entourage filed into the park on the Thursday afternoon. Oliver loved to walk in the park. Cecil, the last man to join the group, had drawn the lot to pull the trigger. The other two would cover. Toope would hand over the Protector. Here in the park in broad daylight a pistol shot to the head would bring down the entire Protectorate regime. One shot. How could it be any simpler? To facilitate their speedy escape the would-be assassins had interfered with the hinges on one of the park gates. This would ensure there was a safe path to freedom beyond after the deed was done. Everything was set. They were all in position. All on horseback.

John Cecil's heart was thumping. He had checked his pistol at least twenty times already that day. Everything became real when the Protector's carriage came into view. Toope was trotting alongside Oliver's carriage. It was up to him to separate the twenty or so lifeguards from the Protector as best he could. He knew the routine. He knew Oliver didn't like his men to be so close when he was taking his walks. Just close enough so they could react should anything untoward happen. Everything was calm in the Protectoral entourage. It was just a routine Thursday afternoon walk. Toope managed to engage his lifeguard comrades in engaging banter as Oliver stepped from the carriage to begin his walk. Toope raised his hat in a big swooping motion as he made his feigned point to the other guards. That was the signal. Oliver was now some yards from his soldiers. It was now or never.

Cecil's plan was not to cause a commotion prior to taking the shot by galloping in. The opportunity was perfect. He slipped his horse past the body of guards and came up behind Oliver. Now he was alongside him. He felt inside his tunic for the pistol. Just one shot in the side of the head. Suddenly the Lord Protector of England, Ireland and Scotland turned and faced him.

'My good man! Is that a Turkoman stallion?' asked Oliver.

John Cecil froze. He was totally thrown. Instinctively he took his hand from his tunic and said, 'Yes, Your Excellency. It is.' Straight away the Protector launched into a conversation about horses. In those split seconds the moment was lost. Cecil lost his nerve. There was no way he could blow this man's brains out now. Meanwhile, Toope and his fellow lifeguard officers had caught up with the Protector and his potential murderer when they saw the two men talking. On their approach, much to Oliver's surprise as he was mid-sentence, Cecil simply trotted off on his Turkoman stallion. The plan was totally scuppered.

Back in the London Bridge cellar that evening, the four men remonstrated with each other. Cecil was castigated by his partners for failing to seize the perfect moment.

'You fucking fopdoodle, John Cecil!' shouted John Toope. 'All you 'ad to do was shoot! What *was* you thinkin'?'

'He just started talkin' to me and I lost me nerve,' replied Cecil.

'We can't give up now,' said Miles. 'We have to persist. We simply have to.'

'Well, 'ave you got any other ideas? asked Toope. 'Cecil 'ere ruined my fucking idea.'

Miles had been thinking about a scheme he had nurtured in his head for days now. He explained it in detail to the other three. Boyes loved the sound of it. Toope was reluctant at first but was happy to go along with it for the glory it would bring him. Cecil was happy to go with the majority. They were going to blow up Whitehall Palace. Burn the place down with Oliver in it. Fuck him.

The day was decided. The time was decided. Boyes was the weapons' man. He had been a master gunner in the royalist army. He knew how to blow up palaces. He had made the explosive out of gunpowder, tar and pitch in the cellar of the shop on London Bridge. It would be strong enough to bring the palace down on Oliver's head. Toope had explained to the others that he would reveal exactly where Oliver would be in the palace on the night. This time they would not fail.

Whitehall Palace. Oliver's favourite daughter, Bettie, was visiting her father along with her husband, John Claypole. Oliver was besotted with Bettie. They were cut from the same cloth. The evening dinner had ended. Bettie always made her father somewhat giddy when she was in his company. After dinner Oliver started throwing cushions in her direction and of course Bettie had the temerity to throw them back. Soon Beth had joined in and there was a full-blown cushion battle in the outrageously opulent dining room of the palace's west wing.

None of the cushion fighters knew that in the chapel that was adjacent to the dining room, a huge bomb had been planted by Miles Sindercombe, William Boyes and John Cecil. All they had to do now was light the fuse and at the very least, the chapel and the dining room would come crashing down in seconds, killing all of the cushion fighters. Fuck them.

John Toope had told his partners in crime exactly where Oliver would be at that time. His information was always accurate. Toope was around the corner from the chapel ten minutes before the time that the fireball would go off. He had to be sure the target was in place. As he passed by the dining room, a flying silk cushion came straight through an open sash window and landed straight in front of him. The Protector stuck his head out of the window and saw Toope. 'How now, my good fellow!' he shouted. 'Toope is it? Would you be kind enough to return that cushion?' Toope obediently picked up the cushion and handed it to the man he was about to see killed. He looked through the window at the happy, smiling faces as Oliver cast the cushion across the room. The Protector had just used his name. He knew him. The humanity of it all suddenly hit him.

He couldn't do it.

He immediately sounded the alarm by shooting his pistol up in the air. Suddenly several other bodyguards arrived to see what had happened.

'Three men have planted a bomb in the chapel,' shouted Toope running towards the chapel door. He was now accompanied by fifteen soldiers, all of whom had been close by. They burst into the chapel and sure enough standing in the knave, they were confronted by three would-be murderers. When the felons saw Toope in military posture they guessed immediately that he had turned on them.

Cecil was easily caught in the first rush. Boyes was quick on his feet. He bolted for the vestry door and in the mayhem he got away by smashing a window with a chair. Miles Sindercome decided to fight his way out and he produced a sword. In a flash one of the soldiers swung a sword at him and his nose fell from his face to the ground in a pool of blood. He gave himself up at that moment.

John Cecil and Miles Sindercome were sent to London Tower. Cecil then had a change of heart. He joined Toope as an informer and told the authorities all he knew. Miles refused to cooperate. He was sentenced to be hanged, drawn and quartered. The night before he was to be executed, his sister brought some poison for him to take so he would not face the awful sentence.

Sindercombe was dead. Yet again, Oliver was safe. For now. The day after Sindercome took his own life, Oliver was sitting at breakfast in Whitehall when Thurloe arrived. He had that stern look on his face that usually indicated something serious was in the air.

'What is it this time?' asked Oliver.

'I do beg for your pardon, but Parliament have concluded that you should name your successor, Your Highness. We have all thanked God that the assassination attempts have failed... thus far. However, who knows what rogues are out there with their plots and their schemes? The royalist army is no more, but the Stuarts have plenty of supporters. It will take but one blow to strike you down. And then, Your Excellency, what would happen? How would it be for Parliament? How would it be for England?'

'Parliament? England? How would it be for *me*?' joked Oliver. 'As usual, John Thurloe, you speak sense. This is an issue that transiently occupies my mind. I am conscious of the possible consequences of which you speak. I must consider this matter diligently. I will then give you my answer. But I must remind you, and indeed Parliament, that I am no king. And the succession question was never part of the Instrument of Government to which I agreed.'

'That is the other matter that I must bring to your attention on this morning,' said Thurloe.

'There is another matter?'

'Yes, Your Highness. Parliament are currently sitting in session. They have requested your presence in the chamber this afternoon.'

'Continue.'

'They want to offer you the crown. Make you king.'

Chapter Twenty-Four

Beth couldn't remember exactly who first suggested that their youngest daughter, Frances, should marry the young Prince Charles. But somebody did. And now the idea had gained significant momentum. It was a Saturday afternoon. Oliver was standing in the middle of the family gathering protesting. The entire Cromwell family were in the Privy Garden at Hampton Court. London was experiencing an unseasonably fine, warm early spring. Henry VIII's gardens were now the exclusive playground of the Cromwells from Huntingdon, lately of Ely and formerly of St Ives. The seats had been arranged in a circle, so a round-table conversation was conducive.

Richard (31) and Henry (29) were not keen on the idea. The young Cromwell ladies, Bridget (33) Bettie (28), Mary (20) were well disposed to their younger sister's regal pretensions. Frances (19) herself was quite taken with the notion of marrying royalty and perhaps eventually becoming a queen. Beth thought that it seemed like a preposterous notion at first. Why would such a thing even be proposed? Surely the idea was to keep the Stuarts away from the throne? But when she thought about it more, aspects of such an arrangement started to make sense. Oliver would not be around forever. If it was orchestrated properly, it was possible that Charles might be controlled by Parliament. Not the other way around. A written constitution could temper his power. With no military overtones, public opinion was bound to be in favour of the return of the Stuarts. The divide between royalist and parliamentarian that had been created by Charles' tyrannical father would be no more.

The conversation was interesting. But Beth was just happy to have her family in the one place at the one time. She admired her two young men. Standing there. Both handsome. Both clever. Both erudite. Her brood of ladies were all pretty. They were embracing the fashions of the day. They were modern young women. By some remarkable quirk of fate, all now princesses. They were similar in temperament. Their religious fervour was well matched. Bettie was a chip off the old block. She was also well able to challenge her father in conversational battles. And he listened to her above the others.

'But, Father,' said Bettie. 'A better expedient might actually be to bring the king back because then you could make what terms you wished with him and you would retain all your present authority.'

'What you say would make sense, Bettie, were the young king not the reprobate that he is. There are things you do not know about this young man. He is much more interested in things carnal than things political. He is so damnably debauched he would undo us all.'

Richard interjected on behalf of his father.

'The whole question of the bachelor monarch across the water has not failed to occupy all of our minds at this moment, Bettie. He is no doubt an energetic and undoubtedly attractive sprig whose claim for a legal right to this business has a solid foundation. But your father is accurate in his assessment. And the most important point of all is this – the young king would *never* forgive our side for his own father's death,' he said.

Beth could see that the conversation was only going to end one way. Once Oliver had taken his position on the issue, the outcome was usually inevitable. The ladies were not going to get their way. Frances would not be marrying Charles Stuart the younger. Beth decided to change the subject to the one that everybody really wanted to discuss.

'Where are your thoughts about the monarchy, Oliver? How do you see it? Is there an argument for your assumption of the office?'

'I am well aware that my position as Protector is not covered by the ancient laws of this kingdom. The title, or indeed, the office of king is more suited to the laws. The principle of monarchy is the mechanism that has made this country great. The world around us would operate much better with a monarchy. And yet, I have my own doubts, my own fears and my own scruples,' said Oliver.

Of all the family now engaged in the discussion, Henry was the one who was most in tune with the reaction that the army would have, should Oliver become king. Henry had become an officer. He had spent the last few years in Ireland. But this was not what they fought for. For Oliver to be king? Surely the army would never agree to this. Oliver had developed a special bond between himself and his men. Without the army Oliver would not be in this position. So this needed to be addressed.

'I think you must know that the army would not be in favour of you becoming king, Father,' said Henry.

'My son. I would only accept the kingship if I was quite convinced that I was being drafted at the general wish of the godly and the men who fought under me. There must be no possibility of me ever being accused of accepting this chalice for personal glory. I speak not this to evade the issue, but I speak it in the fear and reverence of God,' replied Oliver.

Beth knew her husband well and was trying desperately to read between the lines. She had always considered their meteoric rise to such heights as precarious. This was a volatile world they inhabited. Given the right set of circumstances, it could come crashing down at any moment. And in her heart of hearts she knew that a king was better for England than a Protector. And Oliver knew this too.

'Then if you have not yet received a sign from heaven, it would seem better that you ought to accept the crown, despite the army's reservations. Is that your position, Oliver?' asked Beth cutting directly to the chase.

'Yes, my dearest. The estate of a man can never be without some incommodity or other. The best that can be done by any form of government or monarchy for the sake of the people is to preserve peace, law and order. Providence appears to be pointing me in the direction of the royal sceptre. I will seek the opinions of the army officers. I am sure that they will see sense.'

The former Huntingdon orchard thief and serial gambler had made up his mind. The Accession Day of King Oliver I was set for Thursday, 7 May, 1657. The ceremony was to start at 11am. It would take place in the Painted Chamber of the House of Commons. Oliver had made his choice. He would be king. There was no decision that was without challenges and becoming king seemed to be the most pragmatic thing he could do. All he had to do now was to convince the army hierarchy that this was the best choice for England. Most definitely not for him.

Two weeks later and Oliver had still not consulted with the army. But he knew that he must. He must convince them of the reasons behind his decision. The day before his coronation he was taking a stroll in his favourite municipal setting of St James's Park when everything changed. His bodyguard of fifteen men were positioned at various locations around the park. Some at the main gates. Others only a few yards from the Protector as he walked. He found solace here. There were many occasions in the past when he had made life-changing decisions in this very park.

Oliver was strolling along the edge of the small lake approaching the Blue Bridge. He was distracted by the waterfowl. Ducks were wonderfully adept at adjusting to their environment, he thought as he watched them frolic about. Some bobbed on the water heading in the one direction as if they had made a plan for the day and they had all agreed. Their legs invisible as they bobbled around the water lilies on their short journey to the West Island. He didn't see the three men enter the park. One or two of the ducks were resting, their long green necks tucked beneath their speckled wings. He stood for a moment enjoying the simplicity of the park wild life until he moved off again.

At the base of the bridge he looked up and saw three silhouetted figures standing there. He could not discern their faces against the bright sky. Immediately, he wondered why his bodyguards had allowed these men to come so close. And yet, he felt no danger. As they drew closer he recognised that they were dressed in army uniforms. His old friends, Generals Desborough, Fleetwood and Lambert were known to the guards and they had been allowed to pass through the park in close proximity to the monarch elect. Oliver knew exactly what the men wanted. It was no coincidence that they were in the park at the exact same time as he was. In fact, he was pleased that he did not now have to seek them out before the coronation.

'Well, you are like the three kings of the gospels,' said Oliver to his former comrades.

'We know that this activity is habitual to you, Oliver,' said Lambert. 'And that is why we have come. Before you formally accept the title of king tomorrow, we need you to know of our position.'

'It is the import of your message that is momentous to me,' replied Oliver. 'I have much to say on the matter.'

'Conversely, we have little to say,' said Lambert. 'It is a definite announcement from all three of us that we will not tolerate your acceptance of this crown. We will not go in to opposition against you but we will all resign our employments. Many officers also feel the same.'

A bright, searing light came into the mind of the Protector at that exact moment. This was the sign that he had been really waiting for. He had fully intended to argue the case with them. But he could now see that there was no point. The decision had already been made on a knife edge. These men reminded him from whence he came. It was clear now. He *must* change his mind.

The weight had been lifted from his shoulders. In the same

way that there were challenges in accepting the crown, there were also challenges in not accepting it. But the three generals made the latter set of challenges more acceptable to him now. It had been two and a half months since he was offered the kingship. But it all came down to this moment. Rather than attend the Painted Chamber at 11am on the following day, Oliver cancelled his audience with Parliament. Instead he spent the day in prayer. He needed to let this decision reversal seep in. It wasn't until the next day, which was Friday, 8 May, at 8pm that evening that he finally attended, having kept the House in the dark all day.

Oliver took his seat in the room. When asked for his answer by the Speaker to the question that was on the entire country's lips, he stood up.

'I cannot undertake this government with the title of king. I would not be an honest man if I did not tell you that I cannot take it. I am persuaded to return this answer to you, and that's my answer to this great weighty business.'

Beth was delighted that Oliver had finally made a decision. They could move on. Now that he had turned down the crown he threw himself into his work. He soon agreed to a new Instrument of Government that Parliament entitled the Humble Petition and Advice. On 26 June, 1657, he was re-invested as Lord Protector. The ceremony was much more of a royal occasion compared to the first one. The 93 Members of Parliament who had been expelled at the election had now taken up their seats. And these men were not supporters of Oliver Cromwell. It was never going to be plain sailing.

One of the first items on the agenda in the weeks after the ceremony was to meet with a delegation from Ireland. These were men who had lost their estates. Land that Oliver had originally agreed that they keep when he was in Ireland. Oliver was constantly exasperated with Parliament's defaulting on agreements that he had made during the wars. His relationship with his parliaments was persistently fractious. He immediately granted these Irish men their land back. Soon word filtered through to Ireland that the Protector was a man of clemency. Others came with similar stories of woe and Oliver unfailingly employed leniency. Eventually it was Parliament who decided not to allow these Irish petitioners to gain an audience with the Protector. Oliver even showed signs that he was against the settlement of Ireland and the brutal way it was being carried out. Parliament on the other hand, continued to cruelly suppress the Irish people who were both Catholic and royalist. In time it would be Oliver's own name that would become attached to that suppression.

Next on the agenda for Oliver was the re-admission of the Jews to England. Oliver's policy of religious toleration became a major feature of his Protectorate. The Jews had been expelled from England in 1290 by Edward I. But Oliver re-admitted them and allowed them to practise their faith openly.

As the months of 1657 passed, Oliver's health deteriorated. Members of Parliament began to call him 'Old Oliver'. Those who saw him regularly noticed that Oliver's right hand had begun to shake as old age infested his body. He began to spend most of his time at Hampton Court. He was suffering from painful catarrhs. Beth began to send more time with her husband and the focus was firmly on him. How much longer could he continue with all of the day-to-day pressure of executive duties and all that this entailed?

It was a long time since the Cromwells had had a major reverse in their lives. With Oliver's failing health, the signs were that this was not going to endure. As the months passed he deteriorated further and was confined to bed a lot. It seemed that death might finally come to take another Cromwell away. The shock, when it came was utterly devastating. Because it wasn't Oliver that God wanted this time.

It was his favourite daughter, Bettie.

Chapter Twenty-Five

Dr George Bate wasn't the kind of physician who had an affable disposition. He was egotistical and aloof. He had graduated as an MD from St Edmund Hall, Oxford, in 1637. Since he had acquired a superior knowledge to both educated and uneducated men, patronising all ordinary members of society was the gift that he bestowed on the world. Being superior to Lord Protectors and their families was a privilege that just came with the job. He had also treated Charles I when he was ill. Bate was fundamentally a royalist. But when duty called, and duty could pay his exorbitant bills, politics easily took second place.

As far as Beth was concerned Bate was employed because he came with a reputation of being the best in the business. It was the summer of 1658. Bettie was experiencing agonising stomach pains. She had moved her own small family into Hampton Court Palace on the orders of the renowned Dr Bate, so he could treat her. The country air and the proximity to his surgery nearby, he deemed, would be of enormous advantage to her in her current state. Bate had also recommended the invigorating waters of Tunbridge Wells to mollify the illness that was now engulfing Bettie.

Beth was distraught. Bate had been engaged to treat her husband. But Oliver's discomfort was clearly not as acute as his daughter's. Bettie soon became the focus of attention. Oliver's most darling child.

As she watched the arrogant doctor descend the grand stairway following his first visit to Bettie's chamber, thoughts of the two sons that she had lost, Robert and Oliver, flooded her mind. The years may have dulled the pain, but the ache would persevere for life. She knew that Bettie's pain was unyielding. But she daren't consider that she could lose Bettie now. She was only twenty-nine. Surely God would not take Bettie from her as well?

Bate was small of stature. He wasn't much taller than Beth. His lack of height had infused his personality with added conceit. Others may be taller than him, but the upper hand was always his. He stood on the last stair on purpose, just to create the illusion of height. It was one of many tricks he had adopted throughout his life in social circumstances to compensate for being vertically challenged.

'Can you tell what the ailment is, Doctor Bate?' asked Beth.

'Of course, my dear Lady Protectress, I know precisely what the disorder is. That is my job,' replied Bate, who couldn't help himself. Despite the gravity of his prognosis.

'Well, Doctor, will she recover soon? These pains in her stomach, will they abate? Can you provide medication to ease her agony?'

Delivering bad news exasperated the good doctor. He was always uncomfortable with the emotional side of his work. If only people would ask him for medical details about the clinical aspects of each case. How he came to the diagnosis. Why an ordinary physician might struggle, unlike him. How his training and experience had led him to understand so much about medicine. That sort of thing. It would make a huge difference. He had seen this condition so often in the past. By this time the young lady upstairs was in the throes of the sickness, there was no hope. He stopped to consider his next sentence. He tried his best to deliver the blow as gently as he could.

'I'm afraid your daughter is not far from death. She is suffering from a terminal impostume of the stomach. The only thing I can do now is to make her passage to the next world as comfortable as possible. There are potions we can procure. Tonics and remedies that might help with the pain. But this malignance is strong. The disease will overcome her. I am sorry,' said Bate.

Bate might easily have slapped Beth hard across the face. Her worst thoughts were immediately realised. The doctor's words came as a huge shock. This time there were no screams. No shrieks. She simply sank to her knees and put her face in her hands. Almost silently, she began to sob.

Bate was now uncomfortable. He looked around to see if any of the palace staff were close by. A woman would be best. But nobody was near. It wasn't his place to provide comfort. It was his place to impart information. He stepped forward hesitantly. Surely there was somebody close. Beth had sunk lower to the floor now and was sobbing uncontrollably. The situation was intolerable. He couldn't just walk out the door. And yet, the door was only a few yards away.

Of the two human beings experiencing the crisis, it was Beth who came to the doctor's aid. Displaying the stoicism that had characterised her very existence, she realised that the doctor was incapable of expressing compassion. She wiped her eyes with her fingers and she somehow managed to get to her feet. Controlling her faculties with immense difficulty, she offered the doctor a way out of his awkward predicament.

'I am so sorry, Doctor Bate, I am sure you have appointments that you need to attend to,' she sobbed, uselessly apologising. Do not let me keep you any longer than necessary.'

Bate made some noise in acknowledgement of Beth's noble gesture and departed through the enormous gothic arch of the palace's main entrance. It was only as he climbed into his carriage a few minutes later that he began to appreciate the enormity of the lady's actions. He was not immune to an appreciation of the capability of the human condition. This woman may well have infiltrated the home of his former king. But he had just witnessed an act from a person of enviable rectitude. And for one of the few times in his life, he felt a pang of emotion. It was not a feeling that he liked. But as the carriage wended its way down the massive gravel driveway he developed a new-found respect for the matriarch of Hampton Court Palace. He found himself hoping that Bettie's death would come quickly. That she would not suffer. That was not like him at all.

Oliver couldn't bear the idea of losing Bettie. He prayed every day and he maintained a constant overnight vigil in her room, despite his own health issues. Bettie made every effort to stifle her pain so as not to alarm her father too much. A total gloom was cast over the entire Protectoral Court. Oliver was disinclined to attend to his duties. Ambassadors would have to wait. Meetings were put on hold. Parents usually reap their joy from the youth and vigour of their children. To say goodbye to them was an abomination. But cancer was a relentless killer.

In the early hours of 6 August, 1658, peace finally came to Bettie. Her father collapsed completely when he realised that she had ceased breathing. He stayed in the first stage of grief denial for days. He was unable to accept her death. He simply couldn't understand how this beautiful little creature, whom he loved so much could be taken away so cruelly. So full of life. So full of promise. Not yet thirty years old. Oliver and Beth were still too distressed to attend Bettie's funeral four days later. It took place in the evening. Her body was placed on a barge at the pier. On a serene twilight August evening the barge solemnly made its way down the Thames to Westminster Abbey. A flotilla of boats filled with silent courtiers accompanied the body on its mournful journey. It was eleven o'clock at night when the barge reached the steps of the Abbey where she lay in state for an hour. At midnight the procession wound on to the Henry VII Chapel, where Bettie was interred.

In the coming days, those closest to Oliver could see that he had become completely withdrawn. He was totally shattered. Thurloe and the Council of State were of the mind that they should offer him the crown again. It was a pragmatic decision, since Oliver had still not named his successor. If he became king, his eldest son Richard would automatically ascend to the seat of power. He might also have chosen Henry, who would have had a much better temperament and acumen to follow in the footsteps of their illustrious father.

Ten days after her passing, Oliver was sitting in Bettie's empty bed chamber at Hampton Court staring out the window. There was a double-door that opened on to a terrace overlooking the tennis court, that had been installed on the instructions of Henry VIII. The room was pleasantly decorated with colourful tapestries of Artimesia and Orlando. The plethora of chairs, couches and stools around the room were covered in sky-blue taffeta and embroidered in both silk and gold. The four poster bed sat on a hand-woven Persian rug that was characterised by a tight even pile and was woven in rich harmonious colours.

Thurloe appeared at the terrace door. He knew where he would find Oliver.

'Imagine, she has seen God by now,' said Oliver looking wistfully towards Thurloe.

'She will bring her own charms to the Lord and he will be able to refuse her nothing,' replied Thurloe smiling. 'She will also be a favourite in the place that she now dwells as well as the place she has come from. We all loved her. You see if she's not.'

'I can do all things through Christ, who strengthens me, John. But this thing seems too big. I must strive to draw comfort from the well of salvation and Christ's covenant of grace,' said Oliver.

'There will be a happy celestial reunion at some future time, Your Highness. The hour of death of each mortal is indicated by God and God alone. And if you'll forgive me, I must raise a matter with you, which is of much import to the future of England. The crown is being offered to you again. The Master of the Wardrobe has had two velvet caps, purple and crimson fashioned for Your Highness. There are now more factions agreeable that you assume the monarchy.'

'I must take my own resolutions as I see fit. And I will proceed according to my own satisfaction. I hope and wait for an intervention from the Lord and I expect he will reveal himself again on this issue. It is trying for me that the matter is raised yet again. But I understand why.'

'Also, Your Highness, as Parliament has granted you the power to name your successor, irrespective of the issue of the crown, it would seem prudent for you to do so soon. Although I am sure that God will not call you for many years yet.'

Oliver rummaged in his pocket and pulled out a sealed white envelope. He brandished it in the air, and he managed to force a grimace at his Secretary of State.

'I have the name of my successor written down in this envelope. I carry it with me most days. But I tell you now, John, from this day on I shall store it in my office at Whitehall when I return there. I do not believe that the time has yet come to reveal this. There would be too much acrimony caused and of course it is not at all necessary as far as I see it.'

Thurloe was happy that at least Oliver had decided on which son to choose. The pacifist Richard would clearly be ineffectual as head-of-state and the Protector must surely choose the more manly Henry. Oliver stood up and made to place the envelope back in his pocket. He was suddenly struck by a sharp pain in his back and he collapsed on the ground. Thurloe screamed 'Oliver!' and ran towards his master. There was blood trickling out of Oliver's mouth and he was completely unconscious. He was lying face down on the floor. His face pressed down on the Persian rug. Thurloe pulled the velvet bell chain that was hanging at the side of the bed. He turned the limp Protector over on to his back. Oliver groaned in pain. He was still alive. At least he was still alive. A servant came into the room and between the two of them they managed to get the Protector sitting up against one of the bed posts.

'Your Highness, can you hear me?' asked Thurloe. Oliver said nothing. But he was obviously breathing. In minutes, Beth had arrived. She was panic-stricken as soon as she saw her husband sitting on the floor in an almost comatose state. It was an hour before Doctor George Bate arrived in the room. The Protector was by now lying on the bed in which his daughter had died just over a week earlier.

Bate entered the room as if he were the one with the most power there. In his mind that's exactly what the dynamics were. He examined the patient, who was now lucid and in minutes he had made his diagnosis. As far as the doctor was concerned, Oliver had just had a back muscle spasm that had caused him to fall. He had then lost consciousness when he his head hit the floor. There was nothing to be unduly worried about, he told both the Lady Protectress and the Secretary of State. Yes, the Protector was a certain age but there was life in the old dog yet. He was of a robust constitution. He had more time left in him yet. If the Lord is good to him. He must get as much rest as possible for the moment. And soon he would be up and about in no time at all.

As he departed the palace that day, Dr Bate congratulated himself on yet another accurate diagnosis. If the Protectorate family keep him going like this, he will not need any other patients. There was plenty more opportunity for financial gain here at Hampton Court and at Whitehall. He began to work out the figures in his head. Imagine if the Protector was to last, say, another five years.

But for one of the few times in his life Dr George was way off the mark. It was not a muscle spasm that had caused the Protector to fall. It was something much more sinister than that. As Bate was adding up the money he might make in the carriage on the way home, the Lord Protector of England, Ireland and Scotland, the orchard thief of Huntingdon, the destroyer of Drogheda, the killer of the king, would be dead within a fortnight.

Chapter Twenty-Six

The tempest came like a manic opera from the skies, the elements determined to sing out, the trees and grasses as their percussion. Even the torrential rain came in orchestrated rhythm. Waves on the Thames were an unusual occurrence. But they came from the depths of the river this night. It was a Monday. The second last day of August. The storm was severe and perilous. Water crashed onto the river banks where no water had crashed in hundreds of years. The waves danced to the rhythm of heaven's drum. The sky was black as coal. The birds had all disappeared. They seemed to know to take shelter. The wind whined through the trees. Through the streets of London. Window shutters rattled violently everywhere. Looser roof slates were lifted and flung into the air like dead leaves. Centuries-old trees were uprooted like saplings and crashed to the ground. Extinguished in a turbulent instant. The storm seemed to already know that the wind and rain it wrought would echo for eternity.

Later the royalists would claim that the storm was the harbinger of death, the devil coming for Oliver Cromwell. But for now nobody in the country thought for a moment that their Protector was going to die, least of all Oliver. He didn't believe that his time had come yet. By the close of the month he was still completely grief-stricken. He ate little, slept little, worked little. Those in the inner sanctum at Whitehall believed that, given time, he would get over Bettie's death. It wasn't long before he began to take fits. His body would shake violently. The grief had turned into something else. A team of doctors was engaged. There was talk of a stone. For the malarial attacks, he was prescribed the Peruvian *quina-quina*, the bark of a tree that had been found to be efficacious. But the attacks kept coming. Nothing seemed to work. Soon the doctors were beginning to worry whether he would continue to surmount such ordeals.

On the Tuesday morning John Thurloe was particularly stressed. Oliver had not yet named his successor. He had now deteriorated to a point where it seemed impossible for him to focus on any matter save his breathing and his pain. In a rare, lucid moment the Protector convinced Thurloe that he had hidden the sealed envelope in Whitehall. And that Thurloe should go and find it. But he had turned the place upside down and could not find it anywhere. He had servants search in every possible nook, every possible cranny where Oliver might have been expected to store it, but still the envelope was not to be found. Who had Oliver chosen to succeed him?

In the afternoon Thurloe sent a servant to both Richard and Henry's lodgings. He decided that this matter must be faced down. He met the two Cromwell boys in his office just off the Painted Chamber at Westminster. There were four other members of the Council of State in the room. Richard was doleful. Henry was bullish.

'Why must we have this conversation at this juncture? When our father might yet live. We know nothing really of these medical ailments. The doctors may not be accurate. God might well allow him to improve,' said Richard.

'I realise that this is a difficult time for all of the family, Richard,' said Thurloe. 'But it behoves us in the Council of State to be practical in these matters. Yes, what you propose is certainly the case. The Protector is a man of great strength. But should the worst happen, we should be prepared for it.'

Henry was pacing the room. The dogs on the street knew that he should be the one to inherit the role. But nobody could be sure. His father was a traditionalist. This was the question that had preoccupied Henry's mind for some weeks now. In the last couple of years Richard had begun to show more interest in politics and, thanks to his father, Richard had begun to take an active role in government. 'Yes, Richard,' said Henry. 'I agree with John. Imagine what the young Charles is capable of, if we fail to act. The transition must be seamless. The royalists must not be presented with any opportunities to unsettle the regime. Everything we have fought for could still be yet undone.'

'Everything *you* have fought for, Henry. I did not have the glowing military career that you have had. I prefer to keep my light hidden under the bushel.'

Conscious of the way the conversation was going, Thurloe needed to get the answers he needed, so he decided to cut directly to the chase.

'Richard Cromwell, I must ask you here and now, should you be nominated as the Protector's successor, will you agree to taking up the role?' The other men in the room leaned forward in anticipation of his answer.

'If my father has trust in me to take on so momentous a position, then who am I to refuse the Lord Protector's wishes,' said Richard. 'The answer is yes.'

Thurloe looked at Henry. 'The same question to you, Henry.'

'My response is also in the affirmative,' replied Henry. 'And may the best man win,' he joked as he held out his hand to his elder brother.

At least Thurloe had his answer. Both men were willing to take up the role. But what if the Protector wasn't able to verbalise his decision? Thurloe might have to fabricate that envelope and make the decision himself.

A successor to Oliver's throne was the last thing on Beth's mind at that moment. She had just lost a precious daughter, one of her babies, and now her life partner was sinking fast. Just how much sorrow could God throw at one of his poor wretched creatures at a time? For the first time in her life her thoughts began to stray to a world without Oliver. How could she possibly endure were he to expire? He was her everything. He was larger than life itself. During their lives together they had taken on and conquered challenges that would have defeated so many others. Somehow Oliver had seemed immortal. It slowly began to dawn on Beth that this time Oliver might not survive. The doctors were insistent. They were also unanimous. He did not have long to live.

She stayed by his bedside continuously. As Oliver had done for Bettie, just weeks earlier. On the Wednesday morning Oliver opened his eyes and called for Beth.

'I'm here, my dearest,' she said as she clasped her hand in his. He was weak. She knew that hand so well. It was the hand that did things that used to make her crave him. The hand that used to gently push back her hair, so he could kiss her shoulder. The hand of the anxious young boy she had taken in marriage all those years ago. The grip. The strong grip. The hand was the same. But the strength was gone. It was the grip of a dying man.

'Soon I will leave you, darling Beth. Man can do nothing unaided,' he said. 'But God can do what he wills. Yet I take comfort from the fact that the Lord has filled me with assurances of His pardon and love.'

'You have always been an advocate of the Father, Jesus Christ, so you have nothing whatever to fear,' said Beth, the tears slowly falling down her face.

'Live like Christians,' he said, turning towards all in the room. His family was there. His doctors. Men of God. 'And I leave you the covenant to feed upon.' Then turning to a minister who was there, he asked, 'Tell me, is it possible to fall from grace?'

The minister shook his head and replied, 'Not in your case, Your Highness. Not in your case.'

Oliver rallied somewhat on the Thursday morning and Thurloe decided that it was now or never. They needed to know. He gathered the same four men from the Council of State. Four of Oliver's closest allies. Perhaps with these austere men asking him for an answer, something innate might help Oliver to respond. They sat down by the Protector's side. Two men on each side of the bed.

But Oliver had drifted in and out of consciousness all day and it was impossible for them to get him to focus. Soon they were beginning to panic that they had left it too late. How could this have happened? Thurloe stood at the foot of the bed, trying to catch the Protector's eyes should he open them at all.

'Your Highness, we must know the name of the next Protector,' said Thurloe on one occasion when he thought Oliver had seen him. Oliver was too drowsy to answer.

'Your Highness,' began Thurloe again. Nothing.

Beth then intervened. 'Perhaps, John, if you mentioned a name, he might answer with a nod. Or a shake of the head,' she said. If I know my husband, he will not let England down even if his body is contriving against him.'

'Your Highness,' said Thurloe again. 'Is it Richard? Is Richard the one?'

Nothing.

'Is it Henry?' said Thurloe again. This time the Protector opened his eyes and caught Thurloe's attention. He smiled. He shook his head. It was not Henry.

Thurloe looked around the room to make sure that everybody had seen what had just happened. 'Is it Richard?' he asked again. Oliver nodded his head. Yes. It was Richard. The next Protector of England, Ireland and Scotland would be Richard Cromwell. There was no doubt about it.

Oliver's last night on earth came after he had revealed his successor. Beth was half asleep on the bed beside him. She thought they'd have so many more years. She wasn't finished. She wasn't ready to let him go. Oliver suddenly began to talk and the whole room was gripped by the moment. He was awake. He was coherent. He looked around and he smiled at everybody. 'Truly God is good indeed,' said Oliver. 'He will not leave me.' Beth took both of his hands in hers and squeezed them together. Maybe the doctors were wrong. Maybe this was the beginning of the recovery. She had heard of stories like this.

People being so close to death and suddenly the deterioration was reversed. Why could it not happen now? To Oliver?

Her husband, on the other hand had simply accepted his fate. Like many dying people at the very last, he suddenly found himself able to communicate. He had formulated the thoughts in his head as he lay there. He began to speak. It was a prayer:

'Lord, though I am but a miserable and wretched creature, I am in covenant with thee through grace. My work is done but God will be with his people. Thou hast made me though, very unworthy, a mean instrument to do them some good, and thee service, and many of them have set too high a value upon me, though others wish, and would be glad of my death. Lord, however thou do dispose of me, continue to do good for them.'

'Oliver,' said Beth. 'Would you like a drink of water? Is your throat dry?'

'It is not my design to drink or sleep, but my design is to make what haste I can to be gone,' replied Oliver. He looked around the room at the faces. Again, he smiled. He noticed the morose moods of the three doctors that were in the room. 'Why do you all look so sad?' he asked.

'It is the weight of the Protector's life upon us,' replied one of the doctors.

'You physicians think I shall die,' said Oliver grasping Beth's hand. 'I tell you I shall not die this hour. I am sure on it.'

Oliver was right. He didn't die that hour. He died the next day. Thursday passed into Friday. For those last hours he was rarely conscious. He was still fighting the illnesses that had engulfed his body.

On the Friday morning he rallied again. He raised his head from the pillow, and he said, 'Go on cheerfully. Banish sadness altogether. Treat my death as no more to you than that of a serving-man.'

He fell back to sleep. Nobody in the room went anywhere. The family could not bear to be away from their patriarch.

They needed to be there. There was an air of expectancy. An expectancy of imminent bereavement. A bereavement that would echo worldwide. Today would be the day that Oliver would die.

Oliver closed his eyes. He was back on the farm in Huntingdon. His mother and father were sitting each side of the hearth of the old homestead. That old familiar kitchen. He knew every nook. Elizabeth looked up and smiled at him. His father, Robert, was busy whittling a stick for some practical use or other around the house. He winked. His two boys Robert and Oliver were sitting at the table engrossed in conversation. They both looked up and greeted him, beaming. A little girl sat singing a nursery rhyme gently in the corner. She was surrounded by daisies. She was making a daisy chain. Bettie suddenly appeared alongside him and slipped her hand into his. And there was something else. Oliver couldn't quite identify what it was. It was big. He tried to focus on the big thing. There was an atmosphere, a mood, a character. It was oppressive. Overwhelming, almost. He couldn't quite comprehend it. What could it possibly be? Oh yes. He knew now. It was death. It was his death.

At three o'clock on the Friday afternoon, Oliver Cromwell finally passed away. He lost his final battle. This time it was for his life. His watch was over at last. He was in his fifty-ninth year. It was 3 September, 1658. The anniversary of his great victories of Dunbar and Worcester. Oliver's lucky day.

Chapter Twenty-Seven

The main problem for Richard Cromwell was that as head of state he was now solely in charge of the entire English army. Of course Richard had spent little or no time in the army. He had absolutely no idea how the whole thing worked. At the beginning of the wars, with pressure from his other brothers, he had tried his hand at being a soldier. But very quickly it turned out not to be for him. He played no meaningful part in the military conflict. He went off, got married, settled down and lived life as a civilian. To those who knew him he seemed to have no ambition or drive. His future was certainly as far away from the army that it could possibly be. So it was quite a surprise to everybody – especially the army – when Richard insisted as ruler on being personally in charge of the military. Richard had also inherited a crumbling and unstable republic that was in serious financial difficulty. And most especially so because the army pay was in serious arrears.

A month after Oliver's death, John Thurloe walked past a plethora of marble statues of English monarchs in the grand corridor of Whitehall. He was heading for Richard's chamber. He knew that there was a tremendous burden on his own shoulders. He now had to be the glue between the new Protector, parliament and the army. In his hands he had the speech ready. It had taken a couple of days to prepare, but if Richard was to address the army, Thurloe knew what to say. And especially what not to say. Richard had agreed that Thurloe write the speech.

He entered the new Protector's room. 'Good morrow, Your Highness,' he said walking across the room. Richard was reading a book about the fruits of the world. 'Ah, John Thurloe,' said Richard. 'Did you know that there is a sweet fruit as big as a turnip but even sweeter than an apple. And they call it a pine apple? It looks like a pine cone, has yellow innards, and a tough exterior skin that must not be ingested.'

'Yes, Your Highness,' replied Thurloe quite surprised that Richard did not know what he knew. 'Pineapples are now being imported from the West Indies into England. In fact, your late father was the first person in this country to taste one. A few years ago now it was. Indeed, I remember it was too sweet for his palate. He did not quite take to the pine apple, as you call it.'

'Well, like so many other new things I am learning of late, that has also passed me by,' said Richard. 'So will you organise to get some for the Protectorate kitchen, so I can see for myself if this fruit agrees with me? I find exotic fruits quite fascinating, don't you?'

'Yes, Your Highness. I will pass your request on to one of the courtiers in due course. Now, if you would be good enough, I have some more pressing issues to discuss with Your Highness.'

But Richard wasn't quite finished. 'In the next couple of days, if possible. I would like to taste the various fruits of West Indian culture that is described in this publication. English food is fine in its place. It has done me good thus far. But I think now as a potentate, an international diet might suit my position in life better.'

Thurloe was irritated with the Protector's predilection for avoidance of the details of governance. This did not auger well. Richard's personality had started to emerge in the first weeks. Thurloe needed to get down to the business at hand. 'I have your speech ready for the army officers, Your Highness. They are waiting for you. But I must warn you, there are rumblings of discontent. Sometimes the fires seem to be out but sometimes they rekindle again. And today they have rekindled.'

'How so? Is there something in particular that I should know?' asked Richard.

'Well, they do not believe that you should be commander-in-chief of the entire army. They feel that an experienced officer should take that role and that you should remain in the background. Since you have no military experience,' said Thurloe.

'Well, then they will be disappointed, will they not? I assume you have made it clear in my speech that I fully intend to be in total control?'

'I am not so sure that this is a wise course of action, Your Highness.'

'There is simply no other way that this will work,' said Richard moving across the room and snatching the document from his Secretary of State's hand.

Ten minutes later, Richard walked into the room of the palace where the army officers were waiting for him. They looked at him with suspicion. But Richard noticed none of the negative nuances. He was not a reader of men, like his father. He launched into his speech in which he professed his pursuit of liberty and godliness and his desire to keep the army in the hands of godly men. He sought the loyalty, support, and prayers of the army. He pledged that he would do all he could to clear the military arrears and ensure prompter payment henceforth. Then he told them that his role as commander-in-chief of the army was a fait accompli. This did not go down well. The officers left the room murmuring their discontent. Richard thought he had won their minds. It was only a matter of time before their hearts would come around. It was nice being in full control of everything. People kowtowed universally. Whatever he said went. Being the Lord Protector would certainly take some getting used to. But at least things seemed to be going quite well so far.

This lifestyle was a far cry from the lifestyle that he had led prior to ascending to the role. Richard took to the high life very easily. In the past, his father had often chided him for his idleness. He had always enjoyed hunting and country pursuits. As a private citizen, he had also amassed debts totaling twenty-six thousand pounds. But now that he was the Lord Protector, surely the wherewithal could be found to keep his creditors at bay. Thurloe was a clever man. Something was bound to be worked out. Yes, this was all going very well for Richard Cromwell. There were challenges, certainly. But nothing that could not be overcome by applying logical solutions.

Five months later Richard was under house arrest. His short reign was over. It had been an unmitigated disaster. The Commonwealth was in complete crisis. The republic was heavily in debt. There was nothing but acrimony between the army and Parliament. Richard was completely inept. Logical solutions did not apply to reality.

The military had feared that the army would be reduced and the religious freedom that the country enjoyed under Oliver would be chipped away. When Parliament made overtures to reduce and reorganise the army, and take a tighter grip on it, the senior officers had demanded that the Protector dissolve parliament. Richard refused. Going against the army was never something his father had done. But Richard was no Oliver. And so, the army flexed their considerable muscles. Richard immediately buckled. He realised his limitations and dissolved parliament. Under house arrest, he was then prevented from leaving Whitehall by the army.

A deal was soon ironed out. On May 14, 1659, Richard's great seal as Lord Protector was acrimoniously smashed to bits in the House of Commons. Parliament agreed to pay his debts and he resigned his position. The second Lord Protector ever in the history of the country went into exile. The House of Cromwell had crumbled.

The 29 May, 1660, was the young Charles Stuart's thirtieth birthday. His birthday present was to enter the city of London to wild acclaim and put his royal seat on the throne of England. He was crowned King of England, Ireland and Scotland on 23 April, 1660. The army had gone looking for him. They found him willing to take his lawful place as king. The monarchy was restored. Albeit with reduced powers. Parliament weren't going to make that mistake again. The capricious Charles II didn't seem to care. His first order of business was vengeance. All evidence of Oliver's republic was to be wiped out. It would be as if it had never happened. The previous nineteen years ignored. Normality was resumed. The Stuarts were back in town.

It was over a year now since Beth had departed from Whitehall. On her last day in the palace, she had sat one last time on the massive staircase in the gigantic foyer and pondered her life. She was an imposter here. That much she was sure of. Oliver was gone. Richard was deposed. She had always known that the family's grip on those regal heights was precarious. Now living in modest accommodation, she was past fretting about all that. John Thurloe had ensured that she would be looked after. She descended the stairs for the last time and walked out into the world no longer a woman of stately substance.

January 26, 1661, was a bitterly cold morning. Beth made her way to Westminster Abbey. She liked to call to see Oliver most days. Tell him the news. Ask him to look after her. There was a lot of solace in that. She knew that the new king was engaging in a witch hunt for all of those regicides who had signed his father's death warrant. There was nowhere to hide. Even those who went abroad were hunted like dogs across the New World, across Europe. It was relentless. Unswerving. And when they were found they were mostly all executed or imprisoned for life.

Beth was so thankful that Oliver was well beyond the king's reach. He was two and a half years dead. Nothing could harm him now. She had created a comforting routine visiting him here. She felt quite immune to the hostile activities that were going on in the outside world. All of that was for others to deal with. She had done her time. National politics played no more part in her life. It was also made clear to her that this new king would leave her remaining family unmolested. At least she and her children, including Richard, did not have to be looking over their shoulders for the rest of their lives.

Her breath fogged in rhythm with her steady footsteps as she made her way through the cobbled streets. She had given up keeping her head down. Like she used to do in the early days. 'There goes the Lady Protectress,' they'd say. But now nobody cared who she was anymore. She scaled the steps of the cathedral as she usually did. Entering the enormous gothic arena, the sound of the street outside dulled. She turned towards the Henry VII chapel. She could immediately hear banging noises and a lot of commotion coming from that direction. She was totally perplexed. She presumed that a burial was taking place. However, the ruckus was far too crude to be a funeral. Since she had come this far, her curiosity got the better of her, so she kept going. Stepping inside the small chapel she was completely horrified by what she saw.

The marble vault that Oliver had been interred in was shattered into pieces. The lid of his coffin was lying on the tiled floor. A group of soldiers, two with spades were taking their turns spitting on his embalmed corpse. Swearing obscenities at the dead body. Some stamped on his groin area to the amusement of their peers. Another empty coffin lay discarded in a corner. An officer who seemed to be in charge noticed that there was a woman in their vicinity. He approached Beth. ''Ere madam. You probably shouldn't be in 'ere right now,' he said curtly. 'We is takin' the old bastard Cromwell away to give 'im what he deserves. The old fucker thought he 'ad escaped justice. Oh no 'e 'asn't. We've already fucked 'is mother's corpse in a pit outside. She deserves it an all fer spawnin' that monster.' He then made a repellent sound that Beth interpreted as a repulsive laugh.

Beth tried hard to hide her shock, her revulsion, her tears. This was the love of her life. The man with whom she had shared everything. She couldn't believe that the royalists were still trying to get at him now that he was dead. What good could it possibly do? Desecrating his body? And Elizabeth? Her mother-in-law? But Beth had badly underestimated the depths to which Charles II was willing to go to exact his revenge.

She was too afraid to reveal her identity. She turned, put her hands to her mouth and ran from the chapel. The tears came in floods when she reached the street. What was she going to do now? Her daily visits to her dead husband, so cruelly taken away. And what about her Bettie? She was also buried close by. Her beautiful daughter. Would the royalist soldiers defile her body as well? She was totally distraught. How could any human being do this to another? Elizabeth was dead. Oliver was dead. Why can they not let them rest in peace?

The next morning Beth was still struggling. It was like she had lost Oliver all over again. Just when she was finding her feet. Just when she was managing to find the ability to carry on. Images of her husband's corpse and what the soldiers had done to it invaded her thoughts all through the night. She barely slept.

It was still early. She soon became aware of a hubbub out on the street. It got louder as she lay there. There was some cheering and shouting. She went to the window. She pulled up the lower sash. There was a small mob outside. A grotesque procession was passing by. Three horses were drawing three hurdles. Three dead bodies were fastened to the wooden panels. She recognised Oliver's corpse. The other two bodies were of Henry Ireton and John Bradshaw, two other regicides.

The gallows at Tyburn was only a few corners away. Beth couldn't help herself. She had to go wherever her husband was going. That was her policy in life. And now in death. She quickly got dressed and tore down the stairs. The spectacle was well out of sight by the time that she got to the street. But she knew exactly where they were headed. She had seen many a hurdle pass by her front door in recent years.

She turned the corner into the square at Tyburn. She was

just in time to see her husband's body being pulled by a rope around the neck on the infamous hanging tree of Tyburn. She turned away. The people there cheered. They waved. They sneered. The usurper was finally getting his punishment.

Beth was utterly confounded. How could God do this now to his loving and faithful servant Oliver? It was then that she noticed the old man. He was standing just to the left staring at her face. Like her, his head was covered with the hood of his cape. He had a long grey beard. There seemed to be wisdom in his kindly eyes. She knew immediately who it was. 'Valentine Walton,' she exclaimed, and she ran to embrace her husband's old friend. 'Beth!' said Valentine.

'I had heard you were in somewhere in Europe. Was it Germany?' asked Beth.

'Yes, I have had to flee. I am only here for a few days. It is not safe for me to be around. As you know, I signed the king's death warrant. I must remain incognito,' said Valentine. 'Is not this business despicable? You should not be seeing this Beth.'

Suddenly there was an uproar behind them. Oliver's body was cut down by one of the soldiers. An axe appeared from somewhere. He began to chop off the head of the dead Protector. The final ignominy. It took eight blows to sever his embalmed head from his body. Valentine put his arm around Beth and pulled her away. They walked slowly away from the contemptable, grisly pageant. Nobody realised that the departing old couple were the former Lady Protectress and a prominent regicide.

'You know, Beth. We used to laugh a lot about the monkey story back in the old days in Huntingdon, Oliver and I. We had some really fine adventures when we were young orchard thieves.'

Beth knew what Valentine was doing.

'Yes, Valentine,' she said composing herself. 'He often regaled the chimpanzee tale to me. Perhaps it was from this strange incident as an infant that he interpreted he was special.'

'A tiny quirk of fate. Things could have been so much different in the world,' said Valentine.

They both managed a smile.

'I don't think it will be possible for Oliver's name to endure when Charles II has finished wiping it off the face of the earth. I expect his legacy will be totally disregarded,' said Beth.

'It is very sad, but there is no doubt what you say is true,' replied Valentine.

They couldn't have been more wrong.

The End. (Or so it seemed.)

Epilogue

The disinterment of Oliver's body turned out to have the opposite effect of that which was originally intended. It could be said that it brought back to the political stage the very person that the Stuart regime sought to forget. Despite the jubilation with which Charles II was received on his coronation, the Stuarts could not simply pick up where they had left off before his father was executed. The climate had changed. The mystique of the monarchy was gone. Oliver's revival in death metaphorically brought him back from the dead. Following his exhumation and mock execution, the newspapers of the day focused heavily on his life after death. The lengths to which the Restoration regime went to erase the Interregnum from history did nothing to affect the attention levels to which it would be subjected among students of history in posterity. As the centuries passed, it was Oliver's notorious legacy, not that of Charles II that would be forensically scrutinised – for better or for worse.

As in life, the tales surrounding Oliver in death are remarkable. More so the head than the actual body. The body was buried immediately after the posthumous decapitation. Despite many myths and legends of various burial places of the body across England, it is most likely that it was thrown in a pit at Tyburn. And there it stayed. Today, the location is near to Marble Arch, London.

The three heads that were chopped off that day were all erected on the wooden railings of Westminster Hall. Oliver's was the one that lasted the longest duration. In fact, his reign on the railings outlasted the reign of Charles II on the throne. There his head remained impaled on a pointy wooden upright looking down on passers-by until 1685. Even in death, he was defiant. This time it was towards the elements: the hot, humid summers and the bitter cold winters of the London climate.

Not long after Charles died, another storm hit London. The oak upright on which the head had been stuck snapped off in the howling wind. A solitary sentinel who was guarding the nearby Exchequer Office was stunned when the head landed at his feet. Knowing exactly what it was, he picked it up, stuck it under his cloak and brought it home. There, he hid it in the chimney. Soon when it was realised that Oliver's head was missing from Westminster Hall, the authorities posted bills all over the town in an effort to have it retrieved. There was a considerable reward offered for its return. The sentinel panicked and told no one about his find. He didn't reveal his secret until he was on his deathbed when he told his daughter about it. She had no such compunction and she immediately sold it.

Around 1710, it appeared at a London museum. It was then in the ownership of a Claudius Du Puy, a Swiss-French collector of curiosities. By the late eighteenth century, following Du Puy's death it was owned by a comic actor named Samuel Russell. Goldsmith, clockmaker and toy-man James Cox then bought it from Russell but not before Russell had abused the head by passing it around at social gatherings, leading to a significant erosion of its features.

In 1799 Cox sold the head to a trio of speculators, the Hughes brothers for £230 (or £30,000 in 2021 money). They put on an exhibition of Cromwell memorabilia. But doubts surrounding the authenticity of the head rendered the exhibition a failure. A daughter of one of the Hughes' brothers then sold the head to Josiah Henry Wilkinson in 1815. It remained in the Wilkinson family until its burial.

After a full examination in 1911, archaeologists dismissed the head as a fake. The absence of firm evidence of its whereabouts in the early years made them wary about declaring the head genuine. They concluded their study unable to verify or refute the head's identity. The uncertainty increased public demand for a full scientific examination. A member of the family,

Horace Wilkinson, eventually reluctantly allowed the head to be taken for examination by the eugenicist Karl Pearson and the anthropologist Geoffrey Morant. Their 109-page report concluded that there was a 'moral certainty' that the Wilkinson head was that of Oliver Cromwell.

In March, 1960, Horace Wilkinson (a son of the first Horace) bequeathed the head to Sidney Sussex College in Cambridge, the one Oliver had attended as a youth. There it was finally buried at a secret location on campus. In fact, the announcement that it was buried was not revealed until October, 1962. There is a plaque in the chapel of the college referring to the burial but not revealing its location. The exact spot is only known to the dean of the college. The information is passed down from dean to dean.

It is interesting to note that at the same time as Oliver was finally making his exit out this world forever, this writer was making his entrance into it – March, 1960.

Note to Reader

For a book that must be placed in the fiction category, it is critical to know that this story is virtually all non-fiction. At least, there are primary sources for almost every incident. Some minor liberties have been taken to take the reader on a chronological journey of events as they actually happened. Otherwise, the narrative would have looked something like this; 'And then this happened... and then... and then... and then...'

The monkey story is famously associated with Oliver, as is the river rescue carried out by the curate. As far as his promiscuous proclivities are concerned there is a contemporary source that refers to Oliver sexually assaulting women on the street in Huntingdon during this time. Albeit a royalist one, which may have no basis in truth. However, there is too much evidence of a somewhat debauched adolescence to completely ignore. The gambling and the anxiety come from his own words. The death of Oliver's older sister, Joan, at the age of seven is the first of several child or young adult deaths that was indicative of a perilous time before antibiotics. Child mortality was pervasive and life expectancy for an adult was about forty years of age.

The fact that the Restoration writers declared open season on the preceding republic needs to be added to the mix. A literary free-for-all ensued, and the polemic discourse began. So, exaggerations and untruths are inextricably interwoven with the facts. For instance, Dr George Bate went on to treat Charles II and in later life penned his autobiography. He had turned totally against Oliver by this time. In his narrative he alleges that Oliver massacred over 4,000 people at Drogheda including innocent civilians. Like many other contemporary contributors to this debate, Bate was probably never in Drogheda in his life. This would be laughable if it were not for the fact that Bate's ludicrous assertion has often been used as contemporary evidence against Oliver in academic circles throughout the centuries. During the Restoration, Bate also claimed that he had poisoned the Protector to curry favour with the prevailing regime. It was only at the Restoration that erroneous royalist stories of civilian atrocities in Ireland began to gain traction. None of these allegations accord with either the facts, Oliver's moral compass, or most especially – the available evidence.

This is the Oliver Cromwell that the author has found in the history books. Others might research his life and find a different one. But the available evidence fully facilitates this depiction of the man. Diverse opinions of Cromwell abound. It's history. It's a matter of interpretation.

It may occasion surprise when it is realised that the author is a native of Drogheda, the siege of which is the biggest blot on Oliver's career. According to many, he is alleged to have massacred thousands of the author's ancestors in cold blood (at best hundreds); unarmed men, women and children to boot. Tom Reilly's previous books, *Cromwell at Drogheda, Cromwell:*

An Honourable Enemy, and *Cromwell was Framed* have together proven that Oliver was not responsible for the wholesale and deliberate deaths of unarmed civilians while he was on Irish soil. It's high time this huge miscarriage of historical justice was redressed.

The author is also responsible for the publication in 2021 of *Cromwell in Ireland: New Perspectives.* An assemblage of academics has submitted a collection of essays here to discuss his Irish campaign in a fresh light. Throughout Ireland a timeworn bitterness still simmers over the punitive 'Cromwellian' policies, for which Oliver is largely held personally responsible as Lord Protector during the 1650s. It is Cromwell's name that history has attached to the settlement of Ireland by Parliament. This particular book attempts to extricate the word 'Cromwell' from the 'Cromwellian' settlement. Led by Prof Martyn Bennett, a team of period experts re-examine the military campaign with a long overdue shift of focus to other parliamentarian leaders. The facts are skilfully marshalled throughout, presented impartially and it is difficult not to conclude that Cromwell's roles in both the alleged atrocities of the military campaign and the implementation of the Irish land settlement have to date been greatly overstated.

Often labelled as one of history's greatest enigmas, it is clear that Oliver retains the ability to surprise us still. It remains to be seen if the more passive Cromwell that is now emerging will in any way assuage the vile caricature of the man that Irish history, tradition and folklore have all long since accepted.

The author has made several challenges to historians all over the world to prove that Oliver deliberately massacred large numbers of innocent civilians in Ireland – the clear verdict of history to date. So far, no one has risen to the challenge. The author repeats his challenge again here.

With the exception of some minor bit-part roles (the chandler, the lawyer, the prostitute, the gambler, the house-buyer) all of the characters depicted here were real people with real names. They have been cast in the exact role that they played in Oliver's life. Oliver's (reported) own words from contemporary sources are used often.

Oliver has been accused of many things. His hatred of Catholics being one of them. The author hopes that he has articulated that it is clear from the evidence that it was the Catholic shepherds and not the flock where his animosity was directed. Some might be also surprised to learn that he fostered a philosophy of religious toleration throughout his life, which is encapsulated in his religious settlement of 1653. Re-admitting the Jews to England was just one aspect of this. He was also very lenient towards the challenges of both Baptists and Quakers, where others were not. Some might also find it surprising to learn that Catholics in England were not persecuted during the Interregnum. Despite Catholicism being a banned religion, for the most part they were allowed to practise their faith. It is also clear from the evidence that it was Parliament who implemented the retributive policies in Ireland and not Oliver. So, by focusing on him, we let those really responsible for the brutal subjugation of Ireland off the hook.

* * *

It might be heartening to learn that Bettie's body was never desecrated by the royalists. She still lies in the same vault in Westminster Abbey today where she was placed on that balmy August evening in 1658. In July, 1660, Richard left England and went in exile to France. He would never see his wife again. Returning to England around 1680, he lived off income from his estate in Hursley. He died at the ripe old age of 85 in 1712. He is interred in a vault beneath All Saints' Parish Church, Hursley, where a memorial tablet to him has been placed in recent years. He was the longest-lived British head of state, until Elizabeth

II overtook him in 2012. After the Restoration, Oliver's wife, Elizabeth (Beth), moved to Wales to get away from the turmoil. She died in 1665 and is buried in Northborough Church, Cambridgeshire. Henry Cromwell managed to convince Charles II that his actions had been dictated by familial duty. He died in 1674 in the forty-seventh year of his age. He is buried at Wicken Church also in Cambridgeshire. Valentine Walton went into exile in Germany and eventually ended up masquerading as a gardener in Flanders, hiding from the regicide hunters. He died there in 1661, escaping the gallows.

* * *

The southern boundary wall of the property the author lives in today was once the ancient town wall of Drogheda. It was precisely here that Oliver entered the author's home town on the third assault that fractious September evening. Had he not succeeded in taking Drogheda, Anglo-Irish history might easily have taken a totally different direction. Such are the fine lines of historical destiny.

The author's earnest hope is that his ongoing work on Oliver Cromwell will encourage further study on his life and times. It is only by doing this that reconciliation between Ireland and England regarding the Cromwellian period can be further enhanced. Historians have perennially made excuses for the apparent callous nature of his Irish campaign. Now that he has been declared innocent of crimes against unarmed civilians in Ireland, excuses are no longer necessary. However, he is now and always will be a paradox, within an enigma, within a conundrum.

TOP HAT
BOOKS

Top Hat Books

Historical fiction that lives

We publish fiction that captures the contrasts, the achievements, the optimism and the radicalism of ordinary and extraordinary times across the world.

We're open to all time periods and we strive to go beyond the narrow, foggy slums of Victorian London. Where are the tales of the people of fifteenth century Australasia? The stories of eighth century India? The voices from Africa, Arabia, cities and forests, deserts and towns? Our books thrill, excite, delight and inspire.

The genres will be broad but clear. Whether we're publishing romance, thrillers, crime, or something else entirely, the unifying themes are timescale and enthusiasm. These books will be a celebration of the chaotic power of the human spirit in difficult times. The reader, when they finish, will snap the book closed with a satisfied smile.
If you have enjoyed this book, why not tell other readers by posting a review on your preferred book site.

Recent bestsellers from Tops Hat Books are:

Grendel's Mother
The Saga of the Wyrd-Wife
Susan Signe Morrison
Grendel's mother, a queen from Beowulf, threatens the fragile political stability on this windswept land.
Paperback: 978-1-78535-009-2 ebook: 978-1-78535-010-8

Queen of Sparta
A Novel of Ancient Greece
T.S. Chaudhry
History has relegated her to the role of bystander, what if Gorgo, Queen of Sparta, had played a central role in the Greek resistance to the Persian invasion?
Paperback: 978-1-78279-750-0 ebook: 978-1-78279-749-4

Mercenary
R.J. Connor
Richard Longsword is a mercenary, but this time it's not for money, this time it's for revenge...
Paperback: 978-1-78279-236-9 ebook: 978-1-78279-198-0

Black Tom
Terror on the Hudson
Ron Semple
A tale of sabotage, subterfuge and political shenanigans in Jersey City in 1916; America is on the cusp of war and the fate of the nation hinges on the decision of one young policeman.
Paperback: 978-1-78535-110-5 ebook: 978-1-78535-111-2

Destiny Between Two Worlds
A Novel about Okinawa
Jacques L. Fuqua, Jr.
A fateful October 1944 morning offered no inkling that
the lives of thousands of Okinawans would be profoundly
changed—forever.
Paperback: 978-1-78279-892-7 ebook: 978-1-78279-893-4

Cowards
Trent Portigal
A family's life falls into turmoil when the parents' timid
political dissidence is discovered by their far more enterprising
children.
Paperback: 978-1-78535-070-2 ebook: 978-1-78535-071-9

Godwine Kingmaker
Part One of The Last Great Saxon Earls
Mercedes Rochelle
The life of Earl Godwine is one of the enduring enigmas of
English history. Who was this Godwine, first Earl of Wessex;
unscrupulous schemer or protector of the English? The answer
depends on whom you ask...
Paperback: 978-1-78279-801-9 ebook: 978-1-78279-800-2

The Last Stork Summer
Mary Brigid Surber
Eva, a young Polish child, battles to survive the designation of
"racially worthless" under Hitler's Germanization Program.
Paperback: 978-1-78279-934-4 ebook: 978-1-78279-935-1 $4.99
£2.99

Messiah Love
Music and Malice at a Time of Handel
Sheena Vernon
The tale of Harry Walsh's faltering steps on his journey to
success and happiness, performing in the playhouses of
Georgian London.
Paperback: 978-1-78279-768-5 ebook: 978-1-78279-761-6

A Terrible Unrest
Philip Duke
A young immigrant family must confront the horrors of the
Colorado Coalfield War to live the American Dream.
Paperback: 978-1-78279-437-0 ebook: 978-1-78279-436-3

Readers of ebooks can buy or view any of these bestsellers by
clicking on the live link in the title. Most titles are published
in paperback and as an ebook. Paperbacks are available in
traditional bookshops. Both print and ebook formats are
available online.

Find more titles and sign up to our readers' newsletter at
http://www.johnhuntpublishing.com/fiction

Follow us on Facebook at https://www.facebook.com/
JHPfiction and Twitter at https://twitter.com/JHPFiction